So Silver Bright

So Silver Bright

LISA MANTCHEV

Feiwel and Friends
NEW YORK

A FEIWEL AND FRIENDS BOOK
An Imprint of Macmillan

SO SILVER BRIGHT. Copyright © 2011 by Lisa Mantchev.
All rights reserved. Printed in August 2011 in the United States of America by
R. R. Donnelley & Sons Company, Harrisonburg, Virginia. For information,
address Feiwel and Friends, 175 Fifth Avenue, New York, N.Y. 10010.

Library of Congress Cataloging-in-Publication Data Available

ISBN: 978-0-312-38098-4

Book design by April Ward

Feiwel and Friends logo designed by Filomena Tuosto

First Edition: 2011

10 9 8 7 6 5 4 3 2 1

macteenbooks.com

For Amélie, who is princess
and pirate both, and for Xavier,
who agreed it should be "never jam today"

So Silver Bright

CAST LIST

MEMBERS OF BEATRICE SHAKESPEARE SMITH & CO.
Beatrice (Bertie) Shakespeare Smith, a seventeen-year-old girl

Peaseblossom
Cobweb
Moth
Mustardseed
} the fairies from *A Midsummer Night's Dream*

Ariel, an airy spirit from *The Tempest*
Nate, a pirate from *The Little Mermaid*
Waschbär, a sneak-thief
Varvara, a fire-dancer

AT THE CARAVANSERAI
The Scrimshander, Bertie's father
Serefina, an herb-seller
Aleksandr, Leader of the Innamorati
Valentijn, Keeper of the Innamorati Costumes
Various Innamorati performers

AT THE DISTANT CASTLE
Her Gracious Majesty, the Queen
Fenek, a servitor

AT THE THÉÂTRE ILLUMINATA

Ophelia, daughter of Polonius in *Hamlet,* and Bertie's mother

The Theater Manager

The Stage Manager

Mrs. Edith, the Wardrobe Mistress

Mr. Hastings, the Properties Manager

Mr. Tibbs, the Scenic Manager

CHAPTER ONE

We Will Persuade Him, Be It Possible

It is a nipping and an eager air.

Except, for once, Beatrice Shakespeare Smith was thinking of the weather and not Ariel. With a frigid coastal wind tugging at her hair, she sprinted up the stairs set into the White Cliffs. Questions flitted about her mind on the wings of tiny white moths, all drawn to a central, gleaming hope: the chance to have family—*her* family—reunited. She rehearsed her query for the Scrimshander as she raced ever higher:

Will you come with us to the theater? I promised my mother I'd bring you back with me.

Bertie would have made her plea that morning on the beach, fresh from the triumph of rescuing Nate and escaping the Sea Goddess's clutches, except her father had not lingered one moment longer than necessary. Perhaps it was in his avian nature to seek solitude; more likely, Bertie's news that Sedna—his former ladylove—had dissolved into a plethora of tiny sea creatures had come as something of a shock. A few hours had passed since the vengeful deity had tried to kill Bertie, first by drowning, then by strangling, and finally by collapsing her underwater lair, but the Sea Goddess's promise to gather her strength and revisit her vengeance upon them all still reverberated through Bertie's very bones. Trying to escape it, she ducked her head and entered the Scrimshander's Aerie.

"Dad?"

The single word echoed off the walls; it only took a few heartbeats for Bertie to understand something was amiss. Softened by a gray blanket of fog, the meager, midday sunlight did little to illuminate the cavern's depths. Lanterns hung askew, while the embers in the hearth lay dying, the coals abandoned like broken eggshells in a nest. A haphazard assortment of the Scrimshander's carving tools was spread scattershot across the stone floor. The room was a tomb—gloomy, stale, silent—and it was Bertie's hopes that had died.

He's not here.

Bertie circled the cavern, peering into the innermost recesses, praying he'd retired to sleep or retreated to an unknown nook. She moved as a wraith would, gliding from one bit of furniture to another, haunted by the ghosts of a thousand fears but none so terrible as the one confirmed by the tattered scrap of paper she found pierced to the wall above his desk.

I have gone to find her.

The handwriting was nearly illegible, the scrawl trailing off as though the weight of the pronouncement had caused him to drop his pen. On the desk lay a single ink-tipped quill. Bertie picked it up, the fog in her brain clearing enough for her to notice something.

That's not tipped with ink. . . . It's blood. He ripped the feather from his wing to write the note.

Which meant that her father was once more a bird. Once more the creature in love with Sedna. And that he'd abandoned his daughter and his humanity in favor of the Sea Goddess.

I have to call him back.

Perhaps it was for the best that the notebook was tucked into Waschbär's bag for safekeeping; its magic was flawed and subject to creative interpretation at the best of times. Instinctively, Bertie knew something more powerful was needed here: blood-magic, bone-magic, word-magic. Combined, they had helped her escape Sedna's underworld after the cavern walls collapsed atop her, allowed her to return to the surface and to the company of her friends. But could they summon the Scrimshander back on the winds?

The attempt and not the deed confounds us.

She must try.

Taking up one of her father's carving tools, Bertie scored the tip of her finger until a droplet of blood oozed from it, darker than a ruby. "For the blood." Reaching out, she touched the nearest of a hundred carvings etched into the massive whale ribs that formed the Aerie's rafters, then the scrimshaw medallion hanging about her neck. "For the bones."

As for the words, those she held in her mouth, some faceted and glowing like the blood ruby, others delicate and rounded like ivory spellicans: *Let him be summoned.*

The earth thrummed in response, and the floor underfoot shuddered, as though the stone tried to lift her into the very skies. Seconds later came the water, a gift from her mother, Ophelia. It sloshed from abandoned pots and pans, from inky cups and tiny indentations in the floor, mimicking waves swirling about her ankles, inciting the seagulls to gather outside. The winds answered Bertie's command last of all, nudging the birds into a circular pattern, carrying with them the faintest of cries:

"Little one—"

And a second, stronger voice:

"What are you playing at?" Ariel posed his distant query with an interesting mixture of irritation and anxiety. A subsequent puff of wind signaled a hasty approach.

Except it was Bertie's summoned winds that arrived first, roaring into the Aerie and prompting the near-dead coals in the hearth to blaze back to life. Blue and green sparks exploded outward to alight upon furniture, wadded scraps of paper, tattered bits of sailcloth, and oily cotton rags left in forgotten corners. All that had been earth-grown provided sustenance for the fire and, within seconds, the Aerie filled with thick, choking smoke. Trembling like an inferno-trapped sapling, Bertie crouched down in the narrow space where the air was the cleanest and coolest, then tried to bend the fire to her will.

Controlling the earth was simply a matter of filling up the back of her head and the hollow of her throat and the place just behind her eyes with green tendrils and dark soil and crumpled pieces of leaves, and then thinking *please* down to her toes. Soon she realized fire was an altogether different beast, with claws of red and yellow and orange. Bertie tried to catch hold of them, but they twisted out of her reach, as capricious as one of Ariel's spring gales and infinitely more dangerous.

Unable to bear the smoke and the heat any longer, Bertie crawled forward on her belly, trying to locate the Aerie's exit. Tears streamed from her eyes now; when they spattered on the hot stone floor, she half expected them to skitter in all directions like water tossed into a frying pan. A sudden gust of wind shoved the smoky cloak from Bertie's shoulders only seconds before Ariel's slim hand clamped down over her wrist and he towed her out of the Aerie and into his arms.

"I leave you alone for five minutes, and you go up like a Roman candle." With a lazy smile, he decanted clean air into her lungs. "If you wanted to play with fire, milady, you could have simply asked me for a kiss or three."

Bertie tried to tell him she wasn't playing and to let her go, thank you, but all she could manage was a series of coughs into the front of his linen shirt and the words, "My father—"

"Stay put." Ariel pressed her against the cliff face. "I'll get him."

"He's not—" Ye gods, it hurt to breathe, much less speak. "He's not in there."

One raised eyebrow was all the answer she got before there was an ominous crackle of glass. One of the oil lanterns, perhaps, or an unseen cache of sparking powder exploded, and the force of the blast shoved Bertie off the tiny ledge.

CHAPTER TWO

As Confident as Is the Falcon's Flight

Only in Sedna's underworld had Bertie flown before, inadvertently shape-shifting into a bird after slipping off a tightrope. That time, she'd saved herself—and Ariel—from falling into a cauldron of boiling ice.

Similar self-preservation instincts made her cast her arms wide-open again. Every tiny hair upon them stiffened like the nub ends on a thousand quill pens. The rush of air was the same, through her hair, in her ears, but something different emerged in place of feathers. This time, Bertie heard the echoes of wishes never made. Nameless longings leapt inside her heart of hearts like acrobats. Recognizing kindred magic, the scrimshaw medallion hummed against her skin, warming in response—

Seconds before she would have smashed into the rocks,

Ariel caught her about the waist, tethering her body to his chest. He fought the heart-stopping plummet with only a small exhalation of breath to mark his efforts.

His smile was quizzical as they landed. "Did duress get the best of you?"

Thankful that the sands welcomed her feet instead of her face, Bertie couldn't quell the disappointment that burbled up inside her. "I've forgotten the trick of flight, if ever I knew it."

"Given enough time and practice, you'll harness the winds again." Ariel ran his hands down her arms, as though searching for feathers that had refused to manifest. "Especially since you have the best of instructors at your disposal."

"It's not your responsibility to teach me such things." Remembering her father's defection, the words came out harsher than she'd intended. Bertie wrestled to contain her misdirected anger as she looked up at the Scrimshander's Aerie, reduced by distance to a tiny hole in the side of the White Cliffs.

Ariel spared a glance at the cavern's entrance, which was exhaling smoke like the Caterpillar's hookah in *Alice in Wonderland*. "He's gone so soon after your glorious return? That's hardly good manners."

"A lack of manners is the least of his transgressions in my opinion."

"Just say the word, and we'll give chase through the skies."

"And you'll carry me, hanging about your neck like the proverbial albatross? Don't be ridiculous. You'd tire of me before the day was out and drop me in the nearest gully." But sarcasm couldn't stop Bertie's heart from slamming into her ribs as an errant wind howled around them. Deep inside her, all the unnamed longings of her soul raised the question:

What is it you really want?

Nate appeared in the distance, approaching at a run even as Ariel leaned closer, his hand sliding along her arm in invitation.

"I wouldn't, and well you know it."

Bertie gathered up the feathered bits of her mind that knew the joy of flight, carefully tethered them with red thread, and shoved them as far down as she could into the dark earth of her soul. "I can't just leave."

"He's out there somewhere, isn't he? Circling the skies as a fulmar." The air elemental took her hand in his own, threading a bit of wind between their enmeshed fingers like the captured ribbon tail on a kite. "Give chase. You promised Ophelia, didn't you?"

I have gone to find her.

Bertie could picture the Scrimshander's note, though it had surely been reduced to cinders and ash by the fire. "My father made his decision. He's gone after Sedna." Pulling away from Ariel, she clasped her elbows for warmth, suddenly freezing now that she wasn't burning, and began to climb the nearest dune. Half a second later, she slammed into Nate's chest, as solid as an anchor when the world around her was a storm-tossed ocean.

"Are ye hurt?" Without waiting for an answer, he ran his hands over her arms, squeezing to make certain her bones were just where they ought to be. His dark eyes took in her soot-smeared clothes, her no-doubt disheveled hair and face, the blistered skin upon the very end of her nose that even Bertie could see when she went a bit cross-eyed. "I take my eyes off ye fer a second an' the next thing I realize, there's smoke pourin' out o' th' cliffs! I thought ye'd been burnt t' a crisp until I spotted ye on th' beach!"

The worried look on his face shouldn't have irritated her, but it implied everything she hated most about damsels in distress. "The fire was an accident, one that won't be repeated."

Despite three trips to one of the Caravanserai's famed bathhouses, he still smelled of salt and seaweed, Sedna's fragrance yet clinging to him in the way that her starfish hands could not. "Ye shouldn't ha'e wandered off wi'out me."

"Perhaps the Mistress of Revels wanted a moment without her loyal hound nipping at her heels." The air elemental's soft laughter acted like gasoline upon a fire, and Nate flared up.

"She left ye behind as well. Mayhap she wanted a moment wi'out ye makin' cow eyes at her." Nate looked at him as though he could cheerfully tear Ariel's head from his shoulders and stuff it down whatever remained of his neck.

Mustardseed grinned at Bertie. "I was never any good at geometry, but you're stuck in a triangle, aren't you?"

"Shut up," she ordered even as Moth asked, "But what if there were four of them?"

"That's a love rectangle, and five people would be a love pentagon."

"And what are six people in love?" Cobweb demanded.

Mustardseed thought it over a moment. "Manslaughter, I suppose."

"It might yet come to that." Trapped once more between sky and sea, Bertie looked from Ariel to Nate.

I have flown and fallen, and I have swum deep and drowned, but there should be more to love than "I survived it."

Nate spit once in the sand as he turned back to her. "I just wish ye'd be careful."

"Unless you plan on covering me head to foot in cotton

wool"—a notion Bertie didn't put past him—"you're going to have to come to terms with the idea that I might occasionally encounter something dangerous, be it Sea Goddess or wayward fire or questionable meat on a stick."

Here the fairies broke into delighted cries of "Where!?" and "Bugger, she's just trying to illustrate her point" followed by "She's illustrating with meat? Whatever happened to pen-and-ink sketches?"

Ariel contributed nothing to the speculation, instead crossing his arms one over the other. The action recalled his butterfly familiars from the skies, and they flocked to him with eager wing beats.

"Bats!" Moth flailed at the air. "Vampire bats!"

"Don't be ridiculous," Peaseblossom said with a sniff. "Vampire bats don't sparkle."

"They do! They're a great glittery menace!" Moth countered, still cowering behind Cobweb and Mustardseed.

The butterflies disappeared under the collar of Ariel's silk shirt, and if winged insects could shoot withering glances, then surely they disappeared with great disdain. Peaseblossom took advantage of the silence to begin the Inquisition.

"But you haven't told us what happened in the Aerie. Did you try to 'kindle a fire' again?"

"When will you learn the words you write have consequences?" Moth said, wagging a finger under Bertie's nose.

"I didn't write anything." She gestured to Waschbär, standing just behind them. "Our friend still has the journal among his things, I hope."

Despite a long-distance sprint through the sand, the sneak-thief was neither red nor panting. He yet wore his rucksack slung about his impressive shoulders and patted the bag with one dexterous hand. "As you commanded me, good Mistress of Revels."

"But what about the Scrimshander?" Cobweb wanted to know. "Did he turn into a rotisserie chicken?"

Flinching at the suggestion, Bertie shook her head. "No. He was gone before I got there."

"Don't worry!" Peaseblossom hastened to reassure her friend. "He can't stay away forever."

"Sure he can," Moth said, oblivious and cheerful as the boys skimmed about Bertie's head. "He's a wild animal, isn't he?"

Mustardseed and Cobweb added their thoughts, which included, "I guess he could fly until his arms give out" and, "They aren't arms, stupid, they're wings."

Bertie was suddenly very tired: tired of walking, tired of explaining, tired of dealing with her fae friends, and tired of catching the surreptitious glowers exchanged by

Nate and Ariel. As the fatigue seeped inward, it brought with it the mocking laughter of the Sea Goddess. Every breaking wave along the shore seemed to echo her voice, every foam-tipped eddy looked like the crooking of a starfish finger, the strands of seaweed Sedna's vicious tresses. Bertie licked her lips and tasted evil in the air. "She can't have coalesced yet."

Nate's breath came in short pants, as though to reassure himself there was yet air to breathe. "Aye, she's back. I can smell her."

"So can I." Ariel ducked between Bertie and the still-distant shoreline, as though to shield her from view of the water creatures that might lurk in the tide pools. With a muttered oath, Nate did the same, looking aggrieved that he hadn't thought of it first.

"Don't think it protective only o' ye when I suggest we hurry back t' th' Caravanserai," he muttered, jerking his thumb at the massive sandstone outpost. "Fer myself, I don't care t' linger here another moment."

"Nor I," put in the four fairies with one voice.

"It would serve a double purpose to pack the caravan and seek out Aleksandr," Waschbär reminded Bertie. "The Innamorati did want to hire you, good Mistress of Revels, to continue work on their Brand-New Play."

Bertie glanced from the Caravanserai to the much closer and yet-threatening shoreline. "I'm not sure the amphitheater is far enough from the ocean for my taste, but it's better than no plan at all."

Never mind that it saves me from returning to the Théâtre Illuminata—and Ophelia—without the Scrimshander.

Decision made, Bertie began the foot-sucking slog back to the caravan. Resting upon the glittering white sands of the beach, painted wheels and wooden slats looked decidedly out of place. With practiced hands, Ariel tended to the needs, such as they were, of the mechanical horses. Their dull silver flanks gleamed pewter and mercury in the midday light, their amber eyes the same glowing yellow as the sun. Cobweb, Mustardseed, and Moth shoved the detritus from the morning meal between the flowered cotton curtains that covered the caravan's windows despite Peaseblossom's repeated protests that they'd just have to clean it out later. Nate scattered the blackened bits of wood that were the only evidence of their bonfire, but the stench of things-burning wouldn't quit Bertie's nostrils, and every turn of her head brought a fresh wave of acrid smoke.

"You make a particularly fetching chimney sweep, good Mistress," Waschbär noted in passing as he tossed bundles of food and boxes of medical supplies atop their gaily decorated conveyance.

"That bad, is it?" Bertie contemplated her sooty sleeves and could only venture to guess just how dirty her face must be.

"You could paint shadow puppets on the walls with your fingers." He paused in his rapid work to offer her a paw.

A bit puzzled by the gesture, she accepted his hand, only to find a damp handkerchief blossoming in her palm like a water lily. Bertie smiled at him with gratitude in between swipes at her forehead and cheeks until she saw him quiver with ill-suppressed laughter. "I'm just making it worse, aren't I?"

"You are that," came the cheerful confirmation. "Never fear, there are ablutions to be had within the Caravanserai's famed walls."

The sneak-thief's word was golden. Minutes later, the troupe drove the caravan back into the marketplace accompanied by rolling wheels and the tinkle of countless silver bells. Up close, the deceptively beige bricks that composed the walls sparkled with flecks of gold and silver and rose. The scents of unnamed and unknown spices mingled with onions, garlic, and baking breads, prompting the fairies to clamor for sustenance. Ignoring their pleas, Waschbär directed Ariel straight into the Water District, down a narrow roadway peppered with laundry services and bathhouses. In unseen underground rooms, furnaces heated massive copper boilers, their presence marked only by the smoke and steam they belched into the sky. The air here was sultry, damp, and redolent of Mrs. Edith's lavender water and starch. Bertie could feel her hair beginning to frizz as they approached a blue-tiled archway marked by an elaborately scrolled sign:

THERMAEPOLIS
BATHS OF ALL TEMPERATURES
STEAM ROOMS, MASSAGE
BEAUTY TREATMENTS COIFFURES
LADIES ONLY

"There you are," Waschbär said with a flourish when Ariel halted the caravan. "One luxurious bathing experience, as promised."

Though her grubbiness was surely something to behold, Bertie hesitated. Within the Water District, the murmured threats of the Sea Goddess echoed in every puddle. She would have made do with a pitcher and a washcloth, except the building that housed the Thermaepolis included a needle-sharp spire that stabbed at the sky.

Taller yet than a watchtower.

From which she could scan the beach for signs of Sedna's return and the skies for signs of her father. Jumping down from the caravan, Bertie landed on the cobblestones with a thump and a scowl.

The sneak-thief followed, but it was only to offer an unwelcome suggestion. "You might consider postponing your bath long enough to pay a visit to Serefina."

"The herb-seller?" Bertie specified, though she disliked using the misnomer. The woman was far more powerful than any mere apothecary.

Waschbär leaned in a bit and lowered his voice. "She might be able to offer some safeguard against the reappearance of the Sea Goddess."

"Yes, but at what price?" Before he could answer, Bertie changed the subject. "Would you also be so good as to take a message to Aleksandr that I'll be at his disposal within the hour? The rest of you ought to find suitable lodgings for ourselves and our gear in the meantime." She pried a coin off the Mistress of Revels's belt and handed it Nate. "That's for the hotel." She pulled off a second and slipped it into her tattered pocket. "And this is to buy a bit of peace and quiet."

"And soap," Mustardseed advised with a nose wrinkle.

Peaseblossom fretted. "Oughtn't I come with you? I'm a lady, too."

"That is true." Bertie tapped her shoulder in invitation, which the fairy hastened to accept as the caravan rattled down the street and disappeared around the first corner.

"How will we find the others when we're done?" Peaseblossom's frown had tripled until she could hardly see out of her squinched-up eyes.

"Easy," Bertie said, "we'll follow the scent of chaos and destruction."

Professional bathing turned out to be a most complicated process. Bertie was forced to abandon her clothes and possessions—scrimshaw included—in a locker. After she was scrubbed with a combination of sea salt and sugar to rid her of the worst of the ash and soot, the girls were escorted to the steam room. There they were thumped and walloped by someone Bertie inwardly dubbed Brunhild. Almost the exact moment she got accustomed to the pummeling, the beefy woman poured her into a soaking pool.

Disconcerted by the sudden buoyancy of the water, Bertie remembered her ulterior motive in visiting the bathhouse. "I was told you have a marvelous view from the central tower."

"Indeed." Brunhild paused near the door. "The salon is on the top floor. I shall see if there is a stylist available to see you, since you cannot intend to traipse about in public with hair like that."

The observation stung, not in the least because Bertie knew the sun and wind and rain of the previous week had done their worst to her black-and-purple coiffure. She swallowed further protests along with her pride. "My thanks."

Peaseblossom drifted along the surface of the water like a tiny, rose-tipped leaf. "You don't look the least bit relaxed."

"That's because I'm not." Microscopic bubbles clung to

Bertie's skin, each one containing a threat from the Sea Goddess; when they popped, they delivered jagged-edged images of dark water, of starfish fingers wrapped about Bertie's throat, of seaweed hair dragging her down, down, down. "I think I should stick to showers for the time being." Vaulting out of the bath, she hastened under the bracing-cold water spurting from recessed wall fountains and rinsed off with much sputtering and cursing.

Brunhild pursed her lips upon her return, no doubt displeased to find Bertie sitting upon a bench nestled in her robe, teeth chattering but her body mercifully clean. "This way, please. Your stylist is ready."

Pausing only to gather up the extra yards of terry cloth as though they were the skirts of a silk ball gown, Bertie followed their unusual chaperone up a circular staircase. Narrow, open windows punctuated the curving wall at regular intervals, allowing glimpses of the place where earth met water with a lingering kiss. A distant gull cry gave Bertie pause, and she halted midstep.

Dad.

Leaning out the nearest window, she considered the vast expanse of beach. Sand in the metallic shades of coveted coins composed drifts and dunes, wending between palm trees and tufts of pampas grass in fat, serpentine coils. Low-lying fog teased its way ever closer, obscuring the roiling waves that broke on the shore near the White

Cliffs. Putting one knee on the sill, Bertie extended her hand, reaching for the open air. . . .

The attendant reacted with shock to such unorthodox behavior. "Merciful heavens, come down from there before you fall," she ordered with a voice like a trumpet blast.

I'm being ridiculous. That wasn't him. He's off in search of her.

Sedna, who even now threatened to return to corporeal form. Sedna, who would see Bertie dead without so much as batting a salt-spangled eyelash. That the Scrimshander would make such a decision so easily, so *blindly,* filled Bertie with heartache that soon transmogrified into fury. Through a red haze, she scanned the beach, cheeks burning, but saw no sign at all of the Sea Goddess.

To hell with her and to hell with the Scrimshander since he's chosen her.

Scrambling down from her perch, Bertie was firm in her resolve to dye her hair the most eye-blinding shade of magenta there ever was, reasoning that the salon was nearer than a tattoo parlor and even the most horrifying hair color would grow out with time, whereas ink stippled into her skin would be a permanent reminder of this failed day. Seething, she threaded her way through the salon's gracious appointments, over thickly woven rugs, and past potted trees coaxed to bear lemons and limes to fruition even indoors. Once ensconced in a swivel chair, she paged through the vivid hair samples and tried not to note the way the warm hues prophetically gave way to Jade Pendant, Wicked Green, Storm-Tossed Teal, and Midnight Sky.

Turning to Peaseblossom, Bertie mustered a half-hearted smile. "Could you go locate the moderately perturbed pirate, possibly haunting the bathhouse doorstep, and tell him I'll be a little longer than expected? If he hasn't seen to accommodations yet, he should before night-fall. And let Aleksandr know I'll be late as well."

"Of course!" Peaseblossom paused only to give her a cheeky grin. "The tall pirate, yes? Wearing a lot of leather and probably a scowl?"

"That would be the one. Watch out for errant sword swipes." Bertie turned back and nodded to the pixie-like woman with cropped tufts like purple porcupine quills. "Surprise me."

The colorist's eyes widened. "Do you mean to say I should choose on your behalf?"

"I do," Bertie said. "Something extraordinary. The sort of hue that would give one's father a heart attack."

The colorist sorted through the rainbow tresses. "You'd look lovely with Hammered Gold—"

"Cinnamon Stick," cried a second.

"Burning Ember."

As the minutes slid past her like pearls on a knotted string, Bertie did not demur when the attendants offered

sustenance in the form of dewy slices of melon, ruby straw-
berries in cream, and honeyed pastries served with strong
coffee. She occupied her mouth with the sweets and her
eyes with an inky broadsheet, one regaling all the daily
news of the Caravanserai: arrivals, departures, performance
schedules of the various itinerant minstrels, and the decla-
ration that the Innamorati would be opening a Brand-
New Play in the amphitheater in three days' time.

Everything, however, deferred to the headlining news
that Her Gracious Majesty the Queen would be holding a
massive celebration as part of her upcoming birthday fes-
tivities. Many of the salon's patrons had been summoned
to join the Court, it seemed, either as visiting dignitaries
or as performers. Theatrical instinct suggested the best
of the marketplace entertainment surrounded Bertie:
diamond-dancers, now fully clothed, getting new crystals
glued to their finger- and toenails; a snake tamer sitting
under one of the hair dryers; several sword-balancing belly
dancers holding court in the corner. Listening to their excited chatter transported Bertie back through time and
space to the Ladies' Chorus dressing room, only now she
wasn't a troublesome child underfoot and in the way.

"Something to drink?" A servitor offered her water
laced with sunshine slices of lemon.

Accepting, Bertie realized seconds later that liquid

malevolence slicked the surface of the crystal goblet. The glass fell from her hand and shattered on the floor. As Bertie's apologies stuck in a desert-parched throat, the attendants hastened to reassure her it was no trouble at all.

There was no escaping Sedna, even here in Rapunzel's tower, and the urge to flee washed over Bertie in a cold moment of panic. "I have to go—"

Gathering her robe about her, she was immediately stalled by the entrance of a messenger.

"Beatrice Shakespeare Smith?" The girl's braids hung alongside her face like tiny brown silk tassels.

It would hardly be polite to knock the child down the stairs in her haste, so Bertie forced herself to take a deep breath. "Yes?"

"For you." The girl handed over a rectangular box with an impish grin and half a curtsy before bolting back down the stairs at double speed.

Tempted to give chase, Bertie jerked at the parcel's strings and was left to gape at the shimmering chiffon garment and a pair of matching slippers. "Who would send me a dress?"

"Such handiwork is superlative, even for the Caravanserai dressmakers," the nearest stylist observed around the hairpins between her pursed lips.

Some instinct sent Bertie's hand rummaging for a

label. Sure enough, a rectangle of embroidered muslin, hand-sewn into the lining, answered her question:

Moonlight Gown for a Prima Donna Designed by Valentijn for the Innamorati

"The Keeper of the Costumes must have spies every-where to know I'm in need of new attire." Bertie ran a trembling hand over the intricate beading, sewn in swirls and bursts of pale blue and pearl. "And just who does he think he is calling a prima donna, I'd like to know!"

"Never mind that. It's perfection! You must change into it at once." With much clucking and fussing, the at-tendants hustled her behind a silk folding screen, handing over the dainty undergarments nestled in the tissue paper, adjusting the laces on the gown, and adding the silver slip-pers that had accompanied it.

Bertie acquiesced, thinking it faster than fielding their arguments and having to retrieve her ruined clothes from the locker downstairs. Firm in her resolve to perform the speediest quick-change in history, it was only when they escorted her to the trifold mirror that she caught sight of herself and nearly choked. "My hair!"

"Isn't it gorgeous?" the shortest attendant squeaked, overcome by the effect. "It's called Arctic Tempest."

Bertie opened her mouth to respond and found herself entirely deprived of words for once. "It's . . . silver," she finally managed.

The colorist nodded. "And look at the movement it gets." With gentle fingers, she shifted Bertie's hair so that it lifted and resettled around her shoulders, doubly reminiscent of Ariel's wind-tossed tresses. "Extraordinary, is it not?"

"That's the only word for it." Looking at her reflection, Bertie realized just who had thought her a "prima donna," who had met with the Keeper of the Costumes and procured such a dress. Without actually being indecent, the skirts were sheer, the bodice fitted, and the neckline low enough to invite contemplation of the freckles dusting her skin; it was the sort of dress a woman would wear to meet someone significant, with every bead issuing an invitation for a lingering look. Her pulse kicked in her throat as she wondered just what Ariel wanted from her this night and what her answer would be when he asked it of her.

If Sedna gave her a chance to answer at all, that is.

CHAPTER THREE

Thou Shalt Have the Air of Freedom

The moment she stepped foot out of the bathhouse, Bertie set off down the nearest alley at a run and entered a scene crowded with extras: women carrying baskets upon their heads; barefoot children running home to their suppers. Forced to weave her way among them, she glanced up at a sky-ceiling increasingly obscured by wrought-iron balconies, brilliant potted plants, and recently aired rugs. The walls on either side of her narrowed. The sun dipped a degree lower, and what had been bathed in the dusky pink of early evening darkened as though someone had cued the light booth.

Bertie turned a corner and found herself quite alone, at a dead end painted with shadows. Repressing a shudder, she retraced her steps, heels clicking against the cobblestones.

The weight of her beaded skirts shifted, recalling another time, another place, another alley, another dance, except the roses blooming on the walls here were white and instead of Cobalt Flame, her hair was this ridiculous shade of—

"Silver," Ariel said by way of greeting as he emerged from a side street. White butterflies took to the night air, the whisper of their wings hinting at unborn secrets. Soft violin music and guitar song drifted out a nearby window.

Bertie held her breath, knowing it would be only moments before a bandoneón joined them. "It's Arctic Tempest, and it wasn't my idea." But she saw that there was no way to convince him it hadn't been her choice or destiny or some meddling hand of Fate that delivered her to him looking this way.

"'Brandish your crystal tresses in the sky.'" Ariel smiled and offered her a bouquet. The flowers gave off the scent of a forgotten garden at dusk, of lovers meeting in secret under an arbor, of kisses stolen in the half light.

"We don't have time for Victorian niceties—" Bertie started to explain, but Ariel interrupted by pressing his lips to hers. The kiss deepened immediately, his arms encircling her waist as he pulled her against his chest. Fireworks exploded in Bertie's mind, her heart, her gut, burning up every speck of rhyme and reason. Amber sparks she imagined rather than saw sizzled on the cobblestones as Ariel threaded his hands through her newly silvered hair.

"Fire!" someone above them shouted.

Yes, she was on fire, burning like a Roman candle, her head spinning like a Catherine wheel. . . .

"Fire!" the voice screamed again. "Someone call the brigade!"

Another shower of sparks cascaded over Bertie, falling from the balcony overhead. A knotted rug burned merrily, its fringes already reduced to frizzled embers. She stared at it, appalled.

"Tell me I didn't do that."

Ariel's answering laughter summoned the joyous winds, the zephyrs and the mistrals, as he drew her further down the alley, away from the influx of shouting homeowners. "Most likely someone grew careless with a candle or their evening cigar."

"Or the fire got a taste of me in the Aerie, and it's giving chase—"

Overhead, a shrieking housewife tossed a pitcher of dishwater over the flames, spattering the cobblestones below. Occupants of nearby apartments cast the contents of their buckets and basins, provoking hisses and snarls from the fire. Soon, rivulets of water snaked their way between the cobblestones toward Ariel and Bertie.

She took a step back. As though encouraged by her

fear, the water's progress hastened, gathering speed and strength until it oozed about her feet, tracing the tips of her silver slippers with dirty fingers, licking at the fabric with eager, ash-coated tongues. The moment the damp seeped in far enough to make contact with her toes, Bertie heard the faintest of salt-tinged whispers:

"I will destroy everything you love."

Whirling about, Bertie picked up her skirts and ran. The sound of her heels striking the street matched the panicked heartbeat thudding in her ears. Her shoulder slammed into a passerby. He shouted deep blue epithets at her back, but still she didn't slow.

"Bertie!" Ariel called after her.

When she didn't turn to heed him, a sudden gust of wind signaled his pursuit. It was like being caught in a hurricane, her hair and skirts whipped into a frothing frenzy. Then his arms caught her, one about the waist, the other under her knees, and he launched them into the sky.

"I gather something disturbed you?"

As they soared over the Caravanserai, Bertie allowed her arms to slip about him. She tucked her face into the crook of his neck and kicked off her water-dampened slippers, belatedly realizing that at some point Ariel would land. But she told herself she'd rather run barefoot over broken glass and flaming hot coals than wear anything Sedna had touched.

At last she spoke, her lips grazing his skin. "She's getting stronger, Ariel."

"The Sea Goddess?" When Bertie only nodded, his grip upon her tightened. "If you're determined to quit this place, allow me to carry us away to the nearest fairy-tale castle or ancient stone city or temple devoted to the worship of cupcakes."

"A cupcake temple?" Her chest still tight with anxiety, Bertie forced herself to imagine it: bricks of pound cake mortared with buttercream and chocolate ganache, torches like striped birthday candles set into the walls, pilgrims upon the Path of Delectable Righteousness delivering daily tributes of almond paste and raspberry filling. . . .

"If there isn't one already, we could build one," Ariel said, only half teasing until the moment clouds covered the moon and his eyes went dark. "We'll find paradise together, whatever form that might take."

What is it you want? the voices in her heart of hearts demanded, and she knew at least part of the answer.

To quit this place, to let the starshine and blessedly cold night air wash away my every care and trouble, freezing my fears and worries into diamonds I can fling away with both hands.

Inexorable gravity pressed down upon her chest, silent and suffocating.

If this is how Ariel feels all the time, I don't know how he stands it.

Ariel saw the hairline crack in her resolve and set about

breaking her completely by placing his mouth very near her skin when next he spoke. "A whirlwind tour, I think, with each day starting in a different city, you wearing a different silk dress, tasting food the likes of which you cannot even imagine and learning how to weave your word-spells in all the world's languages."

"What about Peaseblossom and the boys?" Bertie only managed the protest with great reluctance, her tongue cleaved to the roof of her mouth as though affixed by sticky toffee candy. "Waschbär?" Her voice dropped a notch when she added, "And Nate? Would you have me just abandon them?"

A curious expression twisted his face into something of a mask. "Never, in all the years that I've known you, have I thought of you as the responsible one, Bertie, so why start now?"

Rather than answer the question—for which she could summon no good rejoinder—Bertie whispered, "Put us down, Ariel."

It came as something of a surprise that the air elemental immediately obeyed, altering his course only slightly to land upon a sand-scattered rooftop. When Bertie found that her legs wobbled more than a dish of blancmange, he held her arm most solicitously until she gathered both her strength and her bearings. Without slippers, her bare feet managed to locate every bit of broken shell and rough tile as she made her way to the low balustrade that encircled the roof. Over the course of their short flight, they'd reached the center of the Caravanserai. The sigil-etched entrance portal winked at them in the distance, and torchlight marked the twisted path that led away from the outer wall, away from the White Cliffs, away from the goddess-haunted waters seeping in from the beach. When a flock of birds took wing, their silhouettes were outlined against the moon.

Bertie tracked their upward journey, her gaze coming to rest on the night sky. Without warning, fresh disappointment settled in her throat, thick and cloying. "He's not coming back, is he?"

"Your father?" The hesitation in Ariel's words came as something of a surprise. "I . . . don't know."

Bertie swayed a bit, unconsciously mimicking the velvet-draped elephants walking trunk to tail on the road just below them. When she spoke, she couldn't keep the pleading note out of her voice, hard as she tried. "You know every breath of wind that stirs as a friend, Ariel. Couldn't you search him out for me? Deliver a message?"

His slow exhalation was like a hand skimming over her bare arm. "As the Mistress of Revels commands, but I would beg one favor first."

"And that would be?"

"I want you to tell me you love me."

Had he betrayed a glimmer of amusement, some hint he was teasing her, Bertie would have laughed and welcomed the release of tension, but there was nothing in his expression to suggest he spoke in jest. "Why would you ask for such a thing?"

Ariel deftly edged around the question, around her. "We both know it to be true."

"I don't deny that it's true," she said, though the admission was made treacle slow. "I just wonder why the words mean so very much to you all of a sudden."

"Indulge a poor fool who would have an even playing field before the scenery shifts about him again."

Bertie wished she could employ a cavalier delivery that would indicate he was a ridiculous boy for demanding such a thing of her, but the words came only with great reluctance, as though she pulled stitches from some part of her soul to give them over to him. "I love you."

The three words separated them for an infinite moment, then Ariel stepped forward. He stood close enough that Bertie's curls discharged blue-white static electricity every time they made contact with the longest tendrils of his own silver hair. A new flavor of panic coated the back of her throat when she saw the haunted look in his eyes.

"I thought there would be more to it than this," he finally said.

Frost settled on Bertie's bare shoulders and upturned

face, and she almost welcomed the cold as her cheeks went numb. "More to it than what?"

Tiny bits of wind rushed over Ariel's shoulders, carrying incoming fog that swirled about him to create the illusion of wings before the imagined feathers were dispersed. "Have you ever seen a falcon, hooded and jessed for the hunt?"

Bertie's lips were so dry that she thought they might crack and bleed when she answered, "No."

"You wear a light glove, milady, but you've no need of straps to bind. It's love that tethers me to you." He tilted his head back; though the muscles in his throat worked, he couldn't seem to swallow, and his next words were hoarse. "Do you have any idea how much it pains me to remain at your side when my soul longs to be airborne?"

The question hit her as hard as a physical blow to the middle. The cravings in her heart of hearts were probably nothing at all compared to what he must endure every moment he spent upon the ground . . . at her side . . . by choice. "A mirror reflection only of what you feel, but I think I can imagine it."

Ariel looked at her then, instead of the sky, instead of the horizon that surely beckoned to him. "Out of a thousand different winds, I think I can resist nine hundred and ninety-nine of them."

Now she was the one unable to swallow. "And the last one?"

"That one wrenches the beating heart from my chest, the blood from my veins, the marrow from my bones." Grasping her hand, he brought it up to his face and rubbed it against his cheek. Pain radiated from his pale skin, from his eyes, from his lips when they grazed her knuckles. "You've two birds to do your bidding, my fair huntress, but I want you to choose me, to love me above all others, to make the pain in my soul worthwhile . . . or I would be free of you."

The very idea that he would leave caused electrical charges to pop and snap in a halo around her head. Thinking she might conjure lightning bolts for earrings at any second and frizzle them both to a crisp, Bertie forced her mind to go carefully blank. The expression she summoned was deceptively serene as she imagined the death masks of Sedna's Guardians, felt the cool glass slide into place over her features. "I don't want you to be in pain. The next time that one in a thousand winds calls to you, heed it if you must, and come back if you desire it."

Ariel went similarly still, all winds disappearing into some unseen, dark place inside him. His eyes were a glassy black, though not with anger. Bertie had witnessed Ariel's temper before, strong enough to shatter glass, or subtle with a cutting edge; this was more frightening than that. "The illusion of freedom is just another sort of prison—"

But whatever else he might have said, the words were

silenced by the sudden and disconcerting appearance of Waschbär at Bertie's elbow. A droplet of sweat—a portent most ominous—trickled down the side of the sneak-thief's whisker-bristled face.

"I apologize for interrupting, but you're wanted in the main square," he said, very nearly out of breath. "The Queen has sent a messenger for you."

CHAPTER FOUR

Another Spur to My Departure

"Come!" Waschbär continued, infecting both of them with his urgency. "Nate and the others are waiting in the central marketplace!"

Bertie trailed him down the nearest set of stairs, casting a desperate glance over her shoulder to see if Ariel followed, but the air elemental had turned away, his hands clenched and shoulders hunched.

Is tonight the night he'll scent that one-in-a-thousand wind and leave for good?

She would have turned back to ask, but the sneak-thief had a death grip upon her elbow and gave every indication he would toss her bodily over his shoulder if she resisted. Dozens of childhood memories surfaced of the Stage Manager hauling her off to the Theater Manager's Office while uttering no end of dire threats and recriminations, usually warranted. Dread and guilt formed a sickly ball in her middle as Bertie wondered what sort of crime she might have inadvertently committed.

"What does the Queen's Messenger want with me?" she finally demanded.

"A better question is what Her Gracious Majesty wants with you." Reaching the street, Waschbär avoided all the lesser-trafficked walkways in favor of a main thoroughfare, clogged though it was with late-night diners, eager merchants, and moonlit performance artists.

"That's no reason to be nervous," Bertie said through clenched teeth when a bit of rough stone scraped the bottom of her bare foot. "Plenty of royalty graced the seats at the theater. One queen can't be that different from the others I've met."

Waschbär stopped then, only to turn on her, a near snarl raising one corner of his mouth. "Pah! Those queens were mere shadows of Her Gracious Majesty, reflections cast by mirror and glass and water."

"It's not like I could know that!" Wholly taken aback by his unusual behavior, Bertie drew herself up to her fullest height and gave him the sternest of her Mistress of Revels expressions, which, considering the knocking of her knees, wasn't as impressive as it might have been. Still, this queen wasn't the only one who could manage imperious behavior with little notice. "And you won't speak to me in that tone again if you value your place in the troupe. Now kindly remove your hand from my person."

He obeyed, albeit with visible reluctance. "We oughtn't keep her messenger waiting." Another turn, and snapping banners overhead announced their arrival at the innermost heart of the Caravanserai.

"Understood, but neither will I be dragged into the marketplace like a criminal before the magistrate." Bertie took a moment to smooth down her dress and regret her castaway shoes; bare feet certainly did suggest she was more pickpocket than playwright!

Nudging aside a small clot of traders haggling over the price of a horse and sidestepping a woman carrying a tray of steaming meat pies, Nate appeared before the two of them. "I've been lookin' everywhere fer ye." Despite his words, he didn't look all that happy to see her. "What ha'e ye done t' yer head?"

"Silver wasn't my choice. I made the mistake of giving the colorist carte blanche to do as she liked."

He took her by the arm; though the gesture was a gentle one, the roughened patches of skin on his palms still caught the fine threads of the moonlight dress as they continued through the marketplace.

"Say something," Bertie demanded, unable to suffer the walk in silence.

"I've seen yer head blue an' black, pink an' red, an' everythin' in between, an' no color's ever given me pause before. It's like . . ." Though his steps didn't falter, Nate's voice did, either because he couldn't find the words to finish, or they were too terrible to voice aloud.

"Like I'm a stranger?" The thought terrified Bertie, opening a dark place in her stomach and her heart both.

"Worse."

The horrible feeling expanded, and her voice dropped another notch. "Like I'm the enemy?"

"Ariel's not my enemy, lass. I can call him by a lot o' names, but that wouldn't be one o' them."

"I think you *have* called him a lot of names over recent months." She meant it to sound lighthearted, to derail the serious turn the conversation had taken, but she didn't quite manage it.

"Ne'er mind him now, we ha'e enough t' deal wi' as it is." Reaching the edge of an enormous crowd, Nate began clearing a path for her.

Bertie followed him, hardly able to believe the number of people crammed into the central square. The usual dance of buying, selling, and coaxing coins from pockets had stilled, an eerie quiet settling over the throng as she approached. A bewigged courier, dressed in immaculate white and gold livery, waited at the decorative fountain. A row of similarly attired personages stood behind him, their gazes fixed upon her most disconcertingly.

Oblivious to the solemnity of the occasion, the fairies arrived on the scene carrying a large skewer of meat between them and arguing over the top of their charred prize.

"Don't you blame me for this," Peaseblossom was saying, "I wanted deep-fried yogurt doughnuts with jam!"

"But I *told* him I didn't want sauce on my bit."

"It's just the smallest helping!"

"Yeah, of hellfire-hot, melt-your-mouth sauce! I'll be farting flames for a week—" Here, Cobweb broke off his diatribe, nose and eyes streaming, to contemplate Bertie. "Good grief, you look just like Ariel!"

"Not now!" She issued the command between clenched teeth as she joined Nate at the front of the crowd.

Waschbär surprised them all by giving the Messenger a most courtly bow, remaining folded in half while he spoke to the man's knees. "Permit me the grand and glorious honor of announcing you are in the presence of Beatrice Shakespeare Smith, Mistress of Revels, Emissary of the Théâtre Illuminata."

The Messenger matched the sneak-thief's bow, inch for inch. Straightening, he lifted a polished brass trumpet to his lips and issued a precise blast of air and noise directly in Bertie's face. She only heard his next words through the tinny ringing in her ears.

"From Her Gracious Majesty the Queen!" The courier extended a thick parchment envelope, sealed with a great deal of wax bearing the royal crest and satin ribbon embroidered with the same.

Nate leaned in to stage-whisper, "I hope 'tisn't an invitation fer a game o' croquet, because ye can't play wi'out cheatin'."

"I highly doubt it." The Mistress of Revels received missives from royalty all the time, so it must have been Bertie's hands doing the shaking when she broke the seal on the parchment. She tilted it toward the irregular torchlight to make out the gilt-engraved words.

Her Gracious Majesty
hereby requests the presence of
and a performance by
Beatrice Shakespeare Smith & Company
at her Birthday Festival,
the Grand Occasion commencing Saturday

"For the Queen's pleasure," the courier added, righting his hairpiece, "she has invited performers and minstrels from the four corners of her lands."

"To the Distant Castle?" Even though it took him

three tries to read the invitation over her shoulder, Mustardseed sounded awed.

Bertie peered at him. "The what?"

"The Distant Castle." When she didn't respond, the fairy fisted his hands on his hips. "It was in *your* play . . . *How Bertie Came to the Theater.*"

Before he even finished speaking, the memory already prickled on the back of her throat.

VERENA

I am the Mistress of Revels, Rhymer, Singer, and Teller of Tales on my way to a distant castle to perform for the Royal Family.

Bertie had composed the line as part of her script, and then, dressed as the Mistress of Revels, she'd repeated the words to a farmwife without thinking twice about them, without wondering at their meaning.

Script in haste, repent at leisure, it seems.

"Her stronghold sits at the very center of this great country," the courier said, "and the terrain is easily enough traveled in a few days' time, but you should consider an immediate departure."

On the very long list of Things She Needed to Do Immediately, Bertie had not counted among them dropping everything to travel to the Queen's stronghold. "I fear I have nothing worthy of performing before Her Gracious Majesty. This invitation would be better delivered to Aleksandr and the Innamorati."

"They have already received their summons as well as permission for more rehearsal time," the Messenger said with a disapproving twitch, though whether it was the circus troupe or their need for an extension that displeased him, Bertie could not be certain. "In any case, the Queen was most specific that the invitation be delivered to you."

Bertie could feel the quicksand gathering about her feet that began with an invitation and ended with her clapped in chains in a drippy-dank dungeon for offending Her Gracious Majesty with a Performance Most Heinous. "But—"

"You would be wise to realize that you cannot gainsay Her Gracious Majesty's desires or her timing." The Messenger stowed his trumpet in some unseen pocket.

"Of course!" Peaseblossom said with a squeak. "We wouldn't like to insult the Queen by arriving late!"

"What kind of insulted are we talking about? Lock us in the tower insulted? Hang us by our thumbnails insulted?" It wasn't immediately clear from Moth's tone if he were excited by or fearful of such a notion.

Mustardseed felt compelled to contribute. "Chop-off-our-heads insulted?"

"Executions are rare this time of year"—the Messenger cleared his throat before adding—"but the Queen has made it quite clear that the gates will be locked two days hence."

"Why would she do that," Bertie wanted to know, "if she wants us there so very badly?"

"Deadlines are a tradition," the Messenger deigned to answer. "'The first morning after marriage' and midnight carriages turned back into pumpkins. The Queen has chosen tea-time for hers. Performers arriving late will be denied both the pleasure of her patronage and the chance to win a boon to be bestowed upon the artist or troupe with the most pleasing performance."

Waschbär stiffened as though a cupid dart had struck him in the posterior. "What sort of boon?"

"The sort that has not been granted for countless years." The Messenger gave the sneak-thief a knowing sort of look.

"I don't really fancy myself a duchess," Bertie started to say, but the laugh that had been building in the back of her throat turned to sand the moment Waschbär flashed her a fierce smile.

"He is not speaking of a paper title, make no mistake. . . . He means a wish-come-true." When Bertie started to make a disbelieving noise, he gave her arm a subtle shake. "Think upon the possibilities of such a gift."

"A wish-come-true?" Realization scrambled up Bertie's spine and hit her in the back of the head with a big, rubber mallet. "And if she chooses our performance, the wishing of it would be ours?"

"To do with what you will." Waschbär's words tripped over themselves in their haste to exit his mouth. "With a mere thought, you could summon all the gold and jewels in the realm, a castle of your own—"

My family reunited. The happily ever after I can't manage to write.

Bertie dared not utter the longing aloud; it was like a birthday-candle wish that, once vocalized, might never come true.

Cobweb spared her from saying anything by crowing, "So it's like winning a wish from a genie in a bottle!"

"No one better expect me to rub an old lamp," Mustardseed muttered. "Mr. Hastings tricked me into polishing most of the brass in the Properties Department once, using that line."

"You're missing the point!" Moth cavorted in the air nearest Bertie's left ear. "We could make it rain cupcakes from the sky! Raspberry-jam pies would grow on trees, and chocolate rabbits would poop chocolate buttons!"

"Bertie can do all that without using a wish-come-true," Peaseblossom said. "Never mind we don't need you chasing after rabbits for their droppings!"

It was true; all Bertie required was a carefully written sentence or two to conjure anything she liked.

I never thought of writing a wish-come-true.

She pulled the silk-wrapped journal from Waschbär's pack, but the sneak-thief wouldn't be pickpocketed.

"This is neither the time nor the place for such magics," he cautioned.

A double-edged truth: Not only would she make a spectacle of herself before the Queen's emissary, but an ill-chosen word could inadvertently set her friends on fire—*again*—or create a Harrowing Journey they'd be forced to undertake.

"I must make haste. I have delayed the Queen's business too long." The Messenger proffered a gold-hinged box of modest size and significant weight. Nestled inside like eggs in the velvet lining of a very odd nest sat four pairs of gold-tooled binoculars; further examination revealed another four pairs, rendered in miniature, the perfect size for the fairies. "Glasses for you and the members of your party, good Mistress of Revels. You'll need them to find your way."

"Of course," Bertie said, trying to resign herself to the unexpected journey. "Magic spectacles are commonplace on a venture such as this."

"We need t' leave right away, if ye don't want t' break th' horses t' get there," Nate said.

A preparatory checklist clattered into place inside Bertie's head, lengthening by the moment and a welcome diversion from renewed concern about Ariel. She couldn't help but recall how deftly he'd handled both horses and wagon during the previous leg of their journey; traitorous eyes skimmed the sky as she wondered if he'd left without saying farewell. "Nate, where did you park the caravan?"

"Th' Performers' Alcove next t' th' amphitheater."

Bertie had seen it in passing, just inside the Caravanserai's inner wall, the one separating the giant stone structure from the shoreline and a brisk walk of at least thirty minutes. Glancing down at her bare feet, she scowled mightily, then set off, carefully watching for broken glass and anything else that might injure or maim.

"D'ye want me t' carry ye?"

"I'll be fine."

"What happened t' yer shoes?"

"Ruined by salt water. We were right. . . . Sedna is already coalescing."

The fairies squeaked and clutched one another. Nate sucked in a breath as though she'd punched him.

"Did ye see her?"

"Only the water, but I heard several whispered threats."

"All th' more reason t' clear out o' here." He snagged the shoulder of a passing rickshaw driver, nearly unseating the poor fellow. With an efficient toss, he put Bertie inside and clambered in after her, giving directions as she leaned out and issued orders of her own.

"Waschbär, find Aleksandr, please? Tell him what's happened and that we leave within the hour."

"It will be done with all due haste, I assure you! There's a wish-come-true to win!" The sneak-thief ducked into the crowd and was out of sight in seconds.

Bertie turned to her fairy companions. "Peaseblossom, you need to go back to the bathhouse and collect my things. Take a coin from the Mistress of Revels's belt and buy provisions. The responsibility for the next week's meals in is your hands, and that means food groups other than *sugar, sugar,* and *yet more sugar.* Is that understood?"

"Aye, Captain!" As they departed, Peaseblossom and the boys started making plans to gather the necessary supplies, which included chocolate-dipped caramel marshmallow pillows, which might or might not be slept upon.

The rickshaw lurched forward as Nate posed a question that was a different sort of sticky. "Where's Ariel?"

"When last I saw him, he was trying to decide whether or not to remain with the troupe." Their cramped conveyance swung around a sudden corner, throwing Bertie against her companion's broad chest.

"Oh, aye?" Only two words, softly spoken into her hair, but Nate's expression said far more.

Struggling to right herself, Bertie tried to sound authoritative, dignified, anything other than equal parts fearful and harassed. "I wouldn't have anyone remain who doesn't wish to be here."

In answer to her unspoken question, he nodded. "When we get to the Performers' Alcove, I'll see t' th' packing an' th' caravan. We'll be able t' depart wi'in th' hour."

"That's good to hear."

They spent the rest of their mercifully brief trip in silence, each keeping their own counsel as wooden wheels clattered over the cobblestones. The driver braked to a sudden but welcome stop between two massive stone columns, and Nate removed his shoes to extract the copper pennies long ago placed in each of the toes for luck. Just beyond the archway, the caravan sat bathed in soft amber light that slanted over the cart, the horses . . .

And the Scrimshander. Standing stiff and silent, he resembled a creature out of the Innamorati's new play, the black glint of his gaze and the sharp angles of his arms and legs more bird than human tonight. His thickly muscled chest heaved under a thin cotton shirt; the awkward way it draped his shoulders and the shortness of the sleeves indicated he most likely pulled it off an untended laundry line.

Hope surged through Bertie's chest as though the gold chain of blood and bone yet connected them, tugging her toward him.

He changed his mind.

After a single step she halted.

Or he's come to say a final good-bye.

She didn't want to hear those words. Like a child, she wanted to clap her hands over her ears and flee. Years ago, she would have crawled under the main stage, into the dark and narrow place under the floorboards where she was safe in her solitude. She could sit, arms wrapped about her knees and mouth filled to bulging with purloined butter-toffee candies and hazelnut chocolates. She could render the candy a bit salty with tears that dribbled, unheeded, down her nose and cheeks and chin. There, she was queen, with no one to gainsay her.

Just now she was neither child nor queen, neither Mistress of Revels nor wordsmith, only Bertie, very much afraid her father might abandon her yet again. Taking an inadvertent step forward, she shoved her trepidation down. "Nate, I'll be right back."

Nate's sharp glance immediately took in both her expression and the Scrimshander waiting for her within the alcove. "D'ye want me t' come wi' ye?"

"I'll be all right." She gave his arm an appreciative squeeze and turned, quickly bridging the space that separated her from her father. Deciding to be preemptive, Bertie opened the dialogue with "I owe you an apology."

The Scrimshander jerked with surprise, perhaps expecting remonstrations rather than olive branches. "You do?"

"I don't know if you've seen the Aerie? . . ."

"Yes, the Aerie. I did wonder what happened there—"

The hollow clang of an unseen bell interrupted the Scrimshander, and the alcove filled with members of the Innamorati taking a break from the evening rehearsal. Their laughter was raucous and their gestures flamboyant. The performers greeted Bertie with small cries and affected cheek kissing, creating as much noise as a flock of pigeons crowded about a bit of bread. The Scrimshander shuddered when careless passersby grazed his unseen wings. The moment a space cleared around Bertie, he stepped into it and dipped his mouth nearer her ear.

"Might we find somewhere more conducive to private conversation?" He indicated a restaurant across the street.

Bertie nodded, extricated herself from the crowd, and followed him. Everything she wanted to say clogged her throat at once as they crossed a small patio crowded with diners, their glittering evening attire tempered by the fire- and candlelight. Her father didn't pause at any of the tables, instead making his way up a long, narrow staircase, threading through servitors who moved in a saffron-tinted dance of shadows. Their whispers were no louder than the gentle breeze that brought the scent of salt to the verandah where the Scrimshander turned to her.

"Beatrice." Her name on his lips contained a lifetime of

defeat, echoed by the angle of his head and the slump of his powerful upper body.

Afraid of what he might say, Bertie leapt in with "We've been summoned to the Distant Castle to perform for Her Gracious Majesty. Though I wish it were not so, we must leave as soon we can make the caravan ready for the journey."

"Ah." He nodded, a jerking bob of the head that reminded her of a bird dipping down to drink.

Bertie took a step toward him and shuddered, wishing he'd picked some other venue, someplace more secluded, with a less breathtaking view than the gracious sandstone balcony overlooking the sea. She could hardly bring herself to go any nearer the water, father or no.

"I want you to come with us." The invitation gushed out of her mouth with the burble of warm froth that comes just before drowning. "We'll pay our respects to the Queen, and then we'll go back to the theater. I promised . . ." Desperate, Bertie managed to gasp in enough air to finish, "I promised Ophelia I would bring you back to her."

The Scrimshander reached out a hand and traced the shape of her face with rough fingertips, as though to memorize the look of her. Work-scarred, his skin told the story of his struggle to remain human in the face of his wild-bird instincts. The world around them—the ocean view, the scream of the gulls, a bit of distant laughter—filled Bertie's head so that she could hardly make out his next words.

"I will not go back to that place again."

They were softly uttered, featherlight, but disappointment lanced through Bertie like a glass blade cutting across her middle, the pain of it tempered only by the sudden and immediate flare of her anger.

"Why the hell not?" She shoved his hand away, feeling as though he'd slapped her. Indeed, the blood surged to her face like the sap in a spring-awakened tree, and she could feel red-rose livid spots of color blooming on her cheeks.

"Not that I won't, but that I cannot."

"Of course you can! All I ask for is a short journey, a single meeting, a few minutes' pleasantries with the woman you once loved!"

"Beatrice—" he tried to interrupt, but she shouted over the top of him.

"I've asked nothing at all of you for seventeen years!"

"Beatrice—"

"And the moment I make a request, you deny me—"

He broke in again to say, "I was just there, Beatrice. At your Théâtre Illuminata."

That brought her to a sputtering halt, the words of her tirade jerked out of her mouth like fish from the ocean. "You were?" The word-fish gaped, trying to suck in water, drowning in the air about them. "But when . . . how?"

He turned toward the sea, shoulders hunched. Fingertips curved into talons, they gripped the balcony railing and gouged it in ten places. "I flew hard soon after leaving you upon the beach, and the winds were in my favor. I left you a note, although perhaps you did not have the chance to read it before the destruction of the Aerie."

I have gone to fetch her.

"Not Sedna?" Bertie's tongue felt thick and rum addled, except she'd had nothing to drink. "I thought you meant you were going to be with her."

"With the Sea Goddess who nearly killed you?" Her father's face tightened, a sailor's knot tied in his forehead and others appearing in the corded muscles of his neck. "Do you really think me capable of such a thing?"

"Do I know you at all?" Her temper flared to match his. "You're no more than a stranger to me, and you gave me no word of farewell, only a cryptic note I might just as easily have overlooked as misunderstood!"

Her father twitched as though she'd ruffled every one of his feathers. "Then let me hasten to reassure you that I did not go to seek out Sedna." When he paused, the silence filled with everything that had ever gone unsaid between them, crowding Bertie back against the railing until the stone dug unmercifully into her back. She didn't think it possible, but his next words made her thankful it was there to hold her up. "I went to fetch your mother."

Bertie's head filled with a roar similar to the thunderous applause during a standing ovation. "Where is she?"

He shook his head. "There was nothing for me there."

And all that was hope and joy burst like a soap bubble against a needle. "Did you not seek her out? Wouldn't she come with you?" Bertie suddenly understood the terror of a winged creature, batting at the bars of a cage too small.

"Forgive me. . . . The words do not come naturally when I am so recently changed back into this form." One hand clutched his ill-fitting shirt, the other curled into a fist at his side. "The theater was closed to me—"

"Do you mean the doors were locked?" As Bertie watched him struggle to answer, she lost her grip on her patience. "Did you try the front door? The Stage Door? Breaking a window? You couldn't have tried much of anything if your only souvenir is a handful of sorry excuses."

The Scrimshander shook his head, radiating sadness and—worse yet—resignation. "You are blessed to be a daughter of the earth who is ever growing and ever changing, but creatures of the air are caught between freedom and our abilities to fight the headwinds. Sometimes we must bow our heads and permit the currents to take us where they will."

As though to prove his point, a sudden breeze swept over the balcony, bringing with it the scent of the sand, of the sea, of lands distant and beckoning.

Nearly overwhelmed by the desire to fling herself onto the back of the wind, to use the stars as stepping stones, to search out Ariel, to run away, Bertie wondered if she could manage it this time or if she'd only fall again. "I might be a daughter of the earth, but I am bird enough that if I fly again, I will fly where I will."

"What do you mean, fly *again*?" The Scrimshander twitched, shoulder blades immediately aquiver. As though to echo the question, the landing shuddered underfoot, accompanied by the terrible rumble of stone scraping stone. "Get back from the ledge!" He reached out and caught her by the arm, trying to pull her into the doorway as a wet wheezing noise filled the air: the death rattle of every mariner that ever drowned. "It's an earthquake!"

Bertie shook off her father's grip and stared at the beachfront, her arms breaking out in gooseflesh as her gaze traveled over the spot where waves should have crashed and foamed. The sand there glistened like a wet, open wound. Newly exposed rocks jutted into the sky, pointing accusing fingers at the moon. The silver suggestion of fish jerked and flopped in a *danse macabre*. "Where did the water go?"

Before he could croak a response, she had her answer. An immense wave was gathering just off the shallows and building to a seemingly impossible height, and a sudden gust of salt-mist brought with it a familiar noise, one that turned Bertie's very bones to ice: the triumphant laugh of the Sea Goddess, launching her attack.

CHAPTER FIVE

So Quick Bright Things Come to Confusion

"We must fly!" The Scrimshander launched himself into the air even as he grasped Bertie's wrist, towing her after him.

Skin once more prickling with the promise of feathers, Bertie gained a foothold upon the sky before her ability to fly was plucked from her mind like a weed from a rose garden. Her father scrabbled to hold on to her, but weighted down by all terror, she fell for the second time today, plummeting to the sand-strewn beach below. She cracked her head with such force on impact that only twinkling stars decorated the landscape. They recalled a sudden and vivid image of Bertie's Mother, the Player who'd taken part in *How Bertie Came to the Theater,* with the sequin-dance of light in her eyes. Then the mental slide show shifted to

Ophelia reaching for Bertie from the glow of the quick-change corner.

"Run, dear heart," her mother whispered, no more than a ghost as the blue light faded. "You must pick yourself up and run."

Before Bertie could obey, the tsunami overtook the beach. The ocean enveloped her in angry arms, shoving her against the Caravanserai's outer wall with a bone-cracking thud, twisting her about, heaving her up. As salty as the Dead Sea and twice as dark, every taste of the water on Bertie's lips was like a death kiss from Sedna.

Go back to hell, Bertie tried to command her, but the words were only bubbles as she flailed against her unseen foe. Hands outstretched, Bertie's fingers closed around what felt like the restaurant's balcony. Bits of kelp lashed about her ankles, a vicious undertow trying to drag her deep, but the Sea Goddess as yet had not the strength to persevere. Bertie clung to the sandstone like a limpet until the water began a reluctant retreat, trickles running off through open windows and pooling upon the beach.

Clambering over the railing and onto the verandah, Bertie landed hard upon her knees. Silver hair swirling about her shoulders, she spit water from her mouth and cleared it from her nose, coughing one moment and retching the next. As though in homage to Ophelia, she dripped as her mother usually did, with a gentle pitter-patter that mimicked rain or perhaps a leaky faucet. There was no doubting it now: Sedna was gathering her strength, and soon it wouldn't be a single wave, but a flood . . . the way she had filled the Aerie, trying to kill Ophelia. The way she'd filled the theater's auditorium to the ceiling before kidnapping Nate.

"Dad?" Bertie pulled herself up and scanned the beach for any signs of her father. A sliver of moon cut the edge of sky, but there was nothing of man or bird anywhere to be seen. With an oath, she turned and ran for the exit, noting that water had sluiced down the stairwell, extinguished torches, and broken the lanterns hanging upon the walls. The courtyard below was sloshing damp. Trays and crockery littered the ground. Dazed servitors picked themselves up off the sandstone floor. Frightened patrons huddled in groups, all of them muttering over the terrors of the last few minutes. Guilt stabbed Bertie in her vitals.

We have to leave before Sedna strikes again. I won't have anyone else hurt because of me.

Thankfully, the rest of the Caravanserai looked none the worse for the Sea Goddess's attack, though the news spread almost as fast as the water had. As a result, Bertie's damp appearance drew looks of varying curiosity and concern. A few called out questions, but she only waved her hand at them in passing, keeping her eyes lowered and her head tucked down, uncertain how much time she might have before the next attack.

Bertie had one stop to make before they departed, a stop that couldn't be skipped.

The braziers and torches set at regular intervals did wonders for the thin silk of the gown and her fantastically colored hair. Within minutes, Bertie was presentably dry, if wrinkled of dress and tousled of curls, much like a washrag wrung out and left dangling on the line. A chill wind whistled down the alleyway, tugging at the filmy overskirt of the moonlit dress. Fervently wishing Ariel's taste in clothing had leaned toward something warmer, she tasked herself to search the luggage for a thick, woolen cloak before they drove into another freak snowstorm.

Thoughts thus occupied, Bertie negotiated the Caravanserai's labyrinthine passages until she reached the desired stall where faded print curtains shifted to reveal the crystal facets of bottles and beakers.

"Come in," the herb-seller commanded when Bertie was still several feet away. One plant-stained hand adjusted the draperies, and Serefina came into view. Lavender steam unfurled from the spout of the brass kettle in her hand, though she turned around to pour its contents into a teacup rather than the faceted bottles she used for her various elixirs and potions. "It's a good thing you came directly here, my silver-haired fox, or I would have sent someone to fetch you."

"Did you want me for my charming companionship, or

have you heard about the freak tsunami that crashed into the Caravanserai's outermost wall?"

Rather than answering, Serefina handed Bertie a cup brimming with liquid the color of amethysts. "Drink this while it's hot."

Bertie sniffed at it cautiously and tried to identify the curious aroma, which smelled not of flowers nor herbs nor any sort of tea she'd ever consumed. That the surface of the brew was iridescent, like an oil slick on water, also gave her a moment's pause. "I'm afraid I haven't time for refreshments."

"You have time for this."

"What is it?"

"Nothing that will harm you." Serefina sat across from her, pouring her own cup and adding a spoonful of something Bertie knew probably wasn't sugar. The liquid fizzled up with foam the color of ripe blackberries, then settled back a darker purple than before. Serefina drank, her gaze an unspoken challenge to do the same. "It should help clear your head and give you a bit of much-needed strength."

"So you know about Sedna." The brew tasted of salt and bitterness, and Bertie couldn't help screwing her face up with displeasure. "That wave was her doing."

"Obviously." When the herb-seller took another sip, the deepest wrinkles around her eyes smoothed out and the lines about her mouth were suddenly less severe.

But surely it's a trick of the firelight?

Bertie resisted the urge to scrub at her own eyes like a tired child, instead taking another swallow. "Perhaps you also know about our summons to the Distant Castle? We have to pay our respects to Her Gracious Majesty and perform for her birthday celebration." She sipped again, pleasantly surprised when the not-tea mellowed into tones of vanilla and buttercream frosting. With the immediate future no longer tasting of panic and salt water, Bertie remembered the wish-come-true and her resolve sharpened once more to the point of a serrated cake knife.

"Queen summoned and Goddess pursued? You'll need to depart with all due haste." Serefina rose from the table, moving to the shelves to collect an assortment of bottles and packets. "Though of the two, I don't know which presents the greater threat. The use of 'Gracious' in Her Majesty's title can be something of a misnomer."

"Right now I'll take the trouble I don't know for the trouble I do, thanks." Though Bertie scanned the stall's interior shelves, she could not locate the crystal flask she'd filled with words in exchange for the return of the scrimshaw medallion. The corners of her mouth tightened at the memory of Ariel yanking it from her neck. But physical pain had scored his face when he spoke of being tethered to her. Although she might fault him for the theft, now she could empathize with his torment. "What are you looking for?"

Serefina's fingers moved over the shelves like skittering spiders. "You'll need a few things. Medicines for fevers, powders for headaches." She sorted through packets, their labels written in darkest red script on the parchment. "Do those fairies of yours ever suffer from stomach gripes?"

"They've intestines of cast iron." Given the perfect opening, Bertie leaned forward. "And their innards aren't the reason I came to see you. I need to trade for a bit of protection."

Hand hovering over a wax-paper envelope of seeds, Serefina nodded. "You're thinking you're too young to be a mother."

The herb-seller's words registered beyond their consonants and vowels, and Bertie blinked. "No! I mean, that's not why I came. I meant protection from Sedna."

Serefina made a noncommittal sort of noise in the back of her throat. "When a girl keeps the company of not one but two handsome lads, she ought to be prepared."

Bertie lifted her chin, though her cheeks burned as hot as the cooking fire. "I won't be like Ophelia, knowing motherhood before I even know myself."

"Nevertheless." Serefina selected an additional container from the shelves. "A spoonful of this every day will keep your belly as empty as a drunkard's flask at the end of a night's carousing." She took Bertie by the hand and placed the cool glass in her palm. "It will not, I regret to say, safeguard against anything else that may ail you as a result: broken hearts, broken trust, broken dreams."

Thinking the herb-seller might as well have handed her a bottle labeled UNTOLD IMPLICATIONS, Bertie set it on the table before her with all the careful consideration due a ticking bomb. "Understood. And what will you have for payment for the medicines?"

"I told you before I've no need of money." Serefina slid into a chair and narrowed her gaze. "Not for such trifles. Protection from the Sea Goddess is an entirely different matter, though."

"Then what would such protection cost me?"

"A mere token . . . something you shouldn't mind bartering. Something I already know is unwanted, by way of your own words."

Bertie twisted her fingers in the tablecloth's fringe. "An unwanted thing? That sounds like a business transaction for Waschbär."

"He is the expert in such matters, but not even his power of thievery can steal something that doesn't yet exist." Serefina's gaze slid from the flask upon the table to Bertie's midsection. "I want the child you'll never have."

The demand hit Bertie in precisely the place where a baby might grow. Several seconds passed before she was able to drag a ragged breath into her lungs, and only then did she manage to wheeze, "Absolutely not, and you're a horrible creature for even suggesting such a thing." She fell back from the table as though it was aflame, nearly knocking over the chair in her haste to escape.

The herb-seller's next words brought Bertie to a standstill. "Protection from the Sea Goddess is a costly magic indeed. And what is it to you, a faceless, nameless child?"

"I spent seventeen years wondering who I was and where I belonged!" The temper that rolled through Bertie surprised her, sending blood coursing to her cheeks until she thought her head might explode. "What makes you think I'd wish the same upon a child of my own?"

Serefina slapped her palm on the table. "I'm not asking for a true child, you silly wretch, but the idea of a child. The life-spark of a person who will never exist."

"How can there be such a thing?" Thinking over the proposition was like trying to gift wrap an octopus without putting it in a box first. "I am a playwright, a teller of tales whose words become reality. There's little difference between the idea of a child and the reality of one, if I so wish."

"This isn't about your word-magic! Someday you will choose one of your handsome lads over the other or someone else altogether or no one at all, and all those decisions will create children-that-will-never-be. The living almost never notice their tiny shades. They mistake their laughter for water or wind or rustling leaves, their tears for errant rainfall. . . ." Now Serefina's voice seemed to reach Bertie from a great distance, from a place where small, shimmering bodies moved with unhindered freedom like so many dust motes caught in a brilliant beam of light. "Too many years ago to count, I was one of those children, pulled from a place of never-was to this world of always-has-been. The time has come for me to train my replacement, and I must have another such child to take my place."

"Then you can jolly well get 'another such child' from someone else—"

Distant screams interrupted Bertie's refusal, replaced seconds later by the tidal shriek of an angry goddess. The sound of rushing water spurred Serefina into action. She leapt to her feet and slapped her hands against the stone wall.

"Oh, no, Sea Witch," she said, her shoulders trembling with tremendous effort, "now you are pushing things too far."

The water thundering down the alley dissipated the moment it passed the herb-seller's stall with only a gush of foam left to spatter the cotton curtain that served as a door. Whether that was due to Serefina's strength or Sedna's weakness, Bertie couldn't tell, but turning back the tide had greatly cost the herb-seller. Serefina sat down hard upon the stone hearth, the lines about her eyes and mouth back in evidence and deeper than before. Her skin was ashen and her breathing ragged.

Rushing to her side, Bertie grasped the other woman's hand; it felt like onion skin, papery and thin, but it was slicked with a thin sheen of sweat that glistened in the firelight. "You're feverish." She turned to the wall of crystal vials in desperation. "Tell me which of these will help."

"Not a one." Serefina leaned back against the wall, her iron key ring dragging against the floor with dead weight. "My elements are out of balance. The fire inside me grows stronger, fanned by the wind. The water dries, the earth erodes. I must have the child to take my place. I can live long enough to teach her the potions and powders and draughts, to train her in the art of the healing magic. Someone must be here..." She traced the stones nearest her with golden fingertips. "To ensure the Caravanserai yet stands."

Bertie's earth-magic sang in response. "You're the reason this sand castle doesn't crumble into the sea."

"Now you know the truth of it." Serefina pointed at the table. "Bring me the kettle. Add two spoonfuls of powder this time."

Stumbling to the tea service, Bertie poured the liquid, now tepid and pale pink. She spilled a bit on the cloth, muttered an apology to both her hostess and the linen, and reached for the herbal spoon. The odd powder caused it to bubble up twice more, this time the color of raspberries.

Carrying the cup carefully to the hearth, Bertie knelt and pressed its rim to Serefina's mouth.

The herb-seller swallowed deep and grimaced. "It works better when it's hot." But the moment she finished drinking, she was able to stand. "What say you now to my proposal, earth daughter?"

Even crouched next to the hearth, Bertie couldn't get warm. "I . . . I cannot give up even the idea of a child. I'm sorry. It's a turning-straw-into-gold sort of bargain, something I would surely regret later."

"What of your other talents?" Serefina's questions drifted down to settle on Bertie's shoulders with the weight of falling snow. "You can breathe water into your lungs without dying and ride the winds like a bird. Would you trade me either of those?"

Bertie reflected upon the abilities she'd inherited from her parents, which had saved her on her journey through Sedna's underworld. "To be quite honest, I'm not certain I can do either of those things when not in the clutches of the Sea Goddess, but I can't trade them either."

"There is little, it seems, you are willing to give for the sake of safety, then."

Bertie heard the wheezing rattle of the wind in the woman's chest, the slosh of water behind her eyes. "What you need most is a bit of my strength. Enough to tide you over until you get the wish-child you seek."

Serefina made a noise so small that it was only the suggestion of a sigh. "I will take your strength and thank you for it. Clever thing you are for offering it to me, for I think such a trade will also safeguard you from Sedna." The herb-seller drew a small hand mirror out of her pocket, its silver backing scratched and pockmarked. "We all wear masks. They start out plain, decorated with the various small artifices of childhood, an innocent lie or two. As the years pass, we add laughter born without humor, tears shed for the sake of those watching."

Without thinking, Bertie took the mirror and peered into it. Only her own puzzled visage peered back at her, though it was still a shock to see herself with silver hair. "What's that to do with Sedna?"

"The Sea Goddess tracks you through the water like a shark, drawn to the scent of your deceptions. Once you remove the mask you wear, she will find it much more difficult to recognize you."

"But I can always build another mask." When Bertie spoke, it was equal parts statement and question.

Serefina smiled. "True enough, wordsmith, but the one you give up today will not be the one you wear tomorrow or the day after that."

Though such an idea gave Bertie pause, it seemed a small price to pay for her safety and, by proxy, the safety of the troupe and the Caravanserai.

Especially in comparison to Serefina's other requests.

Hand shaking just a bit, Bertie raised the mirror again. Ophelia's eyes looked back at her—*you have your mother's eyes*—but everything else wavered. What was left of Bertie's eyeliner formed ridges under thickly painted eyebrows. Traces of glittering eye shadow crystallized into fog-smudged half-moons. And, perhaps most disconcerting, the silver of her hair ran in rivulets down her face to form a translucent mask, glass-trapping her features.

"Lift it from your skin, child," Serefina murmured.

Bertie obeyed, sliding her fingernails under the mask's knife-thin edge and lifting it as one would the lid from Pandora's box. There was a blast of frigid air, and the object in her hand was as much ice as it was glass. Fingers trembling, Bertie held it out in offering to Serefina.

The herb-seller hastily wrapped the mask in a length of silk that smelled of sandalwood and secrets. "My thanks." Her voice was already stronger, clearer, ringing with the brass-tenor of a gong.

In stark contrast, Bertie's knees wobbled. "My apologies that I couldn't do more."

Or wouldn't.

"This will suffice for the time being." Serefina tilted her head to one side. "How does it feel to be without your various artifices, wordsmith?"

Bertie lifted her hand to her face, suddenly self-conscious. "No different—"

But she couldn't finish voicing the falsehood, not when her skin felt softer than Opening-Night roses. There was a disconnect, as if she touched the flesh of another, or perhaps the fingers grazing her cheek were not her own. When she dropped her hand, other sensations rushed at her: the heat from the fire suddenly a dozen degrees warmer; steam from the hissing kettle as moist upon her face as though she'd walked into vapors of the theater's fog machine.

Raising the mirror to look at herself again, Bertie was somehow unsurprised by the anxiety shimmering on the surface of her skin. Though Ophelia's eyes yet peered back at her, though her nose had the same impudent tilt at the end, though her freckles were as much in evidence as ever, rising panic revealed itself in the flare of her nostrils and the twist of her mouth. Try as she might to tame it, to shove it below the surface, to smile, to grimace, to summon any facial expression that would have belied her inner turmoil, Bertie couldn't manage it. There was nothing there behind which she could hide, and the terror of it settled into her very bones.

"I look naked," she whispered, "like my soul is shining out."

"That's because it is." Serefina rose from her place and removed the mirror from Bertie's reluctant hand. "Tarry not. The longer you linger here, the more apt Sedna is to discover you. You've shed deception and falsehood for the time being, but honesty won't trick her forever." When Bertie made no move to leave, the herb-seller gave her arm a shake. "Do you understand? You must get back to your friends and depart as quick as you can. The sooner you're gone from the Caravanserai, the safer everyone will be."

"Of course." Bertie stumbled over her feet as she rose, the hands-not-hers accepting the bundle of packets and bottles of medicine Serefina handed to her.

"Safe travels to you," the herb-seller said in parting. "Should you ever reconsider, you know where to find me."

"I do."

But I won't reconsider such a thing.

Ducking into the Performers' Alcove adjacent to the massive, echoing amphitheater, Bertie came nose to nose with the mechanical horses. Stoic and stalwart, with metal plating and gear-driven innards, the steeds stood ready for departure.

More than a bit damp around the neckline and

underarms, Nate now sorted bits of leather straps tumbling out of a broken box and muttered to himself. "This is worse tangled than a length o' sea-soaked rigging!" He jerked upon the extra reins, setting the silver bells jangling like those of a demented sleigh. "Whoever stowed this needs t' make th' acquaintance o' a cat-o'-nine-tails."

Half hidden by the caravan, Bertie watched him struggle, his muscles clenched and straining under his shirt. A dribble of sweat worked its way down his cheek, slipping under the strong line of his jaw and down the full length of his neck. . . .

I bet he tastes salty sweet.

Two seconds later, reality kicked her in the backside.

And the fact that I think that no doubt shows on my face!

Indeed, a hot blush already suffused her cheeks, and she ducked around the far side of the wagon. Before Serefina traded her for the mask, Bertie certainly hadn't considered the notion that she was as much an actress as any Player at the Théâtre Illuminata, but now she had the proof of it. She forced herself to take one deep breath, then another, her back pressed flat against the caravan until she was nearly felled by a cloth-wrapped slab of bacon.

"Incoming!" Mustardseed yelled several seconds too late. Four little heads appeared overhead, followed by squeals of "Bertie!" and "Look at all the grub we bought!"

Despite the late hour, Peaseblossom and the others had

indeed done their duty. The top of the caravan overflowed with supplies, from waxy wheels of cheese to cotton sacks of dried beans and cornmeal.

"So you cleaned out whatever stalls cater to hearty, raw-boned pioneers traveling by covered wagon?" Even if she'd wanted to look stern, Bertie couldn't help but smile over their thoroughness. "If I've any worries about the journey, they don't include starvation."

Peaseblossom grinned, clearly pleased with herself. "Not only that, but I fetched your things from the bath-house." The fairy retrieved the scrimshaw medallion from the pile of shopping with a ladylike grunt and returned it to Bertie.

As the cool ivory settled back into its proper place between her collarbones, Bertie felt more like herself than she had in hours. "Thanks, Pease."

"Yer back." Approaching from the other side, Nate's appearance nearly jolted Bertie from her traitorous skin.

"I am, and we have to hurry. Sedna's gathering her strength. She's tried to attack me twice with water to-night." Before he could demand a recitation of the story, Bertie shoved the cloth sack Serefina had packed into his arms. "Medicines and other necessaries." She averted her face, trying to school her features. "Your arrow wound probably needs a disinfecting wash, at the very least, and clean rags to bind it—"

"I'll be fine." The pirate leaned in closer, studying her as though she were some sort of odd species of fish that had flopped aboard his vessel. "Ye look different."

"It's just the new hair color."

He shook his head. "That's not it. What else ha'e ye done?"

Bertie turned away, seeking out any and all shadows. "Didn't you ever learn that it's rude to stare?"

Trained in all sorts of armed combat, Nate required only three seconds and as many steps to cut off her retreat. "Some starin' needs t' be done."

"Don't be stubborn for stubborn's sake—"

"Says th' donkey t' th' ass."

"Smart move, there," Mustardseed observed with an ear wiggle, "making yourself the ass."

Nate didn't shift his gaze from Bertie's face when he answered, "I've yet some sense o' self-preservation."

"If that's true, then put a cork in your questions," Bertie said, her consonants clipped. "We need to leave now."

"What about Ariel?" Cobweb asked when Nate didn't.

"If he doesn't resurface within the next five minutes, we leave without him." Bertie raised her voice for the benefit of anyone who might be eavesdropping. "We are not a trifling thing, an ant upon the road to be easily overlooked. A painted caravan, two silver horses, four sugar-hyper fairies. If Ariel has the least desire to find us, he will. . . ."

77

She wanted to sound flippant and devil-may-care, but the strain of making such a decision manifested in a choking noise that echoed off the walls of the alcove. Nate saw something in her expression that gave him reason to clench his jaw, and Bertie wanted to cover her face with her hands, to demand he look away. Instead, she marched up the stairs to the caravan, bringing her bare feet down with far more force than necessary.

"Where are ye goin'?" came the inevitable query behind her.

"To change my clothes! And possibly cut all my hair off so I don't look like him!" The second bit slipped out before she could stop it, and Bertie contemplated banging her head into the sturdy wooden door until she passed out, if only to save herself further embarrassment.

First things first. I have to get out of this ridiculous dress.

Swearing under her breath, Bertie wrestled the garment off. It would have been satisfying to jump up and down upon it, but there was no time for such childish indulgences now, so she settled for flinging it out the door. The silk chiffon drifted away, disappearing like mist on a sunny morning. The only trouble with such a dramatic gesture was that it afforded Nate an unhindered view of her standing in the doorway wearing only her undergarments.

Rather than ducking his head and swearing, as he might have only a short time ago, he caught the dress in one deft hand and headed up the stairs after her. "Ye weren't serious about yer hair, were ye?"

"No. At least, I don't think so. I can't be certain about anything just at the moment." Dragging out the nearest trunk, Bertie set to rummaging, as much for something suitable for road travel as for the opportunity to hide her expression from him. Her jeans sat atop a jumble of velvets and satins; once in them, she felt a bit more herself. The soft crimson pullover added another layer of comfort, as did the hood. Twisting the strands of Arctic Tempest out of her face, Bertie gripped the impromptu chignon and went in search of hair combs.

"I'm already gettin' used to it." Reaching up, Nate coerced Bertie's fingers into loosing her hair. Then, as though it reeled him in, he lowered his head a few inches to inhale the exotic scent of the bathhouse soaps that lingered, even after Sedna's saltwater assault. "Ye smell like th' ocean. An' dessert . . . orange, mint, a bit of vanilla."

Bertie's mouth dried up, wondering what her expression would reveal now that she couldn't hide anything from him, but it was Nate who surprised her again when his lips grazed the side of her neck, his breath wreaking soft havoc upon her ear.

"What would ha'e happened already if he hadn't come between us?"

CHAPTER SIX

I Must Attend Her Majesty's Command

Bertie almost choked on the thought. "My guess is 'nothing much.' You've an unusual sense of propriety for a pirate." She would have pulled away, except Nate's massive arms had shifted so that the left encircled her back and the right cradled the base of her neck; she was well-trapped, and she could hardly breathe for the realization.

"Mayhap ye carved my propriety from my flesh wi' yer arrow." His body was like a bow tightly strung and drawn. The smallest shift in his weight lifted Bertie onto her yet-bare tiptoes, and gentle leverage tilted her head back.

There were protests to be made—Bertie hadn't meant to shoot him when she'd thought she was the Forest Queen, Sedna was on the rampage, Her Gracious Majesty had summoned the troupe—but traitorous lips formed the query "Why don't you shut your piehole and kiss me?" instead.

The invitation, once issued, would not be rescinded. The truth of the matter was that she wanted him to kiss her, that she welcomed the rough feel of his mouth against hers and the light scrape of teeth and the way his arms tightened about her in a vise. She couldn't be swept away by the tides, not while he held her; there was no safer feeling in all the world, and she fell into it headlong, like Alice down the rabbit hole.

By the time Nate was done drowning himself in her, neither of them could breathe properly. The darkness inside the caravan wrapped them in black velvet curtains, the air as thick about them as that of a long-sealed tomb. Bertie had her hands clenched in his shirt, and her breath came in tiny pants; perhaps oxygen deprivation explained the next conversational jewel that dropped from her mouth.

"I want to be with you, but you *are* a pirate, which means you probably have ten sorts of pox, as well as the clap."

That assertion wiped the satisfied look from Nate's face, replacing it with that of an indignant feline whose tail had just gotten caught under a rocking chair. "I don't know any such thing! An' I certainly haven't th' clap! D'ye see any sign o' such on my face or my hands?" As punishment for such an outrageous accusation, he bit her just where her neck met her shoulder.

She retaliated by pinching him somewhere wholly indecent and improper, adding to the assault a long-harbored suspicion. "You've probably bedded dozens of girls from the Ladies' Chorus, no doubt every one of them incubating a different love malady!"

"I ha'e not!" He caught hold of her pinching fingers and pinned them behind her back.

"You haven't had any women, or they haven't given you the gift that keeps on giving?" Her free hand reached out and jabbed him in the midsection.

Rather than take the not-quite-a-game a step further, Nate carefully set her back on her feet before retreating far enough to give her space to breathe, to think. "Why are ye bringin' this up now, lass?"

Unable to determine if she was disappointed or relieved he'd let her go, Bertie turned to the tiny window, jerked it open, and leaned out in search of fresh air. A chill wind snaked its way through the Caravanserai, raising its serpentine head in spine-numbing gusts, and she was grateful to it for clearing the fog in her head. "Because I can't help myself."

"Because yer afraid."

Bertie couldn't lie to him. Not because she'd traded her mask to Serefina, but because she realized she wanted no falsehoods between them. "Yes."

"Because o' Ariel?"

"That's partially it."

"An' what's th' rest?"

She refused to look at him, instead turning her eyes to the night sky. There was still no sign of the Scrimshander, though the crescent moon slanted blue-tinged light over every surface. The events of the day caught up with her all at once, and her teeth started to chatter. "There's something about me, Nate, that drives people away. Ariel. Ophelia. My father."

"I'm still here."

"Until I do or say something completely unforgivable, simply because I can't seem to help myself—" He took a step toward her then, but Bertie shook her head, desperate to make him understand. "I don't mean to be cruel, but I seem to manage it quite nicely on occasion."

"I'm not afraid o' yer words or yer bite, lass. Say what ye like t' me, it won't change what's between us." After a long moment, Nate added, "An' push as hard as ye need t'. I'll give ye as much space as ye want."

"That's a new development," she said, half choking on inappropriate laughter. "You're a champion hoverer."

He ducked his head. "Aye, well, some time spent captive at Sedna's mercy might ha'e somethin' t' do wi' it, never mind ye handled yerself against th' witch wi'out any help from me—"

Tiny hands frantically hammering on the door to the

caravan interrupted whatever else Nate had been about to say.

"Bertie!" Peaseblossom's voice was wood muffled but insistent. "Waschbär is back!"

"The Innamorati are here as well," Mustardseed added with the singsong of a practiced tattletale, "and Aleksandr wants to speak with you!"

"Chef Toroidal brought us a get-lost pie!" called Moth.

"Stupid, it's shoofly," corrected Cobweb.

"Oooooh, I thought that meant good riddance."

"Good riddance pie wouldn't be this sticky," Peaseblossom said, her voice muffled a bit as though her mouth was full. "You don't get rid of someone who's sticky very easily. Speaking of which, get your hands off me, Mustardseed!"

"We should get out there, before one o' them tries t' eat th' arm off th' other." One hand on the doorknob, Nate hesitated. "Did ye mean what ye said about leavin' wi'out Ariel?"

"If I want to win that wish-come-true from the Queen, we need to go now," Bertie answered. It wasn't until Nate turned that she permitted herself to consider the question fully, and the thought of Ariel's absence brought bright-hot tears to her eyes. Hastening to wipe them away, she almost scratched the skin down her cheeks and alongside her nose. At first she thought her fingernails were to blame, but when she studied her hands, Bertie saw that her tears had hardened into sharp-edged crystals that looked suspiciously like diamonds.

"Are ye comin'?" Nate was halfway down the stairs.

She closed her fingers over the jewels and turned back to the open trunk. "I need to find a pair of shoes. Then we can get this demented act on the road."

With an extra pair of Mary Janes located and the diamond-tears tucked into the deepest pocket of her jeans, Bertie followed Nate out into the night. Waschbär was the first to greet her with a chipper salute and then a squint.

"What have you done to yourself?"

I should have known the man who wears a raccoon's mask would notice something amiss!

She tried to sidestep him, but the sneak-thief was dexterous beyond her imagining, and he blocked her at every turn.

"You smell of herbs and intrigue." He sniffed at her again, nose quivering with such enthusiasm that he finally sneezed. Disturbed by the blast, Pip Pip and Cheerio tumbled out of his pockets and clambered onto his shoulders, their tiny black eyes glittering in the half-light from the torches. They sassed Bertie with chitters and squeaks, unintelligibly remonstrating her as Waschbär listened with great intensity, until she was quite certain he knew all about her visit to Serefina, seeking protection from Sedna, and trading her mask.

Bertie glowered at the tattling vermin. "That's hardly polite. And I'd like to know who told you!"

"I won't say anything," Waschbär assured her in an undertone. "Go and make your farewells so we can be on our way."

All the Innamorati performers had turned out for the troupe's sudden departure: the giraffe-girl standing alongside Salt and Sauce, the Pachyderm Professors; aerial acrobats with icicles still a-dangle from their clothes and hair; dozens of specialty performers, their faces thick with white paint and skin encrusted with sequins. Eye-blinding in her frilly gold Columbine skirts, the woman portraying the Sun sniffed into a handkerchief the size of a pillowcase. Her partner, the Harlequin Moon, turned lethargic cartwheels that somehow managed to convey his desolation over their exodus.

Valentijn towered over the assembled crowd. The Keeper of the Costumes looked the sternest Bertie had ever seen him. He carried a battered leather portmanteau, and for one terrifying moment, Bertie thought he might be running away—*who runs away from the circus?*—and wanted to come with them.

But he only pushed the bit of luggage at her. "Several changes of clothes for you, all recently washed and tailored to your measurements. Thankfully, I believe most of them will match your new coloring."

"Thank you, Valentijn." Bertie accepted the proffered suitcase and nearly staggered under its weight. She wouldn't find it the least bit surprising if he had untold powers of packing, with the inside of the portmanteau larger than the outside and containing enough poet-sleeved shirts to costume a dozen wayward playwrights.

"Let me take that, lass." Nate disappeared around the side of the caravan without straining any of his muscles, though he discharged his burden with a grunt and an "oomph."

All the while, the Keeper of the Costumes peered at Bertie, his narrow gaze as piercing as one of his mending needles. "I see more change written upon you than just your hair, young Beatrice. Have you need of more costuming than what I've provided?"

"Considering the weight of that suitcase," she said, "I doubt it."

"Are you certain?" Valentijn pressed her. "A fan, maybe? Or . . . a mask?"

Bertie couldn't prevent the scowl she felt twist up her mouth and forehead. "It's irritating to be read like words upon the page."

"It's my profession to notice details. The skin of your face glows like candlelit silk, and your every thought is a bit of bloodred embroidery stitched upon it." Valentijn pursed his lips in consideration. "What about a veil? I have seven stowed away in the costuming car."

Bertie shook her head. "I would accept your kind offer if I were to remain in the Caravanserai, but such things take time, and I'm afraid we've tarried long enough." She stood on tiptoe and kissed him on either cheek, as was the Innamorati way. "I promise this isn't the last you've seen of me."

"Of course it isn't," he said with a sudden and valiant sniff. "As soon as we are ready, we shall bring the production to the Distant Castle for the Queen's pleasure. After that, perhaps that theater of yours would hire us for a turn."

Bertie had no answer to that, save a small part of her brain exploding with glee over the idea of the Stage Manager forced to deal with three dozen noisy acrobats, pie-flinging august clowns, and Chef Toroidal and his team of Gourmet Gastronomes. She could not prevent the smile that split her face from side to side, nor the snicker of amusement that escaped. "I'll speak to the Management, as I would dearly love to see such a thing come to pass."

"I shall see that it is so," Valentijn said, kissing her once more atop her silver head as the rest of the performers scattered in search of their lodgings, a late-night meal, and other revelries only hinted at by their hand gestures and foreign-tongued exhortations.

Once the last cartwheel-turning acrobat was out of earshot, Aleksandr said, "I would give you use of the In-namorati's train, but since our arrival, we discovered the locomotive's engine appears to have warped." The ring-master flapped his hands a bit, as though he wished sleight of hand could fix matters. "It seems quite an impossibility for a beast of steel and iron, but who am I to question the engineer about such things?"

Though she tried to school her features, Bertie still cringed. She hoped it hadn't been her opportune skipping of the story—and train—forward through the landscape that had ravaged the Innamorati's primary means of transportation. "I hope it can be easily fixed."

"Of that, I have no doubt," he assured her. "And when it is repaired, we shall travel with all due haste to attend upon Her Gracious Majesty, though we are most thankful for the extra time to rehearse, I must tell you." Here, he leaned in to whisper, "Take care with your own performance, good Mistress of Revels. The last storyteller who displeased the Queen was silenced in a most unpleasant fashion—"

"Pardon th' interruption, but I'm afraid we need t' be off now." Lacing his fingers together, Nate made a cradle of his hands. "Up wi' you."

It was a more graceful way to ascend than scrambling or being heaved skyward by Waschbär, so Bertie allowed him to give her a foot up. Right behind her, Nate settled into the seat, the reins resting easy in his hand.

"An' anyone else aboard who's comin' wi' us."

The sneak-thief fit himself between the various bits of the luggage before Nate had even finished the sentence, deftly rearranging boxes and bags so he could see and be seen. The fairies rushed to Bertie's shoulders, all four of them deciding the hood hanging down her back was the warmest and most secure place to sit. Thinking she could pull the strings and effectively seal them in there, should they start to wear on her nerves, Bertie let them be. After a moment's pause and a final round of waving to Aleksandr and Valentijn, the caravan began to roll forward. Wheels dipping in and out of the ruts between the cobblestones, the conveyance marked their departure with merry jingling.

Trying to ignore the clamor of it, Bertie leaned forward to examine the map that spanned the length of the driver's seat. The curious brass-and-gold frame had frozen solid in a snowstorm but appeared to be in working order now. "Did you fix this?"

"Aye, a bit of oil an' polish did th' trick. A good thing, too. It's better than any nautical chart I've ever seen." He tapped the tiny silver caravan that yet marked their position, moving through the delicately rendered sand castle that was the Caravanserai.

Barely touching the parchment, Bertie traced the sepia-painted waves of the ocean to the west, the brushstrokes representing the White Cliffs. The map noted the location of the Scrimshander's Aerie, but the silver bird that would have indicated her father's whereabouts was absent.

He had flown too far, too fast.

There wasn't a marker for Ariel, either. Biting down hard upon her lip, Bertie concentrated on the horses, the narrow roads, the ruts between the cobblestones, anything that would distract her from his absence. Though it seemed like hours passed, it could not have been more than fifteen painful minutes before the exit portal loomed before them. Waschbär kissed his fingertips and reached high enough to tap them against the stone arch as the caravan passed under it.

"Did you find what you were seeking here?" he asked Bertie with a good-natured wink.

Did I?

Bertie had arrived there seeking Nate, her father, and answers to questions she'd asked her whole life. They'd managed to rescue the pirate. She'd met her father, who'd given her answers, none of which had been satisfying. The troupe was departing the Caravanserai without the Scrim-shander, bound for the Distant Castle rather than the Théâtre Illuminata, and Ariel had abandoned them—*yet again*—for the sake of elusive freedom. It seemed something of a draw, all things taken into consideration, but to say so aloud would hurt Nate, and he'd been hurt enough these last few days.

How could she word it so her features wouldn't betray her? "I am thankful beyond measure to have Nate with us again."

"I found what I was seeking, too," Moth said, clambering out of Bertie's hood and diving into the nearest hamper. "Because I was looking for dessert."

"Hey, what do you have there?" Peaseblossom followed him and resurfaced with a suspiciously moist and delicious-looking lump in her hand. "That chocolate cake was for pudding tonight!"

"Pudding tonight, pudding now," he grumbled, licking his fingers without apology. "What's the difference? Only one word!"

"One word can make all the difference," Bertie said before she could stop herself. Wriggling about on the bench, she tried to get comfortable, but Nate and his muscles took up more than his fair share of room. Where Ariel was lithe and lean as a racing hound, the pirate was the solid oak of a ship's mast. The moment Bertie relaxed, her thigh came to rest alongside his, her jeans against his leather breeches. Trying not to jolt, she eased her leg away.

His reaction was one of quiet amusement. "If ye try not t' touch me for th' duration, things are goin' t' be a bit strained, no?"

"I wasn't touching you. I mean, I wasn't trying to touch you. It was inadvertent. . . ." Realizing how that must sound to the passengers in the back, Bertie ordered herself to shut up and calm down. The moment she eased the muscles around her spine, though, she oozed against him.

"I can't tell ye how nice this is," he said into her hair.

Up to their eyeballs in cake, the fairies mistook his meaning.

"You could sing that 'Oh, What a Beautiful Morning' song, except it's not morning, and this isn't a surrey with fringe on the top," said Peaseblossom, who had yielded to the lure of pudding until ganache decorated her eyelashes.

"What a horrifying suggestion," Moth said around a mouthful of milk-chocolate cream. "It's almost like you *want* him to sing."

"He is a lovely tenor," she maintained before she punched Mustardseed in his very model of a modern major general.

"I'm not goin' t' sing," was Nate's wry observance. "Ariel's th' one wi' th' enchanted voice."

Ariel.

Bertie stared at the sky until her eyes watered. This time, the diamond-tears fell before she could stop them.

Nate noticed. "Yer cryin'."

"Maybe just a little." Bertie changed the subject, though it sounded like she was making excuses. "I'm tired. And overwrought."

"Overwrought, my foot." He reached out to touch her face, then hesitated. "Those aren't tears, lass."

"I know." The damn things hurt when they left her eyes, though it was odder still to watch them tumble along the folds of her sweater and rain, crystalline, down to the wooden floorboards. "Maybe I can cry to impress the Queen. Produce enough sparkles to make a nice tiara."

Placing a gentle finger to her face, Nate caught one of the curious tears and held it up, squinting into the lantern light. "What are they, exactly?"

"They look like diamonds," Bertie said, "but it would be just my luck to find out they're rock salt."

By chance or by Fortune's hand, she spoke just as they entered the dark heart of a thicket of elders. In the absence of interfering moonlight, the tiny thing in Nate's palm glowed, the sort of white that implied every other color in all the world at once.

"That's a pretty bit of something," Waschbär said, his shaggy head appearing over the back of the driver's seat.

Bertie slanted a look at Nate. "If that's the opinion of a sneak-thief, my guess is it *is* a diamond."

Nate handed it over to the expert, and Waschbär examined it in turn, finally concluding with a low whistle, "No, not a diamond. It's a star."

"A star?" the fairies chorused.

"Yer cryin' th' stars from yer eyes." Nate's hands on the reins tightened as he added, "Fer Ariel."

"Don't be ridiculous. These can't be stars, and I'm certainly not shedding them over Ariel's absence." But there was no escaping Nate's gaze, not when only a few inches of driver's seat separated them. Compounding her discomfort, the Scrimshander's words echoed in her head.

You have your mother's eyes.

Bertie couldn't help the slip-slide of fear trickling down the back of her throat at the idea that she'd not only traded away her mask, but soon her eyes might no longer resemble Ophelia's. What would be left of her then? Perhaps she was like an hourglass, each tear a grain of sand slipping through the bottleneck, and when they ran out—

Waschbär didn't let her finish the maudlin thought. With a loud clearing of his throat, he inquired, "To the Distant Castle, yes?"

"That's the plan." After giving him a look of bottomless thanks for the distraction, Bertie returned her attention to the map. The road they traveled ran alongside the Reine, a decent-size river that assured the troupe would have fresh water for the duration of the journey. Following its thin black line to the farthest right edge of the map, a building appeared. Rendered in greater detail than the Caravanserai, thrice over larger than that massive Thirteenth Outpost of Beyond, the Distant Castle was surrounded by three sets of stone walls labeled THE TRIPLE CROWN. Though they were still too far to make out the smaller structures between the walls, it appeared that each of the rings about the castle contained its own village.

"Three townships, three walls, three gates we must pass through." Bertie was hardly surprised. Three was a powerful number, be it portents or punch lines.

"We need t' hurry if we want t' arrive before they lock th' gates." Nate pointed off to the side of the road, where a stone mileage marker smugly noted the vast distance they had yet to travel. "Th' courier said 'twas a few days' journey."

"A single rider on horseback might manage that pace," Waschbär concurred, "but not this contraption, loaded down as it is with a year's worth of edibles."

"*Some* of us were of the opinion that no calamity could be greater than running out of food." Peaseblossom shot a significant look at the boys.

"We'll just have to hurry," Bertie said, "riding late as we are now, as long as we can stand it, and getting up early. We have to win that wish-come-true."

"What sort of performance are you planning for Her Gracious Majesty?" Waschbär wanted to know.

Something in Bertie's midsection twisted up at the thought of writing another play. Her last effort, ostensibly for the Innamorati's Brand-New Play, had unfortunately manifested in real life during the perilous journey to rescue Nate from Sedna. "If the Queen has heard enough about us to send a messenger to issue an invitation, my guess is Her Gracious Majesty is expecting something more impressive than a village puppet show."

Moth took offense. "Are you impugning our performance?"

"I'll impugn *you.*" Peaseblossom put up her dukes, then added a duchess for good measure. "I'm not performing with you three cannibals again, after what you did to my Henry." She hadn't mentioned her marzipan paramour recently, but her ire returned over the untimely ingestion of her boyfriend.

"We can perform without you," Mustardseed countered. "No one is irreplaceable."

"Yeah! I can channel Juliet just as well as you." Cobweb jabbed his chest with a maraschino cherry stem.

"You can't perform a secondhand show for the Queen," Waschbär interjected. "You need something prepared in her honor, offering up a reflection of her glory!"

Peaseblossom had even more important things on her mind, it seemed. "What are you going to wear?"

The ruin of the Mistress of Revels's emerald skirts and embroidered bodice commanded a moment of regretful silence. "When we stop to make camp, we'll take a quick inventory of the costumes and properties. Surely Valentijn packed me something suitable for an audience with the Queen."

"You've never suited a queen before," Mustardseed said, his mouth quirking up at the corners. "Or are you forgetting Gertrude?"

Cobweb snickered. "She's not quite a chop-your-head-off ruler, but almost!"

"Shut up, Cobweb." Preferring her head remain just where it was, Bertie refused to think of Her Gracious Majesty as anything remotely resembling the Queen of Hearts. Instead, she closed her eyes and made a vow to herself, to her parents.

I'll win that wish-come-true. For all of us.

CHAPTER SEVEN

If You Do Take a Thief, Let Him Show Himself

Traveling through the night without stopping, by sunrise the troupe caught up with the tail end of a cavalcade headed for the Distant Castle. Wagons and carts ahead were piled high with exotic goods, riders saluted from horseback, and conveyances strange occupied the road: carriages lacquered the shiny red-black of ripened cherries and richly canopied *jinrikisha* pulled by shirtless servant boys in brilliant blue trousers. Though none of the fantastic parade matched the Innamorati for grandeur, the number of troubadours rehearsing their scales rivaled the melodies of the birds in the trees. Some performed solo while others were accompanied by musicians on fantastical stringed instruments, gongs, drums, and panpipes. They greeted Bertie and company with hand gestures, nods, and calls of "Beautiful weather ahead!" and "Lovely morning for traveling!" followed by "No trouble at all this season with brigands and thieves, praise be to Her Gracious Majesty!"

Waschbär made a derisive noise at this revelation. "That simply means they are busy elsewhere."

"And if we chance upon your former comrades?" Bertie's question was a bit garbled, posed around a mouthful of flatbread, spiced beef, and garlic sauce. They'd decided to break their fast while traveling, and she was doing her best to enjoy the sandwich, given it was the last food from the Caravanserai. "Should we let you do the talking?"

The sneak-thief set down his food, looking as though his appetite had fled into the hedgerow. "My hope is we'll be able to avoid such an encounter."

"I take it you didn't part with the brigands on amicable terms." Bertie hoped Peaseblossom wouldn't catch her wiping her mouth on her sleeve. "What did you steal from them?"

"Freedom." Waschbär lingered over the word as another might a mouthful of wine. "An unforgivable theft to such men and women." His voice dropped a notch. "They have done far worse in their careers than plunder and pillage, though I tried to take no part in that. When I could stomach no more of their mercenary acts, I stole away in the dead of night, and I vowed I would never again deprive anyone of valuables they cherished."

"That was when you decided to steal only unwanted things?"

"Yes." Waschbär shifted, perhaps discomfited more by the memories than her question. "I took refuge in the bustle of the Caravanserai, but soon I was drawn beyond its walls to the White Cliffs and your father's Aerie."

"You took the scrimshaw medallion." Bertie reached for it, twisting her fingers in the chain.

He confessed to the theft with a nod. "Once I would have lingered in the marketplace, rife as it was with gold pocket watches and velvet coin purses and fat money clips, but my newly made vow set me on a different path. I sought solace in the long road, traveling until my feet were sore, sleeping under the stars. Eventually, I reached a bustling city. A circuitous route left me in the alleyway behind your Théâtre Illuminata, and Fate led me to a window open in the Properties Department."

"An open window, eh?" Cobweb fisted his hands on his hips. "I can just imagine who opened it!"

Bertie coughed, recalling the incident in which she'd tested the magical barriers of the theater by tossing the aforementioned fairy at the opening, resulting in a frizzling and a decided lack of underpants on his part. "I've no idea what you're talking about."

The sneak-thief didn't notice the conversational footnote, his mind still following the narrative. "I couldn't so much as touch a single item in the Properties Department, though I left the scrimshaw as a gift for your Mr. Hastings. What had drawn me to the theater in the first place yet beckoned, luring me down a long hallway and up a narrow staircase, to a glass-paned door."

And then Bertie could guess the rest of the tale. "The unwanted thing that lured you there was in the Theater Manager's office, wasn't it?"

Waschbär shook his head. "Not one unwanted item, but two: the journal and the opal ring, both cleverly concealed in a hidden drawer of his desk."

"The ring came from the theater as well?" Bertie frowned, not expecting that new puzzle piece. "With every mystery solved, another is born, it seems." Looking down the road, she realized the other travelers had left the troupe in the dust, forging ahead while Waschbär told his tale. "The mechanical horses aren't going to get us there in time, are they?"

Nate consulted the map. "We have enough time t' reach th' gates. Stow yer frettin'."

Bertie leaned forward, putting her head on her knees. "I'm too tired to fret."

"Ye can nap, if ye like." Nate offered his shoulder for a pillow with a welcoming pat. "Rest yer head."

"I've too much thinking to do to sleep. I need to conjure up a dazzling and brilliant performance for the Queen." But every idea seemed more pebble than diamond, especially when Bertie admitted most of them were worries about Ariel: where he might be, whose company he might be keeping now, wondering if he'd care at all that they'd left the Caravanserai without him. Mimicking the mechanical horses, shiny brass gears in her head spun wildly with thoughts of him, each full revolution bringing her back to the beginning of her musings.

Did he scent that one-in-a-thousand wind and leave for good?

"Yer face is fair squinched up," Nate noted. "An' I don't think it's th' sun in yer eyes."

"It's warm, isn't it?" Bertie sidestepped the observation, hoping to compose her features and knowing she didn't quite manage it.

"He chose not t' come wi' us, ye realize?"

"I don't want to talk about that right now." Would that she could have managed the statement with greater conviction! "And I didn't say a thing about Ariel."

"Ye didn't need to." It was almost as though he chose the shortest words possible, pounding them into the wood of the caravan with a voice like a hammer. "Yer every thought crosses yer face. What caused such a thing?"

I should tell him about trading the mask.

Though she wanted no falsehoods between them, secrets were not the same thing as lies, and some part of her desperately needed a secret right now, however small. Bertie hugged it close to her, clinging to it as a child would a stuffed bear or a blanket when the night-light failed and the floorboards creaked. Something brushed over her nose, and she thought it a spiderweb or a bit of mist before realizing the secret had surfaced upon her skin, forming the thinnest of barriers between her soul and the outside world.

Because she wouldn't lie to Nate, she changed the subject. "The herb-seller said Sedna is tracking me through the water like a shark."

He shuddered. "Th' last thing we need is the Sea Goddess givin' chase just now." Nate glanced about them, eyes trained upon the landscape the way he might scan the seas for an incoming squall. "Though there's not much chance o' her manifestin' in th' middle o' this dusty road." He spoke with conviction, but under that ran a murky green thread of fear.

"Was she awful to you?" The moment she spoke, Bertie wanted to take the words back and eat them, no matter how vile they tasted. Nate flinched away from the question as though she'd slapped him hard; indeed, his cheeks reddened and something horrible to look upon filled his eyes.

Before he could speak, she hastened to set things to rights. "Let's strike a bargain and not speak of Ariel or Sedna again today."

Adjusting the reins with visible relief, Nate nodded. "What would ye speak of instead?"

"Anything else. Shoes and ships and ceiling wax—"

"Oh, aye," he said, picking up the rhyme, "an' will ye give a cabbage t' th' Queen?"

The idea teased a laugh from Bertie. "Not a fitting gift. I'll try to think of something other than leafy produce." Then, their heads filled with conjuring tricks, silk flowers, and rabbits pulled from top hats, they fell into the sort of conversation they might have had months ago back at the theater, their words wandering over the landscape just as the caravan did. It was only when Bertie's stomach growled that she realized the sun hung low in the sky, a glowing pink spotlight aimed at their backs.

"My thoughts exactly." Nate guided the caravan off the road near a bend in the river.

"We can't stop now," Bertie protested, despite the fact that after more than a full day's journey, her backside was aching numb.

"That's enough fer now, considerin' we didn't sleep at all last night." The pirate matched her, wince for wince, when he clambered down. "Everyone off afore I chuck ye overboard."

The fairies and Waschbär descended, indefatigable and in good cheer, the former frolicking in the grass like winged puppies and the latter dismounting the conveyance as though it were no more than a hobbyhorse. The sneak-thief turned out his pockets, thus displacing Pip Pip and Cheerio, who tumbled one over the other with squeaks and bites.

"Mind th' vermin," Nate said, lifting one booted foot as they gamboled past him.

Three of the four fairies and Waschbär immediately sought out the nearest trees to relieve themselves. A bit more decorous, Peaseblossom emerged from a nearby thicket a moment later, twisting her little tunic about her hips and looking disconcerted.

"I'd forgotten what it was like on the open road. I think the Lost Boys must have had an easier time of it than Wendy."

Bertie did her best not to laugh. "You're going to wish we'd stayed at the Caravanserai when we're sleeping on the ground tonight instead of in a feather bed."

"Don't speak of the Caravanserai," Mustardseed said with a groan. "I miss the food already."

"Aye, well, if ye want t' eat anytime soon, we'd best get t' it," Nate observed with a glance at the sky. "Waschbär, ye see t' th' fire an' I'll tend t' dinner."

"Will do!" The sneak-thief took a small hand ax into

the trees. When he returned, he carried a stack of logs, each as long and as fat as his forearm. With his usual speed and dexterity, he scraped back the grass, clearing a place for a fire.

The fairies sorted through the food supplies, tossing down flour and salt and the side of bacon. Bertie sliced off pieces of the smoked-and-salted pork while Nate committed the curious alchemy of baking ship's biscuits, rubbing white fat into salted flour and transforming the crumbling mass into small rounds of dough. Peaseblossom had to search the entire caravan to find the necessary pans, but soon bacon frizzled in one skillet and biscuits in another. There was also dried fruit, a wheel of sharp cheese, and a stone jar of pink pickles the fairies thought might be either radishes or beets.

It was full dark by the time they sat down to eat, but they did so by lantern light with good appetite and humor. The metal plates Peaseblossom had unearthed were so thin that when Bertie drew her fingernail about the edge of hers, it sang an odd melody, the vibration of which settled into the empty space at the back of her throat. Bone-tired and her belly full, she thought she could have fallen asleep in the grass quite happily.

"It was a good meal and heartily enjoyed, more so for the company than the viands," was Waschbär's cheerful contribution as he lolled against a well-placed rock, a biscuit clasped in one paw and the ferrets balanced upon the other.

Cobweb looked at him askance. "That didn't stop you shoveling in those viands with remarkable speed! I lost track of how many biscuits you ate!"

"If biscuits were stories," Bertie said, fixing her gaze upon the fire, "I'd bake a pan of piping hot fables right this second."

"Do fables have jam filling?" Moth wanted to know. "Or chocolate?"

"I think it's allegories that have jam filling," Mustardseed said. "And maybe parables."

Not thinking it possible, Bertie realized she still had room for dessert. "Is there any more cake?"

Rummaging in the nearest hamper, Peaseblossom turned up the other half of the chocolate cake. "Here you go."

Bertie broke off a piece and offered it to Nate. Ducking his head, he surprised her by taking the bite not with his hand, but his mouth.

"Ahem!" Peaseblossom said, clearing her throat so hard she dislodged a bit of dessert along with her disapproval.

"Ye ought t' see t' that cough," was Nate's cavalier response. "Before it settles in yer lungs an' th' pneumonia takes ye."

"I don't have pneumonia—"

"Bronchitis, then."

"We have forks," Peaseblossom said, the sternest governess there ever was, "should you require one."

"I'm fine wi' her fingers, seein' as my hands are completely preoccupied wi' tendin' th' fire."

"I'll say the same to you as I said to Ariel," the fairy lectured the pirate. "You'll mind your manners and be respectful, or you'll have to answer to me!"

Bertie said nothing, but when she offered Nate another bite of cake, she let her fingers linger about his mouth, encouraging the second kiss in as many minutes. With her mask left behind as payment to Serefina, she couldn't hide her sudden longing to inhale the scents of soap and ocean on his clothes, to feel the heat radiating from his chest. The third piece of cake she fed him came with a tiny grazing of his teeth across her finger, and she was a sailor's knot nearly undone.

He must have seen it written upon her face, for something flickered over his own features: a promise, perhaps, mixed with determination and some flavor of triumph. Mumbling something about a pressing thirst, Bertie scrambled to her feet, grasped a lantern, and fled. A narrow stretch of grass and a tiny copse of trees separated the campfire and the river, which burbled a pleasant welcome to her. Rinsing the worst of the frosting off, she left her hands in the cold current until her fingers began to go numb. Even then, the places where Nate had kissed her burned like a firebrand.

"Are ye all right?" Of course he'd followed.

Still kneeling, Bertie didn't turn as she splashed the bracing water on her face. "Just needed a bit of a rinse. The chocolate—"

"It's not th' chocolate troublin' ye." Nate stepped toward her, brow knit, and pulled her to her feet. Tiny fireflies gathered about them, glowing with soft pink light and emitting an oddly happy humming noise.

"Just what we need, to be eaten alive by mosquitoes." Bertie swatted at them, but the winged things looped about her shoulders, tracing rosy hearts upon her skin. Mortified, she squeezed her eyes shut and wished either for bug repellent or for a hole to open up and swallow her.

When neither manifested, Nate tilted his head to one side. "Yer silence is like calm water before a squall."

"Complaints, complaints. You said someday you'd have silence from me." It had been the same day they'd reenacted the tango, the same day he'd been kidnapped.

"Well then, mayhap it's time t' collect on th' quiet."

Though Bertie was expecting the kiss, she wasn't expecting the rest of the world to fall away from her. As her eyes closed again, the silence he wanted spread through her until the river, the caravan, and the rest of the troupe faded into a darkness deeper than a blackout, leaving only the two of them. With nothing and no one to stop them this time, Bertie wrapped herself about him.

Chocolate cake be damned—I want him *for dessert.*

Shoving her fingers through Nate's hair, Bertie snapped the leather string holding back his plait. Flickering broken-glass bits of lantern light caressed his jaw, licked over the stubble on his chin, which Bertie realized belatedly accounted for the stinging around her own mouth. When she kissed him again, Nate's hands gripped the back of her sweater, almost as though he'd like to tear it from her, but the next second he made an incoherent noise into her mouth. Bertie felt his balance shift wildly, then he staggered, and they both fell.

They landed in the river before Bertie could so much as squeak out a protest. It was deeper than it looked, and significantly colder than the shore eddies she'd used to wash her hands. With the frigid water working its way into her underwear, it was easy enough to picture ice-fed streams funneling down from snowcapped mountain-sides.

Up to his armpits, Nate shoved the dripping strands of hair from his face. "A rock turned under my foot, curse it t' th' seventh ring o' hell."

Gasping, Bertie flopped over like a fish and headed for the shore. "I would have thought you'd have better balance, being a mariner."

"Forgive me, it's been some time since I kissed a lass aboard a storm-rocked ship."

"How long, exactly?" Her teeth had started to chatter, but even the castanet clatter couldn't disguise the snort of laughter that escaped. It was beyond comprehension that she was amused by the sudden and thorough dunking, but it had been most effective in dousing the fire inside her—for the moment, anyway—permitting a cooler and wetter head to prevail. Offering Nate her hand, she pulled him up and out of the swift-flowing stream. "Perhaps it was for the best."

"An' what d'ye mean by that?" Linen shirt dripping and leather breeches soaked several shades darker than they ought to be, Nate shook his head like a dog after a bath.

"I just meant that there are things to consider before anything else happens between us." Trying to not stare at his mouth, Bertie could feel a flush nearly set her face on fire.

"Such as?" His hands were about her waist now, at once insistent and undemanding.

"Such as being responsible."

He hesitated then asked, "Ye mean th' chance o' children?"

"Aye, children." Mimicking his accent, Bertie couldn't resist putting him in the spotlight. "Do tell, have you left one of those planted in someone's belly before?" She jabbed him in the midsection and summoned a bit of *King Lear.* "'She grew round-womb'd, and had, indeed, sir, a son for her cradle ere she had a husband for her bed.'"

Nate held up his hand, the one marked to match her own. "If it's a husband ye want, a husband ye have."

Bertie's left hand sought out his right so that their handfasting scars met furrow to furrow, and she laced her fingers through his. "I don't want a husband, nor a baby." She didn't mention Serefina's desire for a child-not-born, nor the flask among the medicines that would have served to keep her safe from the other sort of offspring.

"What about Ariel?" Nate asked softly. "D'ye want him?"

"We didn't leave him behind; he chose not to come with us. I am determined not to spare him a thought."

"Mayhap that's what ye want t' believe, but that's not th' story yer face tells." He brought up his other hand, thumb tracing her jaw with a gentle motion intended to erase all thoughts of his rival from her head.

"What story is it telling, then?" Bertie didn't like the idea that there were stories without words; words were unpredictable enough, but this new alternative was even more dangerous.

"Naught I would say aloud, fer fear ye'd shove me back in th' water." Though it looked like he wanted to do much, much more—apparently she wasn't the only one with her story written upon her features—Nate let go of her face and stepped back. "Ye need t' change yer clothes again."

"Sudden dousings seem to be my specialty lately." Bertie shivered from more than the cold. She retreated, as though the river's clear currents were poison that would slough the skin from her bones, the lulling burble transformed into the tattling voices of Sedna's minions. "Do you think the water will carry word of our whereabouts to the Sea Goddess?"

Nate blanched. "We need t' get away from th' river right now. I should ha'e thought o' that." Taking her by the hand, he towed her through the trees separating them from the campfire, muttering all the while. "We need t' douse th' fire an' pack th' gear, move th' campsite well away from th' water—what in th' name o' all th' hells?"

Bertie had to step around him to see what had brought him to an abrupt halt. Waschbär and his ferret cohorts were conspicuously absent, and the unusual tranquility of the night was safeguarded by the fact that the four fairies' mouths were gagged with rag-clots. Tied together and suspended precariously over the fire by a woman of Amazonian proportions, the fairies flailed their feet and squeaked incoherent warnings. Nate must have understood them better than she did.

"Ha'e my back!"

Nate drew his sword as he turned, trusting she would protect his blind side. Years of onstage sparring had honed Bertie's fighting instincts, and she fell in behind him, fists raised. Thirty or so shadows approached from all sides: men and women both, dressed in shades of midnight and onyx, strapped with weapons from ankle to armpit, a few with gold teeth winking in wide smiles. The largest of them leapt at Nate, wielding a knife that flashed silver-red in the firelight.

Taking advantage of Bertie's distraction, a beefy-armed man twice her age and weight reached out and snagged her roughly by the elbow.

"Mind your manners," he admonished her with a leer.

"Mind *this*," Bertie countered as her solid right hook broke his nose with a sickly satisfying crunch. Before she could process the small victory, another arm clamped about her waist and a knife was laid alongside her neck. The world constricted to approximately six inches of incredibly, horrifyingly cold metal.

"Don't move, if you please, or I'll slit your throat," instructed a husky voice. Bertie's captor swung her around to see a new opponent jab the butt end of a gnarled walking stick into Nate's barely healed wound. With a roar, the pirate rushed him, and the two fell arse over teakettle into the dirt.

"He's a talented fighter," Bertie's dance partner

murmured, his breath smelling of tooth rot and smoked meat. "Pity he didn't teach you a trick or two."

There he's very much mistaken.

She followed the thought with an elbow to her captor's gut and a well-placed stamp upon the tiny bones atop his foot. The man holding her hostage retaliated by grasping a handful of her wet silver hair and snapping her head back to expose her neck.

Not, Bertie noted through the red haze of shock and pain at being handled in such a brutal fashion, the way any of the Players would have reacted.

There will be no mustache twirling with this lot.

"I ought to slit your throat and have done with it," her attacker said, digging the tip of his blade in deep enough to bring a whimper to her lips, and the warm trickle that followed indicated he'd drawn blood. "Suppose you change my mind by calling off your hound?"

"Nate," Bertie croaked in compliance.

Heeding her voice, he turned, giving his opponent the advantage. In seconds, the pirate was eating a mouthful of dirt, a boot grinding into his back. His struggles ceased the moment he saw the knife to Bertie's throat, his body going deadly still as his gaze flickered around the clearing.

By then Mustardseed had eaten through his gag. "We tried to warn you!"

"But the big one got the drop on us!" Cobweb squeaked seconds later.

"Shut up, you!" The lady brigand reeled the fairies into her hand and gave them a squeeze. Moth's eyes nearly bugged out of his head with the pressure, and Peaseblossom's face turned as pink as her namesake.

Forgetting she was in no position to issue orders, Bertie barked, "Stop that!"

The woman paused in her tender ministrations, eyes shifting to her Leader before her boa constrictor grip upon the fairies resumed.

Though they'd been tiny, fluttering menaces for all the years Bertie had known them, she had never before stopped to consider what delicate bones her friends must have: hollow, like a bird's, and snapped as easily as campfire kindling. Their struggles began to subside, most likely due to lack of oxygen, and Bertie's fears reached up her throat to similarly choke her. "Make her stop; she'll kill them!"

"Nothing wrong with a bit of incentive, is there?" With his hands still gripping Bertie's hair, the brigands' Leader dragged her closer to the fire.

She wished she could spit in his eye but was fairly certain that, if she attempted it, all she'd do is spatter her own face and perhaps enrage her captor enough to make good his throat-slitting threat. "Just take what you want and go."

"Thank you kindly, we'll do just that," he responded, "the moment you give us the journal."

Bertie stiffened, wishing she could lie but knowing her utter lack of guile would appear upon her face. Still, she attempted it. "What journal?"

"Don't play coy. You were seen with it in the Caravanserai."

Damn. She'd only taken it from Waschbär's pack for a few seconds, but apparently that had been enough.

That didn't mean she would admit it, though. "You must be mistaking me for someone else with silver hair." The lie felt slick on Bertie's mouth and added another thin layer to her new mask.

The man holding her didn't speak, didn't smile, giving no warning before he released her hair and used that same hand to slap her hard across the face. A rippling cascade of pain accompanied the fresh batch of starry tears that fell through Bertie's field of vision, the diamond-brilliant bits pouring from her eyes and pattering into the dirt at her feet.

"Coo, would you look at that?" The lady brigand started to move forward.

"Remember what we were hired to do, if you please," the Leader snarled at her, and the woman leapt back as though scorched. When he returned his attention to Bertie, his features were fragmented into kaleidoscope patterns by her tears. "Perhaps you'd like to consider the difference between stubborn and stupid now?"

"Don't tell him a damn thing—" Nate started to protest before the dirt filled his mouth once more. Not settling for the mud gargle, the brigand standing atop him pulled back his boot and kicked Nate hard in the ribs, just where Bertie's arrow had hit him. Curling over himself, the pirate groaned and went deathly pale.

"Bertie!" Her name was a fire engine's wail on Mustardseed's and Cobweb's lips as the lady brigand held their boots to the flames. Moth was goggle-eyed with fear, and Peaseblossom had passed out completely, hanging limp from her bindings. Even when the tips of her tiny wings began to curl up and smoke at the edges, her eyelids didn't so much as flutter.

Bile boiled up the back of Bertie's throat, and she blurted, "It's in Waschbär's knapsack!"

Her confession prompted the Leader to hold up one finger, and the female brigand lifted the fairies infinitesimally. Tiny droplets of sweat rolled down the sides of the boys' faces, dropping onto the fire with minute sizzles. Peaseblossom still didn't move. Bertie couldn't breathe, couldn't think, and she couldn't answer when the Leader put his nose inches from her own and murmured, "So the hairy little turncoat now travels with you. That's an interesting development."

CHAPTER EIGHT

A Fair Hot Wench in Flame-Colour'd Taffeta

"**D**id you not part on good terms then?" Bertie demanded with as much insolence as she could muster under the circumstances, which lay somewhere between not much and none at all.

A single nod of his head brought the fairies back within flames' reach.

"I'm the one asking the questions right now," the brigands' Leader said, his voice hardly audible over the crackle of the fire and Bertie's heartbeat hammering in her ears. "Just where might his knapsack be?"

"Atop the caravan," she managed, but just barely.

"Unlikely that the sneak-thief would part with his treasures, and yet you've little to gain by lying to me right now." The Leader jerked his chin, and three brigands scaled the sides of the troupe's conveyance with the stealth of ninja assassins. Tossing the travel-scarred bag from person to person, they delivered it with impossible speed to their Leader, who held it out to Bertie. "If you please."

She wanted to sound as defiant and rude as the fairies at their worst, but couldn't manage it, not with three sets of pleading eyes upon her. Not with Peaseblossom looking like a rose petal crushed under a careless foot. "Why me?"

"In case you've any tricks up your dainty sleeve."

Bertie wrenched open the bag. Rummaging about in search of the silk-wrapped notebook, her fingertips brushed over the heavy ring set with an opal and a glass vial containing sand before her hand closed around the wicked-sharp blade of the obsidian knife.

Telltale murderous thoughts must have flickered over Bertie's features. The brigands' Leader clasped her wrist and twisted the weapon from her grasp before she could finish entertaining the thought of plunging it into his right eye. The stone sliver landed in the grass alongside her diamond-tears, its crimson ribbon trailing away with an eerie suggestion of blood spilled.

"Our little mouse thinks to attack the lion," he said, prompting a slosh of laughter from his cohorts. "Try again."

This time, Bertie extracted the journal on the first try. "Take it and be damned—" Before she could finish, before she could so much as blink, it was gone from her hands.

"Such a small thing to be so very wanted." The brigand Leader removed the protective silk to confirm his quarry. Tucking the journal into an unseen pocket, he let the scrap of fabric flutter to the ground.

"It was certainly an unwanted thing when Waschbär took it," Bertie said with a flare of temper. In response, the lady brigand lowered the fairies until the campfire flames tickled their toes. As the boys screeched, Bertie wished she could make their captors spontaneously combust. "Unlike some, he follows a code of honor!"

"But how charming that you think of him so highly!" the Leader chortled with true amusement, the sort reserved for a child who insists the grass is purple and the clouds made of cotton candy. "I would have the location of our former comrade."

"Believe me when I say I haven't the foggiest clue where he's gone." She might have said much more and peppered the diatribe with curses, save the barest stirring of the wind caused Bertie's breath to catch in her throat.

Ariel?

After a long moment, it blew again, breeze enough to fan the fire and move the hair along the nape of her neck. And how she wished for him to manifest, to appear overhead like some avenging angel intent upon smiting . . .

Lots and lots of smiting!

. . . except this time, the wind was merely the wind, no

precursor to the air elemental's entrance. Moments passed before Bertie realized that he wasn't coming, that he hadn't somehow sensed she was in danger and raced to her side. Her disappointment brought more pain than the brigand's second deliberate blow to her cheek.

"As you said yourself," she said with a choking sort of sob, "there's no use lying to you right now."

After a long moment, the Leader nodded to his companions. The woman holding the fairies dropped them, thankfully not into the fire, but onto a patch of weeds. The man responsible for wounding Nate took the pirate's sword as his prize. The others rushed forward to gather the "diamonds" from the dirt and strip the boxes and bags from the caravan. Bertie made no sound of protest when they pulled out Valentijn's parting gift of clothing, nor when they found what remained of the Mistress of Revels's gold coin belt, nor when the fairies' hatbox theater was pitched atop the fire with malicious glee. Within minutes, the cart stood as barren as a vulture-pecked carcass, and Bertie was left holding only Waschbär's knapsack.

"Oughtn't we have that as well?" the lady brigand suggested with a greedy gleam in her eye.

"The contents are unwanted things, even by the likes of us," the Leader responded with a mocking sort of bow. "We got what we came for. It's time to take our leave."

Their exit was something to behold, for they didn't so

much depart as melt into the night, disappearing around trees and ducking between the places rendered silver by moonlight. The Players at the theater couldn't have managed better, not even with their trapdoors and folding screens, but Bertie didn't pause to appreciate the subtle dexterity of it. Instead, she leapt forward to scoop up the fairies in both hands.

"Stop wiggling!" Something in her voice prompted the boys to obey. Releasing them from the twine was the easy bit; seeing Peaseblossom laying limp in her palm after the boys flitted free was not.

Subdued by the sight of their fallen comrade, Mustardseed, Moth, and Cobweb landed on Bertie's shoulders, neither pleading nor screeching their concerns. As she lifted Peaseblossom to her cheek, the boys pulled their elfin caps off, leaving their hair to poke in every which direction. Cobweb sniffed mightily, Mustardseed didn't even heed the tears already rolling down his cheeks, and Moth twisted his little hat so hard that he ripped it right in two.

"Oh, Pease." Bertie stroked a finger over her tiny friend. "Don't be—" She couldn't say it. Saying it might make it so.

A hand clamped down upon her shoulder, but the rasp of Nate's voice accompanied it. "Steady there." He had his other hand pressed to his side, and his face was more than a bit bloodied by the brawl. "She's not—"

"No." Bertie shook her head until she was dizzy. "She

can't be." But the slight movement caused Peaseblossom's singed wings to crumble to ash.

"Shouldn't someone clap?" Mustardseed asked, wiping his eyes and nose on his sleeve. "Clap if we believe?"

"Clap if you think it will do any damn good," Bertie said, cupping her hand around Peaseblossom. "But if the fire took her from us, the fire can jolly well give her back."

Easier if the fire was a person from whom she could wring such a favor. Bertie reached into Waschbär's bag, stirring its contents with her hand until she located the opal ring. Turning toward the dying red and gold flames, she tried to imagine the woman who would wear a piece of jewelry such as this. Once sparked, a story not her own poured out of her mouth with the hiss and pop of the burning wood:

Lava-born, she waits in the heart of a great volcano. Bloodred toe shoes adorn her feet, salamanders slide down her skin to encircle her throat and form a glowing necklace, and her eyes glitter black from edge to edge.

Someone else had put pen to paper to write the description, and a whiff of thin silk and wood, of whiskey and cigarette smoke accompanied it. Before Bertie could place the scents, so tantalizing in their familiarity, the suggestion of a woman emerged from the opal. No more than a wisp of smoke, the curious apparition instantly wavered and began to dissipate. Bertie hastily fed the image bits of her soul: meaningless memories that were oak twigs and dry pine needles, painful ones that were sap-covered branches eagerly devoured by the flames. Though she didn't want to recall the Scrimshander, Bertie nevertheless conjured the memory of flight, of gliding with him upon the wind, the feel of feathers upon her arms, and the ability to soar from the darkness as a bird. Nearly intoxicated by the remembrance, she called the winds to her, directed them at the woman standing before her.

Strengthened, the fire-dancer took several hesitant steps until she stood in the very heart of the campfire. Midsummer lightning suddenly filled the night sky, and apple trees encircled the campsite. Everything burned, from the boughs overhead to the shiny volcanic pebbles that skittered underfoot to the tiny scrap of light, a bit of iridescent nothing with glowing wings that sat upon the fire-dancer's shoulder.

"This isn't some ungodly vision, is it?" Bertie, still cradling Peaseblossom's limp form, whispered to Nate. "You see her, don't you?"

"Aye, I can see her." Nate didn't sound at all happy about it, not that Bertie could blame him. "An' Peaseblossom, too."

That was all the confirmation Bertie needed. She held

out her hand to the newcomer, though the rolling heat exuding from the woman curled the tiny hairs upon Bertie's arm. "Please give back my friend."

The fire-dancer stood, quiet, unmoving save for the softly flaming tendrils of hair that snaked over her shoulders.

Recalling the ring, Bertie held it out. "I would trade something for her—"

With an ear-piercing shriek, the fire-dancer leapt out of the flames, enveloping everyone in a cloud of smoke and cinders and ash. Burning fingers grasped at the ring, scrabbling over Bertie's skin; pain spread up her arm, as though a blacksmith had replaced her very bones with glowing iron rods.

But the tiny lustrous thing on the fire-dancer's shoulder was now within reach. Bertie snatched at Peaseblossom's shimmering doppelgänger while the air swirling about her thickened, gray and choking—

I seem to have a knack for asphyxiating. . . .

—and just when she thought she might suck the smoke into her lungs and die, Bertie summoned the magic of sap running through tree veins, clapped her hands together, and forced the fairy's soul back into her body. An explosion of light and heat and color knocked Bertie flat on her backside, arms akimbo, rendered nearly deaf and blind for several agonizing seconds.

"Pease?" The name was a gasp as Bertie's lungs yet burned. A moment later, a tiny ball of light traveling at approximately one hundred miles per hour hit her directly in the chest. Embracing a fully restored Peaseblossom, Bertie wished there was a way to hug her friend harder without squashing her flat, then gently grasped the fairy and raised her to nose level. "Don't you *ever* die on me again!"

"Not if I can help it!" Along with the exclamation, the fairy exhaled yet-glowing cinders.

"What she said!" The boys rushed forward to deliver their own squeaking remonstrations, clutching an unwilling Peaseblossom to a variety of bosoms—or where bosoms would be if they had any.

"I told you it would take clapping to save her!" Mustardseed crowed as he hugged Peaseblossom's left ankle.

"Bertie." Backlit by the campfire, Nate's head seemed to be surrounded by a nimbus of light, sparking gold off his earring. "Are ye burnt?"

She paused to take inventory, but other than the occasional wheeze, Bertie hadn't sustained any damage from the fire-dancer's touch. "I'm all right."

"That's good. Now, d'ye think there's any way t' take that ring back? Th' moment that creature put it on her finger, yer bit of story became truth."

"Not my story . . . I was mouthing someone else's narrative." Bertie's eyes refocused on the figure crouched before them in the leaves, automatically cataloguing the fire-dancer's transformation-carved details: burgundy-black hair arranged in impossible curls and tiny braids, a heavy gold band encircling her head with an opal as large as a quail's egg dangling from it. "Someone else wrote this creature into existence."

"It's true." The newcomer's pronouncement held a note of finality, like the ringing of a church bell at midnight. "He wrote me into existence and then trapped me inside this stone. Too long have I been imprisoned." When she slid the opal ring onto her finger, the jewel vibrated with unearthly harmony and the nearly dead fire behind her blazed up anew. "You have my deepest thanks."

"Do your deepest thanks come with cake?" Mustard-seed wanted to know.

"Cake?" The fire-dancer looked at Bertie, puzzled, but it was Nate who spoke first and not about dessert.

"Get behind me." He reached for a weapon not there, face drawn and ferocious as his hands curled into fists. "The brigands are comin' back—"

But it was Waschbär who entered the scene, his perturbation manifesting in the rustle of grasses and leaves he normally would have passed through with uncanny silence. Bertie noted with a certain amount of jealousy that his mask was yet intact, that not a trace of surprise or guilt or any number of other emotions were revealed upon his face or in his dark eyes, at least until his gaze alighted upon the fire-dancer.

"And who is this?"

The newcomer answered, "My name is Varvara."

"Never mind her!" Mustardseed, Moth, and Cobweb paused in their ministrations to Peaseblossom to hurl accusations at Waschbär. "You vile betrayer!"

"Turncoat!"

"That horrible woman squeezed Peaseblossom *to death*."

"Her insides were nearly her outsides!"

"Aren't you ashamed of yourself?" Mustardseed's question was the one Bertie would have asked, though she couldn't have delivered the line with as much ire as he did. The fairy sounded two parts appalled grandmother and one part condemning judge and jury, especially when he followed that question with, "What have you to say in your defense?"

"I've no excuse." Waschbär's shoulders slumped forward under the weight of the recriminations. "I can only apologize for my baser instincts, which caused me to flee the moment I realized we were nearly surrounded. I was through the shrubbery and halfway across the field before I realized what I'd done."

"The brigands stole the journal." Bertie pushed the fall of her silver hair from her eyes to better fix Waschbär with her Sternest Gaze. "That cursed thing might have caused great complications and confusion thus far, but I'm sure it will be needed before the telling of this tale is done. We have to get it back."

"An' how d'ye propose t' do that exactly?" Despite Varvara's screech of protest, Nate kicked dirt on the fire and poured water over the smoking coals. Then he went to wind the mechanical horses, turning their keys with grim twists of his hand. "We're not lingerin' here long enough t' ha'e our throats slit or ha'e Sedna catch up wi' us—"

"I'll get the journal back," the sneak-thief interrupted. "Only when I reclaim what's been taken will I be worthy to travel with you again." Bertie would have protested, but he shook his shaggy head. "Don't use your word weapons to argue with me. Every moment I linger here, my quarry draws further afield." He reached out, squeezed her arm in unspoken farewell, then melted into the night. He took the gleaming sets of eyes that were Pip Pip and Cheerio with him, but left his bag of unwanted things for Bertie to shoulder.

Clutching it until she could feel her knuckles protest, Bertie turned troubled eyes to Nate. "He oughtn't to go after them alone."

"Don't be daft. Ye want it back, an' there's no one else t' spare fer th' job." Nate clambered onto the caravan and hauled Bertie aboard as easily as he might have lifted a pup by the neck scruff. "Everyone up who's comin'."

"Wait for us!" Mustardseed, Moth, and Cobweb immediately made a sling chair of their hands and carried Peaseblossom atop the caravan in a manner most unusually solicitous.

A delicate hand appeared next to Bertie's elbow, holding the discarded scrap of silk that once bound the journal shut. "This is yours, I believe," the fire-dancer said.

Bertie took it from her and shoved it deep into Waschbär's bag. "Thank you."

Without waiting for anyone's permission, Varvara clambered up the caravan's ladder to join them.

"And just what do you think *you* are doing?" Moth wanted to know.

"Coming with you so that I might repay the debt I incurred." The fire-dancer folded her legs under her, looking disconcertingly comfortable even when twisted like a pretzel.

"What debt?" Cobweb took up the inquiry.

"The debt of freedom." Varvara looked over at Bertie. "You'll hardly even know I'm here." Indeed, the next second she seemed to pull her crackling energy and light within her, tamping it down as one would a campfire until only her obsidian-dark eyes signaled she was anything more than another beautiful albeit mysterious performer travel-ing with the troupe.

"I suppose we can't just leave her here, alone." Bertie turned to Nate. "We'll have to take her with us to the Dis-tant Castle. Maybe find a way to work her into the act."

Still ministering to Peaseblossom, Mustardseed balked at the idea. "That's a terrible idea! She could roast us as soon as look at us!"

"You are performing for the Queen?" Subtle red sparks accompanied Varvara's question. "If you seek to impress Her Gracious Majesty, I can surely be of some as-sistance during your performance. I can do more than just dance."

"Like twirl flaming batons?" Moth wanted to know.

"Catherine cartwheels?" Cobweb asked.

"Roasting of marshmallows?" Mustardseed said, fi-nally won over.

With a small chortle that was like liquid amber poured from a thick crystal cup, Varvara nodded. "All of the above and more, I assure you."

Peaseblossom said nothing, merely narrowing her eyes and looking all manner of grim things. Bertie couldn't blame her reticence, given what she'd just endured. A page turned over in Bertie's head, and the next bit of the fire-dancer's narrative came with a warning.

*Never mistake her complacence for the
illusion of control. She is like wildfire,
at once utterly beguiling and wholly untamable.*

This time, the cadence of the stern words was unmistak-able, filled as it was with echoes of the Theater Manager's inflections. The fire-dancer's breath escaped with a low hiss, and Bertie hastened to extract a promise from her. "You'll come with us, and everyone will be on their best behavior, understood?"

Fire-dancer and fairies nodded as one, so Nate sig-naled the horses. With a jolt that set the lanterns swaying, the caravan commenced rattling down the road, without the weight of all the luggage to steady them.

"We'll make better time," was his grim observation, "seein' as how we've been stripped clean o' food an' clothes an' everythin' else."

Irrepressible even in the face of potential nudity and starvation, Bertie managed a smile. "You'll cut our time in half, at this rate."

"More than that," he said, "fer I've no plans t' stay on th' road. We need t' carve our own path, away from th' river an' away from any chance Sedna will find ye."

"It will make it harder for Waschbär to find us as well," Bertie noted, not necessarily thinking of the sneak-thief when she said it.

Nate saw something about the quirk to her mouth that displeased him. "Aye, Waschbär . . . an' anyone else that might be givin' chase."

"The brigands," Bertie retorted. The moment Nate returned his attention to the road, she finished her thought.

And Ariel.

His absence was like a sore tooth her tongue sought over and over again, despite the ache, despite the knowledge that it hurt.

Considering the challenges ahead of them, she ought to plan their performance for the Queen instead of fretting about Ariel. Unhampered by complex affairs of the heart, the fairies huddled down inside Bertie's hood like so many mice in a nest. Feeling at ease if not quite welcome, the fire-dancer hummed a wordless tune under her breath that caused the stars to swim and run like raindrops down a windowpane. Lulled by the noise, Bertie fell into a reluctant and uneasy sleep.

CHAPTER NINE

This Scepter'd Isle,
This Earth of Majesty

The jerking halt of their progress roused her some hours later, and Bertie was appalled to discover that not only was her nose buried in Nate's shirt-sleeve but she'd soaked the linen with drool. Worse yet, there was no surreptitious way to wipe her mouth, not with him already looking down at her, bemused.

"A little spit ne'er hurt anyone."

"A lot of spit never hurt anyone, either!" Mustardseed said, working up something in the back of his throat that sounded potentially life threatening.

"Don't you dare!" Peaseblossom accompanied the command with a solid thump to the back of his head, prompting him to swallow it.

"Why'd we stop?" Moth asked as Mustardseed turned green and keeled over.

"We need to scavenge some breakfast an' find a bit o' drinkable water," the pirate answered, scanning the nearby fields in search of sustenance.

"He's joking, right?" Cobweb looked about them. "There aren't any stores or restaurants for miles!"

"I think he means we should . . . pick things." Mustardseed had recovered enough to wrinkle his tiny nose. "Suppose I accidentally step in a cow pie?"

"Hooray, pie!" cheered Moth.

"Not *that* kind of pie," Peaseblossom said, then enlightened him as to the true nature of a cow pie in disturbingly vivid detail.

"Yeeeeeeew!" Moth said with disconsolate fingers in his ears.

The others immediately began muttering to themselves about the need for pudding and wouldn't a bit of jam tart be lovely about now, especially for poor Peaseblossom, invalid that she was. Determined to remedy the situation, the boys scattered to search the caravan for sweet survivors of the pillaging. A few minutes later, Cobweb crowed with triumph.

"They missed the case with the gold binoculars, Bertie! The box was shoved all the way under the seat!"

"Pity they aren't gold-foil-wrapped chocolate binoculars," Mustardseed said with the saddest sort of sniff.

A breeze gusted around them, an amused exhalation. Nate took no note of it, but Bertie's head whipped around in search of the source. Sleeping like a salamander coiled before a glowing hearth, Varvara's skin ember-glowed with the sudden attention, and she stretched luxuriously.

"Have we reached the Distant Castle already?"

"Not by half," Nate told her, jumping down. "If anyone needs t' visit th' necessary, now's th' time t' do it."

"Of all the things that might be considered necessary at this juncture, peeing on the local foliage isn't one of them," Peaseblossom said, though the boys hastened to do just that.

Bertie, however, was relieved to see her little friend restored to all previous levels of vim, vigor, and vinegar. "You're feeling all right?"

"A bit tattered about the edges," the fairy replied with a grin, "but I'll do." Then, contrary to her mandate, Peaseblossom headed for the nearest set of shrubs.

The next puff of wind brought with it the whisper of her name, and Bertie scrambled down, striking out into a heavily wooded area on the opposite side of the road with a call of "I'll be right back" to the fire-dancer yet sitting atop the caravan. Treading upon bracken and fern released a spicy reek that cleared the last of the smoke from Bertie's sinuses. Distracted by the scents of the forest, she yelped aloud when a hand clamped down upon her elbow and dragged her behind the largest of the pine trees.

"I've been looking *everywhere* for you." Ariel's hair snapped with barely contained fury. "Whatever made you leave the main road?"

"You're one to ask questions!" While adrenaline was not as tasty as a quad-shot cappuccino, it certainly had the same effect upon her body. "The last I saw you, you were on a rooftop at the Caravanserai, declaring your soul-wrenching need for freedom. Didn't you relish the time to yourself?"

"Not nearly as much as I thought I would! And you shouldn't have departed without me!"

"Then you shouldn't have stayed upon the rooftop to sulk! I was terrified you'd never come back." Mouth un-stoppered, the truth poured out of Bertie, brighter than the sunlight that suddenly slanted between the trees. Be-latedly, she remembered her mask, as yet merely the thin-nest film of secrets, and could only guess at the flicker and play of emotions crossing her features.

Indeed, Ariel ducked his head to peer at her. "What have you done to yourself?"

Bertie found it impossible to voice a placating lie. "Taken out a bit of insurance to make certain Sedna can't track me down."

"You need to get to the Queen's stronghold," he said, yet staring at her face. "You'll be safer there, surely."

Looking up at him, Bertie didn't give a fig about the Queen or her stronghold. "So you heard about our summons?"

"I made the necessary inquiries as to your whereabouts when I realized you were gone, yes."

That he'd cared enough to find them, to follow, caused a bright sort of happiness to unfold inside Bertie like a paper lantern catching on fire. "I'm glad you're here."

"That," Ariel answered, leaning forward to kiss her softly, "is abundantly obvious."

He tasted like the very stars, and each movement of his lips against hers was like touching the sky.

The noise that erupted behind them was too small for a supernova but too violent for a mere throat clearing; Bertie leapt away from Ariel to spot Nate standing only a few feet away.

"Not t' be interruptin' anythin', but we need t' get back on th' road." Without another word, he turned and crashed through the underbrush, breaking branches with his wide shoulders and flattening small plants with his boots.

"Damn it all." Bertie watched him go, conflicting emotions twisting her intestines into knots.

Far from looking smug, Ariel's expression clouded. "The

fact that you love us equally might have saved us in Sedna's cavern, but one day soon, you are going to have to make a decision." He took several steps in the opposite direction.

Bertie considered lobbing a rock at the back of his head. "Where are you going now?"

"I'll fly to the Distant Castle. I don't think I can stand the torture of earthbound travels, just at the moment." Indeed, his shoulders shook, either with the effort of remaining on the ground or with temper. "Never fear, the gallant pirate lad will see to your safety."

"Ariel, don't—" She would have argued more, but could think of nothing to say to persuade him to stay. Left standing alone in the clearing, she contemplated climbing into the nearest tree, pulling the moss around her like a shawl, and letting the sap encapsulate her; surely then she would get some much needed peace. "Amber-trapped for a hundred years would do, for a start."

Except Bertie could not abandon her promises to Ophelia, to herself. She returned to the caravan, marginally grateful that Nate waited for her to clamber aboard before he signaled the horses to move out. Her gratitude did not, however, extend to the "breakfast," which consisted of mushrooms, berries, nuts, and assorted greenery Nate had scavenged from the hedges. Convinced they'd be poisoned by salad and toadstools, the fairies refused to touch any of it, breaking instead into a cache of sweets gone undetected by the brigands.

"Not the sort of truffles," Mustardseed had explained with a glower, "you find in the dirt."

"Unless you dropped it there!" Cobweb extracted several pale-green-and-white-striped marshmallows from a paper bag. When the others raised eyebrows at him, he clutched them defensively. "What?"

"You were holding out on us!"

"And if I hadn't held out, the brigands would have taken them!"

Before the boys could start biting one another, Varvara leaned forward, setting one of the confections aflame with her fingertips. As the fairies' arguments trailed off, she offered the caramelized sugar to them.

Thoroughly appeased, Mustardseed jumped up and down. "Oh! Oh! We need graham crackers!"

Cobweb swooned. "I think I love you. Will you marry me?"

Varvara laughed and let him lick her fingers. Something about the fire magic had apparently strengthened her, for now her fingernails glittered with hundreds of tiny rubies.

Moth tapped the toes of his little boots together. "If we still had the journal, Bertie could write us a hail of graham crackers."

"Shut yer gobs," Nate muttered.

"What's the matter with you?" Mustardseed wanted to know.

Instead of elaborating, Nate expressed his disapproval of Bertie's forest tryst by forcibly handing her a scrap of linen containing her share of the food. "Eat that."

Although a welcome diversion from having to discuss her kiss with Ariel, the berries were sour enough to curl her toes. Tempted to spit them overboard, a glance at Nate told her the punishment for such an action might start with keelhauling and end with plank walking.

If yesterday's journey had been a sun-softened choco-late bar, the ensuing hours were a miserable piece of jagged-edged rock candy, liberally coated with purse lint and bits of used tissue. The fairies contributed only complaints and ever-louder stomach rumbles as time advanced alongside the caravan's wheels. Observing the sun's relentless arc over-head, Bertie despaired over their lack of suitable script and costumes.

When he finally spoke, the pirate's tone erred on the side of consolatory, if not contrite.

"Did ye think t' ask th' newcomer why she was ensor-celled int' a bit o' jewelry?"

"I've been too busy panicking about our upcoming performance to ponder what sort of new magic we're deal-ing with," Bertie retorted.

"I know th' sorts o' trouble yer capable o'." Sharp words that could have cut, had Nate placed more anger behind them; the blade was turned aside by a gentle elbow nudge. "An' now there's trouble I don't know."

"I promise to be on my best behavior," came a lilting voice behind them.

Bertie twisted around in her seat. "Apologies. We should have just asked you instead of conjecturing."

"Not to be rude," Mustardseed said, assurance that whatever he was about to say would certainly be less than polite, "but how did you get trapped in that ring?"

"A magician grew frightened of his own word-spells and trapped me there." Varvara pressed her mouth together so hard that sparks leapt from her lips.

"That ring belonged to the Theater Manager, and he certainly is no magician—" Except Bertie remembered a small snippet of a conversation she'd once had with Mr. Hastings.

The Theater Manager had aspired to write a grand opera.

Could Varvara be one of his characters?

Before Bertie could inquire as to such a thing, the fire-dancer tilted her head to one side and said, "I'd prefer not to speak of the past, but rather the future. How much further is the Distant Castle?"

Bertie leaned forward to check the map, and her

stomach dropped at the sight of their progress. Though Nate had managed to cover a surprising amount of terrain, the Queen's stronghold still lay a goodly distance ahead of them. Counted by finger widths, hundreds of miles yet separated them from the Distant Castle. One hard look down the ragged dirt path they traveled confirmed it: A sentinel row of trees grew on the right, craggy mountains flanked them on the left, and between the two rose a silver spire, so distant as to seem impossible to reach in less than a week or two.

"It doesn't matter," Bertie said, tasting fresh despair. "We'll never make it on time."

"I hear th' challenge, an' accept."

She wasn't having any of the optimism Nate was serving. "Even if we do arrive before the gates are locked, we've no act to perform, no props or costumes. Everything was stolen by the brigands." Clutching the sneak-thief's bag to her chest, Bertie wished it held more than silk-rags and sand.

"Ye'll think o' somethin'," Nate said with a weary yet bemused smile. "Ye always do."

"That's hardly reassuring," Bertie shot back, "but far be it from me to dismiss a vote of confidence when we so heartily need one."

"Th' Queen invited ye specially. If she wants t' see ye, it's a matter o' great importance, never mind yer clothes an' yer bits."

"Easy for you to say!" Dressed as he was in leather trousers that wouldn't wrinkle and a linen shirt that looked good even when it was covered in pleats and creases, Nate was still presentable. If Bertie looked as unkempt as she felt, she must resemble a walking rag-bag. "Boys never worry about these things!"

"Men," he corrected her on two counts as he guided the caravan back onto the main road, now devoid of traffic, "know when clothes are important an' when they are not."

Caring less about clothing than candies, the fairies were once again scouring the wagon for crumbs. Bertie reached under the seat and pulled out the binoculars' case. "Here, you little monsters, occupy yourselves."

They promptly abandoned the empty marshmallow bag, each accepting a pair and then trying to determine the best vantage point. Within seconds, they'd decided to sit upon Bertie. Mustardseed assured his place on her left shoulder by clambering over Cobweb's back, though that good fairy retaliated by handily tripping his friend.

"Let me see!" Moth crowded in next to Peaseblossom, who'd wisely moved to Bertie's other shoulder.

"I've left you plenty of room." The fairy's offense was evident in her tone as she indicated a miniscule space near her feet.

"NO ROOM!" he bellowed, though he managed to scrunch up and peer through his glasses. "Oh, look! A castle!"

"Already?" Shifting the horses' reins to his left hand, Nate retrieved another pair of binoculars from the case. When he lifted them to his eyes, a startled noise tumbled out of his mouth. "Ye might want t' see this."

After handing Varvara an extra set of spy glasses, Bertie obeyed. The castle gates snapped into focus, bricks like square pearls forming a massive wall, the archway composed of impossibly twisted glass tendrils. Secondary and tertiary tiers rose above that, like the layers on a wedding cake.

Bertie lowered her glasses, and her exclamation of delighted surprise was transformed into a strangled noise of disbelief. The glasses had done more than magnify the Distant Castle; they'd transported troupe and caravan to the very gates of the Queen's stronghold. Nate drew the mechanical horses up just short of the glass archway. On either side of the closed doors hung a gold-and-white bell-pull, one marked VISITORS and the other SERVANTS.

Vaulting down from the driver's seat, Bertie rang each of them in turn, politely at first and then with greater desperation. "It's no use . . . they've locked the doors, as promised."

The fire-dancer appeared at Bertie's elbow without so much as a stirring of her crimson skirts to mark her graceful movements. "What is glass was once sand and fire." Varvara slanted a playful look at Bertie. "Everything about you suggests you are a daughter of the earth."

"I am, but—"

"Then let us open the doors by means of a method more creative than lock picking." Varvara placed her palms against the wall. "Unless the sands will not obey you?"

The fire-dancer's eyebrow, quirked in challenge, so reminded Bertie of Ariel that she could hardly breathe.

"What are ye doin'?" Nate called from the caravan.

"Breaking and entering," Bertie muttered as she placed her hands alongside Varvara's. "Which means I'm certain to have my head liberated from my shoulders within the hour!"

The fairies shouted a variety of warnings, but their voices faded to a dim murmur when the fire-dancer's ruby fingernails stroked the gates, wrapping the memories of flames about her fingers and drawing them toward her like so many ribbons. Before them, the glass shuddered, and Bertie had to scramble to move the sands aside before they were buried up to their necks. Under her command, the tiny particles of stone swirled through the air like glitter tossed, slowly gathering in drifts on either side of the road. Pressing forward step by careful step, Bertie and Varvara cleared a path wide enough for the caravan to pass.

"Drive through!" Bertie shouted to Nate, hoping he could hear her above the hiss of sand and Varvara's peal of triumphant laughter. The moment he cleared the inner wall, Bertie began the struggle to return every grain of sand to its rightful place. "Put the flames back, Varvara!"

Red-hot salamanders slithered over her skin, hissing with reluctance to be parted from their mistress, and for a moment, it looked as though the fire-dancer would refuse. Finally, Varvara shrugged and flicked the flames at the portal.

Their powers met and merged and fell apart, two dancers in a waltz, and though Bertie did her best to render the gates as they had been, there was no denying the theater's art nouveau influence upon the result. Glowering, she was attempting a second rendering when two guards rounded the corner of a nearby tavern.

"Halt!" They approached at a run, leveling silver-tipped bayonets at her. "Stop what you're doing and put your hands in the air!"

"One second longer," Varvara said, either not recognizing the danger or not caring that she and Bertie were about to be arrested. "My friend improvised a bit with the architecture. We wouldn't want to be accused of artistic license along with breaking and entering, would we?"

"Never mind that!" With a muttered curse, Bertie grabbed the fire-dancer by the arm, severing the connection between the fire magic and the glass gate. "We have to get out of here!"

Nate set the reins to the horses' backs as the girls scrambled onto the caravan. They left the guards in the dust, though Bertie knew it was only a matter of minutes before the troupe was apprehended. There was, after all, only one road: the one leading directly up to the castle.

"I have sand in my ears!" Moth wailed, shaking like a dog.

"And mouth," Cobweb said, spitting far more than necessary.

"I have it somewhere worse," Mustardseed hinted darkly.

"Drive faster, Nate!" Bertie commanded as the caravan rattled through the first tier of Her Gracious Majesty's kingdom, the domain of the Lioness.

"Easier said than done wi' all th' yammering!" he flashed. "The road's as narrow an' bent as a cat's tail."

To prove his point, the mechanical horses raced breakneck around a building of tawny wood. Supported at intervals with rugged cornice pieces carved to resemble paws, the structure loomed over them as though about to pounce. Twisted in her seat to keep an eye on their pursuers, Bertie only caught glimpses of the feline statuary guarding various houses and their smaller cat cousins. Disapproving topaz eyes glinted, and tails twitched in condemnation, as though word of the troupe's transgression had already reached them.

In contrast, Varvara's face was still alight with the salamanders' glow. "That was fun! We ought to do it again sometime soon."

"We are not going to repeat that performance," Bertie said, trying to sound firm.

"An' just what will ye say t' get us out o' this mess?" Nate wanted to know as they approached the second gate. Two rearing unicorns marked this archway, each facing the other, manes forever wind tossed, their golden horns glinting in the last of the day's sunshine.

"I haven't the slightest clue." Bertie gripped Nate's arm as they flashed through the open gate, ignoring the shouts of a new set of guards. The buildings in the second township were painted brilliant white, interspersed with the verdant leaves and brilliant pink flowers of private gardens. Tethered to the dark-fruited mystery of pomegranate trees were small, one-horned white goats, universally tended by young girls who stared goggle-eyed at the caravan as it rattled past.

"Th' road's growin' fair steep," Nate muttered. "If I don't keep th' horses movin' fast enough, we're goin' t' slide back down th' hill an' perish in a pile o' splintered wood. Get ahold o' somethin'." When he whistled to the team, their metallic ears pricked back at the shrill command that no doubt ricocheted inside their silver skulls.

Obliging him, they picked up their pace, approaching the innermost wall of the Queen's stronghold within minutes. At first glance, the vast silvered surface offered no easy entry, and Bertie braced herself for the crash, yet the caravan slid into a sliver of darkness: an almost invisible corridor formed by mirrors set at infinitesimal angles. For a moment, they were trapped in a prism, multiple painted wagons and metallic horses skimming around them. When the troupe finally emerged from the curious tunnel, the road leveled off, but everything continued to suggest a world mirrored. Leaves and blooms of blown glass defied gravity and the limits of real-world landscaping to snake over the very sides of the mountain. The surface of the castle glittered, plated with fish-scale brilliance, each of the tiles a variation on the color scheme: pewter, sterling, and the flat dull gray of the sky before a storm.

The caravan should have made a tremendous rattling noise, crossing a bridge over water so flat that Bertie could see her reflection in it, but the horses' hooves fell silently out of respect for Her Gracious Majesty's abode. Inside the courtyard, performers and wagons and live horses were crammed wheel to wagon next to one another, each jockeying for space near doors guarded by two massive men in white. Nate wrestled with the reins, pinned though they were between a cart of lute players and six itinerant singers balanced atop a single donkey.

"I am Fenek, personal courier to Her Gracious Majesty." A servitor in a feathered cap appeared beside them like something conjured out of a hat. "Might I have your name, please?"

Mindful of the guards from the previous gates closing in at a run, Bertie answered in a rush, "Beatrice Shakespeare Smith and Company."

Fenek snapped to utter attention, his demeanor changing from one of welcome to urgency with the blurred motion of a white-gloved hand to his forehead. "Good Mistress of Revels, you are expected! Her Gracious Majesty feared you hadn't arrived before the gates were locked." Bertie made a noncommittal noise in the back of her throat that ended abruptly when the servitor added, "Please follow me at once! She has said your performance shall take precedence over all others."

"At once?" She glanced over her shoulder, catching sight of their pursuers. "Of course. Lead the way!"

If he was puzzled by her vehemence and swift dismount, the servitor concealed it well. "Do bring your binoculars."

Hurrying behind him, Bertie passed through massive Venetian-mirrored doors. Delicately etched and beveled from floor to ceiling, they fragmented her face into flower petals. The Queen's garden entered the castle with them, bedecking the satin-clad walls of the corridor with ivory butterflies, dragonflies, and rocking horse flies. On the carpet underfoot, tiger lilies nodded to roses, daisies whispered to violets.

Probably muttering their disapproval of my disheveled appearance.

Bertie knew her only option was to explain the circumstances of their arrival and beg the Queen's forgiveness, not only for the gate, but for their lack of preparation. "I have something very important to explain to Her Gracious Majesty—"

"Shhhh," Fenek admonished, his footsteps the scuttling of a nervous rabbit's late for an appointment. "Someone is currently performing. Take care to enter quietly."

But there was no need for the warning. When the Company entered the Grand Hall, Bertie hardly drew a breath, and for once, the fairies weren't making a sound. It was the largest room Bertie had ever seen, larger by far than anything she could have ever imagined. Countless glittering chandeliers descended from a ceiling that seemed to extend to the very heavens, while the floor spread out underfoot in a dozen impossible directions at once. Tiered seating ringed the outer perimeter of the performance space, occupied by countless spectators: courtiers in grand dress the color of black pearls and antique silver coins, performers in gayer costumes that were bright splotches of color against the rest. All eyes were trained upon the countless enormous mirrors that reflected the image of their Queen and the performing singer:

Ariel.

Without the mirrors, it would have been impossible to make him out. Distance reduced the Queen's magnificent dais, encrusted though it was with gold and silver and canopied with white velvet, to something belonging in a doll's house. Her Gracious Majesty was a near-featureless poppet whose presence was the only doorstop preventing the space from expanding forever. Amplified by enormous horn speakers set at intervals, Ariel was mid performance, and more than just the song prickled the hairs along Bertie's arms.

"This way, if you please." With hippity-hopping steps, Fenek led the troupe past chairs toward the performance space, ignoring the curious looks of those around him, the spreading whispers that began as no more than a few words then built in strength and number to rush toward the Queen. Unseen musicians ceased their ministrations to flute and violin.

In the resultant silence, a voice from the dais that could only belong to Her Gracious Majesty bellowed, "What is it, Fenek?"

CHAPTER TEN

Tell O'er Thy Tale Again

Before the servitor could answer, Ariel spoke up. "It is the one for whom you've been waiting, Your Gracious Majesty."

When Bertie raised her binoculars to her eyes, the air elemental's features came sharply into view. Lowering the magical magnifiers with haste, she discovered that she stood only inches from the first step leading up to the dais, transported there much as the caravan had been whisked to the glass outer gates.

Close enough now to take her by the hand, Ariel presented her to the Queen with one of his graceful flourishes. "Permit me the honor, Your Gracious Majesty, of introducing Beatrice Shakespeare Smith and Company."

She immediately dropped into a curtsy. The rest of

the troupe must have employed their binoculars as well, for they appeared like rabbits from a magician's hat behind Bertie with the noiseless pops that accompany surfacing alligators. Varvara executed a most graceful obeisance, and Nate fell to one knee.

"Get down," he muttered to the fairies, neck bowed.

They complied, flinging themselves at the floor and hitting the marble in four noisy belly flops.

"Ow," came the tiny protest from Moth.

Again, the Queen's voice rang out. "Approach, so that we might look upon you."

Swallowing hard, Bertie rose and stepped closer to the dais. Well-meaning streamers of wind teased about the grubby edge of her sweater, tugged at the hasty arrangement of her silver hair. Bertie had yet to look upon Her Gracious Majesty's face, though she could feel the Queen's gaze upon her, at least as sharp as Mrs. Edith's.

"For pity's sake, child, what is so interesting about the floor?"

"Nothing, Your Gracious Majesty, my apologies." Bertie raised her eyes to the person occupying the throne. The Queen was a woman in her middle years, magnificently upholstered in silk taffeta, the fabric embroidered with the unicorn-and-lioness motif. The crown atop her head was thickly jeweled, and Bertie could well imagine seven dwarfs toiling their entire lifetimes to ornament it. For all the grandeur of her trappings, the Queen's regal appearance went far deeper than her clothes. Her Gracious Majesty was, in some indescribable way, entirely different from the other queens Bertie had known at the theater, perhaps merely because the quality of her silence was more impressive than the loudest of Gertrude's shouts.

"Is she a relation of yours, Ariel?" the Queen asked after a long moment. "There is the faintest of resemblances."

He gave her a ghost of a smile. "A relation of sorts, Your Highness. Once upon a time, she was my wife."

Bertie nearly choked. She wanted to protest but swiftly decided that would only make her look the greater idiot.

"Was your wife, but is no longer?" The Queen's interest was piqued. There was the unmistakable rustle of her skirts as she sat up straighter in her chair. "What curious circumstances brought about your separation?"

Though the air elemental looked properly somber, the sharp brightness of his eyes gave every indication he was enjoying himself hugely at Bertie's expense. "At the time I took her to wife, she was already wed to the mariner kneeling before you, Your Gracious Majesty."

A scandalized murmur spread around the edges of the hall. Bertie's cheeks blazed with mortification when she caught bits of whispers that included the words "the little harlot" and "that's a deed most foul!" Behind her, Nate exhaled slowly, his low, water-serpent's hiss filling the air. Though he'd told Bertie Ariel wasn't his enemy, his hackles were raised as he stepped forward to take his place at her side. Bertie's hand immediately sought his, the scars from their handfasting meeting once more.

Don't do anything stupid.

Though she didn't dare speak the words aloud, he must have understood. Shoulders shaking with the effort, Nate forced himself to relax.

Lifting one finger on her right hand, the Queen wrung silence from her subjects. Bertie wished she had similar powers, though she would have taken pleasure in using all ten of her digits to choke the words from Ariel's throat. She turned pleading eyes upon the Queen—

Ask me what really happened. Ask me for the truth of it.

—but Bertie was greatly disappointed when Her Gracious Majesty raised her voice only to note, "She hardly appears woman enough for one man, much less two."

This time, the courtiers responded without fear of repercussion, so their laughter was the roaring of lions and the gentle whickering of one-horned horses. The fairies vibrated with barely concealed temper. Nate's expression suggested the awful things he planned to do to the air elemental, and Bertie wondered through the haze of her humiliation if Ariel would survive to see another dawn.

The Queen marked none of them, her gaze still upon Ariel. "Would you wish that she was still your wife?"

His respectful mask slipped a bit. "I will admit my heart still suffers the wounds of a man denied, but I'm afraid she has parts aplenty to play without also assuming the role of wife, Your Gracious Majesty: the Mistress of Revels, Rhymer, Singer, Teller of Tales, Emissary of the Théâtre Illuminata." He rolled Bertie's many titles about his mouth like marbles before adding, "Forest Queen."

Here, the Queen's penciled eyebrows nearly skidded off her face. "And just who crowned you such a thing, Beatrice Shakespeare Smith?"

The truth spoke itself. "I was born to it. I am a daughter of the earth."

"Yet you presume to call yourself a queen, as well as a handful of other titles that sound altogether very impressive but mean relatively little."

One couldn't exactly be rude to royalty without fear of head choppery, so Bertie only nodded and replied, "Yes, Your Majesty."

The Queen settled back into her throne. "You may tell me how all this came to be." When Bertie hesitated, Her Gracious Majesty smacked her hand against the arm of the throne, causing everyone else in the hall to start as though she'd slapped each of them personally. "Well? What are you waiting for?"

Though it was difficult to manage in jeans, Bertie curtsied again, because it gave her time to sort out her words. "I am afraid we haven't yet had time to prepare a performance, Your Gracious Majesty, and I need to apologize for a mishap at the lower gates—"

"Never mind that now, I'm asking for your story, Teller of Tales." The finality of her tone gave no room for importuning. "Begin at the beginning, go on until you come to the end, then stop."

Bertie swallowed hard and nodded her assent as she knew she must. "Of course, Your Majesty." It was only as she backed away from the dais that she permitted herself to exchange an agonized expression with Nate, that she entertained thoughts of kicking Ariel quite hard in his shins, that she motioned to the fairies to clear the space around her with a smile that didn't reassure anyone.

To stand ill-dressed and even more ill-prepared before an audience was an actor's worst nightmare, really, recalling the velvet-curtain and spot-lit dreams Bertie had experienced as a small child in which she was thrust onstage in a costume not hers to recite lines she didn't know before an audience armed with rotten fruit and moldering tomatoes. It had taken repeated lavender-scented reassurances from Mrs. Edith that such a travesty would never come to pass, that Bertie was a little girl and not a Player, that no one expected her to ever tread the boards.

She was mistaken about that.

At least I'm not naked.

Small consolation, but a steadying one nevertheless. Bertie took a deep breath, caught hold of the audience's attention like ribbon-reins in her hands, and began. "It starts with a meeting most curious."

A dim shape appeared alongside her to suggest Ophelia's water-soaked chiffon and flowers, then the Scrimshander's winged arms bore that young woman to a cavern in the cliffs. In delicate detail, Bertie described the ivory rafters of the Aerie, its scrimmed whale ribs coalescing overhead for everyone to see. The courtiers gasped and clutched one another when the tentacled shadow of Sedna towered over Bertie's parents and flooded the cavern with the suggestion of water. In great gushes, the imagined ocean swirled about the Queen's Great Hall, snaked under the seating, and sluiced across the marble.

The room wasn't the only thing transformed by the telling. Each word Bertie spoke added a flounce upon a dress not there, a bit of embroidery, an inch of lace, a jewel to her hair, throat, fingers, wrists until she stood before the Queen and her court, not in rags, but properly attired as the Mistress of Revels. Power filled Bertie with wildfire. Excitement poured through her veins, rouging her cheeks brilliant pink as she shifted the scenery about them, breaking their hearts as Ophelia's had broken upon her return to the Théâtre Illuminata.

The Mistress of Revels conjured its velvet-and-gilt

grandeur for Her Gracious Majesty's pleasure. Moving among ghostly Players, the years skimmed around Bertie, her childhood passing in a sentence or two. The events of the past month spun out like spiderwebs, threads criss-crossing; some—like Ariel's and Nate's—were stickier than others, trickier for the storyteller to traverse without un-balancing herself. Easier to manage were the mechanical horses, the rollicking caravan, the sandstone of the Cara-vanserai, the terrible glory of Sedna's Hall, their escape from a watery tomb, a journey toward a distant silver spire, the attack by the band of brigands. Peaseblossom's death brought the audience to tears; as the courtiers wept, Bertie wondered how best to bring the performance to a close.

It had to end with Varvara, she decided. Bertie placed a finger to her lips and waited for the utter silence that followed.

"If the fire took her from us, the fire can give her back," she promised them.

About Varvara, Bertie built a massive opal, smooth surfaced and gleaming. All the ethereal lights of the aurora borealis shimmered around the fire-dancer, painting her costume and pointe shoes with sky-burning blues and greens and golds. When she emerged from her jewel co-coon, Peaseblossom clung to her bodice, face puckered with the effort of glowing orange-gold.

As Varvara began a series of pirouettes around her, Bertie caught hold of Peaseblossom and held her aloft. Marigold sparks cascaded over the entire room, pouring from the chandeliers, the mirrors, the very ceiling. Careful not to squish her friend, Bertie brought her hands together with a thunderclap, and when Peaseblossom emerged from an explosion of glitter, the audience leapt to its feet with a collective gasp, bursting into applause for her resurrection.

Such theatrics would have done nicely for a finale, except Ariel exhaled a breath he must have been holding for some time. Varvara immediately flared up with the sort of blast that explodes from a fire-eater's mouth, her skirts and shoes once more the shade of blood on rubies. The enormous mirrors around the hall vibrated, humming in twelve-part harmony until they shattered. Shards rained down toward the marble floor, the courtiers, and the Queen herself.

By some shared instinct, wordsmith and fire-dancer flung out their hands and transformed the lethal needles, separating all that was silvered glass into sand and flames. Varvara called the fire to her and wrapped it about her in an ember-glowing cape, while tiny bits of stone collected in drifts upon the floor around Bertie's feet.

"Only one way to prevent seven years of bad luck," she whispered to Varvara.

The fire-dancer grasped her meaning; with a noise like white thunder, they restored the mirrors as they had the front gates. The silvered surfaces rippled in their frames like waves upon the ocean before solidifying, reflecting countless panting and wild-eyed Berties and just as many silver-haired, impossibly aged Queens.

Breath catching in her throat, Bertie turned to the dais. When the Queen pursed her lips, her face blossomed with countless wrinkles. When she finally spoke, the single word rasped as though dust had settled in the back of her throat.

"Interesting."

It was as though the many years in Bertie's story had all manifested upon Her Gracious Majesty's features at once. Bertie hazarded a glance about the room, but none of the courtiers or servitors seemed to think anything was amiss with the Queen's appearance. Hoping it wouldn't cause offense, she scrubbed at her own eyes, wondering if it was some trick of the light or the result of the countless broken mirrors, but no.

Her surprise banished all that was word-conjured. The massive opal faded. The Mistress of Revels's grand costume fell apart, unraveled thread by thread by the silence. Standing alone before the dais, unmasked once more, Bertie was devoid of words, unable to do more than look up at the regal monarch and wait for what would come next.

"You have pleased me," the Queen finally said. Only then was Bertie able to draw a breath, to relax enough to be able to feel her fingers and toes once more. Her Gracious

Majesty stretched out her arm. Thinking she would be allowed to kiss the Royal Hand, Bertie approached. The Queen's fingers unfurled, and a gleaming broach of rose gold lay in her pale, wrinkled palm. "A token of my esteem."

Bertie stared at it blankly for a moment, realizing it was the same as the bit of jewelry she'd seen pinned to Mrs. Edith's various shirtwaists every day of her growing up.

A gift from the Queen, that's what she always said.

Bertie took the offering and her legs bent of their own accord. "My most humble thanks, and I would humbly beg your forgiveness for what occurred at the front gate."

For a moment, Bertie thought the Queen might take back her broach and her good will, but Her Gracious Majesty only barked a laugh and waved a hand to indicate such things were of little importance to her. "You are forgiven."

Bertie felt her knees go wobbly. "My thanks, Your Gracious Majesty."

The Queen crooked a finger at Bertie, beckoning her closer. "Just what would you do with a wish-come-true, I'd like to know."

The boon. Bertie hadn't even spit enough to lick her lips. "My family, Your Gracious Majesty. I would see us reunited."

After a long moment, the Queen consulted a small, mirrored timepiece that dangled from her taffeta dress, perhaps to see just how many minutes an impertinent snippet of a girl had wasted. "You will have breakfast with me on the morrow in my private chambers, Beatrice Shakespeare Smith." She reached for a walking stick resting upon the side of her throne, then spared a glance for the rest of the Company, all wearing various looks of astonishment except Moth, who was picking his nose. "While we dine, your retinue is free to enjoy the grounds. That will be more peaceful, I think."

Realizing she ought to say something, Bertie gave another deep curtsy and murmured, "Of course, Your Gracious Majesty," even as the fairies muttered about how they always got left out of the fun. Thankfully Nate's low admonishment of "Shut yer mouth!" was lost to the sudden shuffle of feet, the shifting of silk skirts and brocade surcoats as the entire assemblage bowed and curtsied to the Queen when she rose.

Her Gracious Majesty paused by Fenek long enough to say, "Take them to the Imperial Tea Room whilst their accommodations are prepared. The girl looks as though she could use a cup to steady her nerves."

"At once," Fenek said with a low bow and a sidelong glance at Bertie.

Only then did "the girl" realize she vibrated with postperformance energy, much as the mirrors had before breaking. Her nerves jangled with every flicker of light from the chandelier, every reflection upon the marble floor, every whisper of the departing courtiers.

Perhaps I'll shatter as well.

Bertie fisted her hands and bit her lip, trying to get the shaking under control, but that only resulted in half-moons dug into her palms until she nearly bled.

"Does the Tea Room serve food, too?" Mustardseed demanded, pulling out a change purse that should not have fit in his pants. "I saved my coins from the Caravanserai, and I'm starving!"

"You're always starving!" Peaseblossom protested.

"If you know that, you ought to have fed me by now!"

The Queen shook her head. "Partake of my hospitality, no payment is necessary"—here she paused to consider the Fearsome Foursome for a long moment—"save the cost of good table manners."

"I'd rather pay coins and gobble any way I please," Moth said quite truthfully before adding a belated, "Your Majesty."

"Just as I suspected," the Queen answered with a wry smile. "All the same, I will have your manners, or your heads."

The fairies paled and muttered promises about chewing with their mouths shut and refraining from belching at the table. By the time Cobweb included a rash vow about the employment of a napkin, the Queen had disappeared, trailed by two dozen ladies-in-waiting.

In their absence, Ariel moved toward Bertie, hair crackling with static electricity, the silk of his sleeves snapping and billowing. Without realizing it, his fingers sought out the pale flesh at the base of his throat, the place where Bertie's iron collar had settled on his skin when she'd imprisoned him at the theater. "What were you thinking, to summon Fire and trap it within mortal flesh?"

"Varvara isn't trapped in mortal flesh, Ariel. The opal ring was her prison, and I *freed* her." When he started to interrupt, Bertie fixed him with a killing look. "Why must you think the very worst of me?"

Taken aback by her vehemence, Ariel paused a moment to restrain his winds and compose himself. "My apologies, then. I shouldn't have accused you of such a thing."

"Our unguarded reactions are the most honest ones." Bertie wished she could shrug it off, but only now did she realize the sense of hurt and betrayal she carried in place of the journal.

"Ne'er mind that now." Nate broke between them and steered her toward the nearest exit. "We need t' get ye clear o' th' crowd."

"This way!" Fenek said with a jerk of his head and a hippity-hop gait.

Indeed, the courtiers already called to Bertie, catching hold of her sleeves and shaking her by the limp hand, seeking to curry favor with the newcomer. Fenek didn't slow down or mark their attentions. Just behind him, Nate used his imposing stature and his dark expression to clear a path like a ship cutting through the water. Escorted by Ariel, Varvara kept pace with a telltale tapping of her toe shoes upon the marble floor. The fairies struggled to keep up, dodging ladies-in-waiting and gentlemen attendants, finally soaring overhead to avoid the press of bodies.

When Fenek gestured at last to a door, Moth clapped his hands with glee. "I smell cherry pie!"

"Cherry *blossoms*," Peaseblossom corrected. "They smell nothing alike, really."

The sign overhead was in Japanese, but the ornamented door and the impressive amount of gilt paint left no doubt in their minds this was the Imperial Tea Room. By now, Bertie's right eye had begun to twitch in a most disconcerting fashion, and she couldn't stop herself from shivering as though doused in ice water. Upon answering the door, the hostess of the establishment looked askance at her, unpainted lips rounding into an O of surprise. A long moment passed during which the woman glanced from Nate and Ariel, to the four fairies muttering about death by either seppuku or starvation, to the fire-dancer still balanced upon her toes, back to definitively vibrating Bertie.

"Is she well?" was the polite query when, by rights, she could have ordered them back out the door.

"Nothing a little tea won't cure," Fenek told her, backing away. "Her Gracious Majesty bade them come here. I will return to show them to their apartment when it is ready."

"Of course. Please come in." The attendant gave a quick nod, a beautiful bow, and led the troupe into the tea room.

Bertie caught quick glances of paper screens, elegant, stark calligraphy scrolls, and the elaborate knot of fabric at the back of the woman's kimono. The Wardrobe Department had an enormous hutch that housed over a hundred folded kimonos and obis, in brilliant shades of chrysanthemum-stitched orange and plum blossoms painted on lavender. There was one in particular, white butterflies flitting across slate gray, that had always reminded her of Ariel. But none of them compared to the ensemble worn by the hostess. The silk itself was a muted celadon, the threads forming embroidered tea leaves so finely matched that they almost disappeared into the fabric each time she took another sandal-shod step.

The woman slid open a door to a small chamber, empty save for wall paintings and tatami mats upon the floor. When she indicated they should enter, Nate nodded and ducked his head, but Ariel remained with her, speaking in a language that was, Bertie finally realized, the hostess's native tongue.

Nate poured Bertie onto a woven straw mat and settled on his heels beside her. "Ye look like a lit firework, about ready t' explode. That was quite th' tale." He reached out and brushed her hair from her face, trying to peer into her eyes. "Toward th' end, ye were as pale as a ghost an' goin' sharp around th' edges, like a knife honed." Both hands found her jawline, his thumbs tracing over her cheeks. "Fer a moment, I thought ye might be lost t' th' story."

"I didn't feel lost at all." Unable to kneel as he did, Bertie lolled against the nearest wall and hoped she wouldn't fall through it. She recalled the way the words had filled her, as if she were a cup overflowing. "I could have gone on for ages, I think. Stopping was a bit like shoving a cork into a fizzing champagne bottle."

Nate scowled at the idea. "An' now yer twice as limp as a wrung-out rag. Whate'er ye might think, th' tellin' cost ye somethin' . . ." He trailed off when Ariel entered, carrying a lacquered box and an iron pot. "I thought ye were orderin' tea."

The air elemental gave him a withering glance. "I did. Normally this set would be used outside in the gardens, but our hostess was most understanding about both the young lady's incapacity and the need for a privately administered restorative." After arranging a variety of implements in a pattern that pleased him, Ariel began an elaborate ceremony of measuring, pouring, whisking. It was the most beautiful and graceful series of movements Bertie had ever seen, though it went unappreciated by the fairies.

"That's a lot of trouble for a cup of tea!" Moth observed, his tongue poking out the side of his mouth as he diligently folded a bit of silk. A few seconds later, he triumphantly donned the repurposed table linen, now a miniature origami robe.

Bertie narrowed her eyes at him but couldn't halt their mischief, and soon Mustardseed and Cobweb were similarly attired. Thus costumed, they performed a rousing rendition of "Three Little Maids From School Are We," and when they got to the line "pert as a schoolgirl well can be," Moth honked Mustardseed somewhere highly inappropriate, and the three of them went down in a tangle of limbs and napkin-improvised obis.

Peaseblossom fixed her gaze upon the ceiling, her cheeks as pink as her moniker implied. "I can't take you three anywhere."

Ariel merely shook his head and offered Bertie a beautiful vessel filled with steaming green liquid. Breathing in the scent of it, she regained use of her arms and reached for the cup with both hands. A single sip restored her, the tea pouring down her throat like rainwater on parched plants. She felt their roots take hold in her center, pushing new growth out through her arms and legs. Nate made a disconcerted noise, but Bertie managed, "I'm fine," without it sounding like falsehood.

The forest is where I'm strongest. I would do well to remember that.

Ariel sat back, trying not to look pleased with himself and failing utterly. "Normally, you should pass the cup to the second guest, but I think you need that more than anyone else here."

"Aye, it seems t' be working," was the pirate's grudging admission.

Bertie continued to sip at her tea, cupping the delicate porcelain bowl with both hands to better absorb the heat and the scent. Fortified, she turned her attention to the available forest: paintings on rice-paper screens, cherry and plum trees that waved flowered fingertips at her. Like servants with heads bowed, the trees approached when beckoned, transforming the room into a glorious orchard. Padded chairs sprouted underneath Bertie and the others like mushrooms, and twisted branches grew together to form a long, low table covered with almond blossoms. The crockery Ariel had unpacked from the lacquered box multiplied, some of the kettles burgeoning beyond the size of Bertie's head, others no larger than Peaseblossom's thumbnail. Instead of staid biscuit-and-sandwich fare, the tea table treated them to intricate desserts wrought to look like dragonflies on water and tiny pink-nosed rats.

"Here's a place I haven't seen fer a while." The end of Nate's nose had gone pink as well, fuzzy whiskers growing until a veritable March Hare sat alongside Bertie. "Though th' trees were a bit different that time, an' I think I was more myself then." He reached up to scratch at one long ear, still pierced through with a gold hoop earring.

"'Something curious, being strange,'" Bertie said, her gaze drifting down the table to the others. Now dressed in the slate-gray ceremonial kimono embroidered with butterflies, Ariel had passed the second preparation to Varvara. Though the fire-dancer took the offering, she did not immediately drink. Cradled in her hands, the contents of the cup came to a slow simmer, bubbles breaking the surface. Only when it achieved a roiling boil did she deign to lift it to her lips. The fairies, meanwhile, had gone to investigate the nearest plate of sweets.

"What are these things?" Moth didn't wait for an answer, stuffing one in its entirety into his mouth. "Mmm!"

Cobweb investigated the contents of his compatriot's gaping maw. "Looks like sweet bean paste to me."

"For goodness' sake, Moth, chew with your mouth closed," Peaseblossom admonished, nibbling delicately the edge of a thick jellied sweet that wobbled when she glared at him. "Remember your promise to the Queen!"

"I need somethin' less cloyin' myself." Nate extracted a leather-wrapped flask from his pants pocket and poured a dollop of caramel-smooth liquor into an otherwise empty cup.

"Clean cup, move down," Ariel murmured, and he was suddenly sitting next to Bertie. "Do you feel any better?"

She nodded, setting her bowl upon the table. "I do."

"That is most excellent news," Fenek said, popping up

before them like a rabbit out of a hole. Almost at once, the fruit trees returned to their proper place upon the rice-paper screens, and the forest scene disappeared into the steaming fog originating from the single teapot sitting on the rush floor mat.

Bertie blinked, hardly able to fathom the rapidity and thoroughness of the scene change, but Fenek had already backed into the hall with a nervous twitch of his nose. The servitor bowed thrice to the hostess, who returned the gesture with graceful aplomb.

"Follow me?" He didn't wait for them to answer, already halfway down the adjacent hallway by the time Bertie found her feet and staggered to the door. "Your rooms are prepared at last, thank the mirrors, with hot baths and supper delivered. Also, clothing and supplies to replace what was stolen from you."

"Would that everything could be replaced," Bertie said, her thoughts turning to the journal and to Waschbär. Only now, with the command performance well behind her, did the terror of the brigands' attack return to haunt her. "The thieves took more than our supplies."

"Yeah, what about our peace of mind?" Despite carrying the significant weight of a purloined dumpling atop his head, Mustardseed kept pace with them as Fenek began to climb a set of massive curving stairs.

"And our dignity!" added Cobweb.

"What dignity?!" Moth wanted to know.

"Shhh," Cobweb said with a well-timed jab of the elbow, "we might be able to get some dignity out of this, if we play our cards right."

After another two interminable flights, Bertie almost asked Nate to carry her piggyback. Only pride and Ariel's presence, like a silver-trimmed shadow behind them, prevented her. Ahead of them, Fenek opened a door with a twist and a flourish.

"I hope these will do."

One cursory glance at the grand accommodations, boasting multiple bedrooms, a central parlor, enormous windows set into the walls, and mirrors—always mirrors— and Bertie indicated her approval by sinking onto the nearest chaise. "It certainly will."

"Look at the dinner!" Peaseblossom cried. A vast table was already set with delicacies both hearty and dainty, and within seconds, the fairy was happily knee-deep in what appeared to be honey custard.

"You have to try some of this!" Mustardseed had crawled up the back end of a roast chicken, head popping out the departed bird's neck hole, his cheeks bedecked with rosemary, lemon twists, and buttery smears.

"Who needs fowl most foul when there's cake?" Moth and Cobweb had located a dozen varieties, each frosted and decorated within an inch of their sugary lives.

Fenek spared them a quiet look of horror before turning to Bertie. "I will return for you in the morning. Please do be ready . . . you don't ever want to keep Her Gracious Majesty waiting." Bowing and scraping, the servitor backed himself out of the room and closed the door behind him with a click.

"Ye need to rest." Nate managed to get in the first word with lightning rapidity.

"It's nothing some food and a hot bath won't fix." Bertie strived to sound cavalier and almost managed it. Another thin skimming of protection surfaced upon her face, but it wasn't enough for her taste, not with Nate and Ariel both eyeing her like the fairies would a chocolate-coated caramel. She longed to bury herself in the bedclothes and sleep until her features were obscured by a mask as thick as painted papier-mâché.

Food first.

Piling cheese and fruit atop a plate the size of her head, she added an obscenely large chunk of chocolate cake just as the bell next to the door rang. Nate opened it to reveal servitors bearing cauldrons of scented, steaming bathwater. Plate in hand, Bertie followed the bucket brigade into the largest of the bedrooms. The moment the servants departed, she disrobed, climbed into the copper tub, and consumed her take-away meal while sitting up to her chin in blessedly hot water. Peaseblossom and the boys were already asleep upon her pillow by the time the bath had gone cold, their hands and faces wiped mostly clean with the corner of a towel and their tummies tubbed out with food.

After wrestling on a nightdress dripping waterfalls of lace, Bertie clambered onto the boat of a bed and touched each of them in turn with a gentle fingertip. She lingered over Peaseblossom, who snored loudest of them all, and then pulled the coverlet up. A breeze from the open window carried the scent of glass-fragile flowers and moonlight, the occasional trill of a night-wary bird, the burble of the river that snaked its way past Her Gracious Majesty's abode with deference. Despite bone-shattering fatigue, Bertie's thoughts strayed to Nate and Ariel.

Her hands told the story: The boys were abed, the air elemental sleeping in the chamber on her right, and the pirate in the room on the left. Her arms extended of their own volition in either direction under the crisp, cool sheets, each of the handfasting scars aligned with the man who'd made it. Though both wounds had healed, Bertie's palms stung with the memories of two weddings, one forest-bound, the other an impossibly cold ice ceremony in the underground lair of the Sea Goddess.

Nothing save marriage, she reflected before tumbling into a dreamless sleep, could have ruined two friendships more thoroughly.

CHAPTER ELEVEN

Her Acts Being Seven Ages

Upon the morrow, Bertie woke with a start. Unable to remember where she was for several long minutes, she stared without comprehension at the grand appointments of the room. The pale-blue silk bedding was piled about her like wrapping paper torn off a gift, and what little she could see of the floor was lushly carpeted. Grasping the coverlet, Bertie wrapped it about her shoulders and slid from the bed, trying to banish the chill in her bones. Only coals glowed in the hearth now, like lions' eyes peering through jungle leaves, and the fairies had deserted her.

"A good mornin' t' ye, lass," said a voice from the doorway. "I thought I heard th' dulcet sounds o' ye wakin' . . . an' by that, I mean th' snorin' stopped."

"Snoring?" Bertie turned and couldn't help but smile at

the picture Nate made in her doorway, filling it almost edge to edge. He'd exchanged his soiled shirt for one of immaculate white and polished his boots until the leather gleamed, though he'd yet to shave. Behind him, sunlight streamed in the windows, gold-catching his earring. He wore a new cutlass at his waist, peace-tied, Bertie noticed, but present nevertheless. "That's hardly a gentlemanly observation."

"Neither are th' other observations I'm entertainin' at th' moment." Uncrossing his arms, he stepped into the room.

It would be childish to scarper, to flee with a squeak like a mouse pursed by a ruggedly handsome cat, and so she stood her ground. "I haven't time for wordplay this morning. I've an audience with the Queen, remember?"

"Ye look fine." Another step taken to close the space between them.

"Then you've gone quite blind as well as daft." The words, far more lighthearted and teasing than she'd intended, formed another layer of her new mask, one that sought to safeguard not only the thoughts in her head but the feelings of her heart.

Nate must have heard the new tone in her voice; though he didn't touch her, his next statement reached for her just the same. "Now that Ariel's back, yer havin' second thoughts about us."

She struggled to lift the mask, to give him the honesty he deserved. "I haven't had time to breathe, much less contemplate you, or me, or the idea of an 'us' in any sort of detail."

"Fair enough, I suppose, but I won't let ye push me away fer long. An' let me be clear after witnessin' that display in th' trees: Th' only one I want ye t' kiss is me." Now he did reach out, hands finding her waist even under her bulky coverlet, drawing her against him so he could cover her mouth with his. When Bertie glanced at the open bedroom door, he added, "Ariel's taken yer fire-dancer t' th' gardens, neither o' them wantin' food."

Twitching at the tickle of his as-yet-unshaved face against her neck, she issued the halfhearted protest, "Stop making a meal of me and have some breakfast."

"I'd rather have somethin' else."

"Will you make explanations and apologies to Her Gracious Majesty if I am late?" Not a question Bertie could pose every day, and she wasn't altogether sure she was grateful for it now.

Nate gave her a narrow look that said more than the words he swallowed, then led the way into the main parlor. There, the fairies sat upon a round table inlaid with a chessboard that was hardly visible for the plates and cups and trays heaped upon its gleaming surface.

"There's bacon!" Moth piped up.

"Not as much as there was a minute ago," Mustardseed said quite truthfully, "but we can call for more!"

"Look! Croissants!"

"They *are* like soft, buttery pillows!"

Thinking their duty done in alerting Bertie to the offerings, they resumed shoveling in pastry and coddled eggs as fast as their little hands could go.

"Yer goin' t' choke, if ye keep at it like that." Nate sat down and removed temptation in the form of a stack of toast from the fairies' reach.

Unable to resist to the lure of croissants, Bertie took the other chair. "One won't take up much room, and then I'll still be able to eat with the Queen."

A steady stream of servitors appeared after that, delivering hot water for washing up and more food for the fairies, who had a seemingly endless appetite for a certain cherry tart that was a specialty of the Queen's kitchen. A soft knock at the door marked Fenek's arrival, and he entered bearing a grand bit of attire on a crooked finger: a near reproduction of the Mistress of Revels's costume.

"It was thought you required something appropriate to wear for an audience with Her Gracious Majesty."

Dropping the rest of her pastry, much to Mustardseed's and Moth's delight, Bertie wiped fruit from her fingers. "My thanks. I wasn't relishing the idea of appearing in my nightdress."

"Perish the very thought," Fenek said. "The Queen's Dressmaker worked upon this all night to re-create your magic-summoned garments from yesterday. I hope they are to your liking."

Bertie managed a dignified "A multitude of thanks," and an inclination of her head. It wasn't until she ducked into the safety and relative quiet of her room that she permitted herself a happy chortle as she dressed. The Royal Dressmaker had thoroughly outdone herself, employing countless yards of rich green fabric that shimmered with the gray luster of a costly pearl. Perhaps to show off a bit, she'd also added lace frills to the underskirts and tiny silver flowers embroidered along the hemline.

As a final touch, Bertie pinned the rose-gold broach to the bodice. Stepping before the mirror to admire the rich gleam of the metal, she discovered toiletries set out for her use on the dressing table alongside Waschbär's knapsack. Her fingers traced over the pots and tins, selecting colors and brushes with care, realizing the pink-glitter shadow and rouge, kohl pencil and eyelash paint formed another sort of mask. Arranging her hair as best she could with the comb and the hot tongs, Bertie took a deep breath, and studied her image in the mirror for a long moment.

"Posture," she admonished herself because Mrs. Edith wasn't there to do so, then she hastened to rejoin the others.

The breakfast had been cleared from the table, the fairies now engaged in a game of chess, with Cobweb, Moth, and Mustardseed battling each other for the right to play the kings and Peaseblossom reigning as a croissant-bedecked queen. They waved cheerfully to Bertie as she passed, calling out, "Break a leg!" and "Break an arm and a leg!" followed by, "What about a pelvis? Is it lucky to break a pelvis?" so that Bertie departed for her audience accompanied by a gale of their giggles and the low, nearly missed admonishment from Nate to "Mind yer words."

"Come, we mustn't dally." Fenek skipped, fleet-footed, down the stairs.

After descending, they turned into a gallery, one side lined with lead-glass windows, the other with portraits of the various monarchs; all women, Bertie noted, and none painted at the same age. Drawn to the view from the windows, she caught sight of figures, small as paper dolls, moving through the gardens. Courtiers mingled with the troubadours and minstrels, gardeners with guards. In the very center of a perfectly symmetrical mirror-image hedge maze, Ariel and Varvara promenaded together. From this distance, it should have been impossible to tell it was them, except silver hair glinted in the sunlight, and the fire-dancer sent up sparks with every step.

Bertie chewed her lip, tasting the very expensive rouge she'd painted on her mouth only minutes ago. They were much alike in some ways: mercurial, unpredictable. Air surely had more in common with fire than it did with earth. Indeed, speaking with Varvara had brought an unearthly glow to Ariel's skin. Just now, he was gesturing with great animation to the sky, his entire being alight with enthusiasm and joy . . .

. . . and a yearning that was more clear at this distance than when Bertie stood just inches from him.

It took Fenek clearing his throat to realize she'd stopped moving.

"This way, if you please," he said.

"Oh, yes. My apologies." A blush joined her face paint, as though Varvara had placed burning hands upon both of Bertie's cheeks.

Ten paces later, they stood before a door marked with a golden crown inset in frosted glass. Arranging her skirts and smoothing her hair, Bertie tried to take a deep breath as the servitor lifted his hand to ring the bellpull, but a colossal noise from within the royal chambers startled them both.

"I shan't tell you again!" came a shrill, almost childlike shout from within. "Take it away, the horrid, nasty stuff!"

Muffled strains of "At once!" and "Our apologies!" gave way to scrapes of pottery and the clink of broken glass. When the door opened, two food-bedaubed maids exited, carrying a tray of soiled napkins and smashed bits of porcelain.

"Mind her temper this morning!" the first said in passing.

"Fetch me an omelet AT ONCE, DO YOU HEAR?!" preceded another dish skimming past the end of Fenek's nose and shattering against the far wall.

"Your Gracious Majesty," he said, displaying the courage of lions, "the Mistress of Revels is here, at your behest."

Bertie half hoped the shouting monarch would send her away, but after a long moment of silence during which no more plates were broken, a haughty voice issued a command. "Show her in."

Letting Fenek act as her shield, Bertie entered the Queen's apartment behind him. Except, instead of the Queen, an eight-year-old girl sat in a large, tufted armchair, dolefully swinging her slippered feet and glaring at them both. She wore skirts of darkest blue, with the same royal cut and crest embroidered into the heavy velvet. Bertie recognized her from one of the portraits in the gallery.

She must be the Princess.

Bertie hastened to curtsy, though her gaze flickered about the room in search of the Queen. "Your Highness."

The child did not mark the greeting, preoccupied as she was with glowering at the door. "I told them I wouldn't eat porridge. Did they think me such a child that I wouldn't remember my own proclamation?" She reached up to adjust a thickly jeweled crown, too large for her dainty brow.

Bertie stared harder at her then, at the impudent tilt of her nose, at the thick curls falling on either side of her face. . . .

It isn't possible!

But Fenek, finding nothing at all amiss, bowed and said, "My Queen, you asked for the Teller of Tales to wait upon you this morning?"

"I remember that as well." The childlike Queen spared Bertie a glance. "Your mouth is hanging open, Mistress of Revels. Have I a spot on my nose?"

"No. That is, you do have a bit of porridge, just there." Bertie indicated the corner of her mouth. "But you must forgive me. I'd no idea—"

"You may go!" the Queen bellowed at the servitor. Only when Fenek hastily bowed and backed himself out of the room did she bounce from her chair and grab Bertie by both hands. "Come! We must hurry, before the maids return with my omelet!"

Bertie nearly fell, trying to keep up with her. "Where are we going?"

Her Gracious Majesty smothered an infectious giggle as she towed Bertie to the wall. What appeared to be a landscape painting of a large, rose-filled garden slid aside with a touch of the Queen's ring-adorned finger, revealing a narrow hallway. "Down this way! I've something you must see."

"Yes, Your Gracious Majesty?"

The Queen gave a breathless sort of laugh over her shoulder, running even faster, if that were possible. Instead of answering Bertie's question, she tossed words over her shoulder like pearls. "The boon, silly! Remember? You wanted it for your family."

"Yes, Your Majesty?" Puzzled, Bertie tried to keep up, her sandaled feet making a *slap! slap! slap!* against the polished floor.

The Queen's curls bounced like bedsprings as she ran. "Yesterday I checked the tiny mirror on my pocket watch and wanted to say something that very moment, but that would have been too irresponsible for my older self. So I had to wait for the morning, when I started over as a child. Not too early, mind you, for babies aren't any use at all, but I imagined that near breakfast time I would be able to help, and so I am!"

Such a stream of nonsense! Bertie couldn't fully comprehend the reality of a queen who started her every day over again as an infant and aged with the passing hours. "Help me with what, if I might be so bold as to ask, Your Majesty?"

"It won't work to wish your family back together," the Queen said as the corridor ended in a small chamber filled with mirrors turned against themselves. "The way things are right now, not even my magic can help you."

"The way things are? . . ." Either the room was cold, or the Queen's pronouncement slid ice down Bertie's spine.

"It will be easier just to show you." Her Gracious Majesty jockeyed Bertie into the space on the floor marked with bits of mirror inset to form a star. "Stand just here, peer into the looking glasses, and tell me what you see."

"I see only myself, Your Majesty, and you." But the moment she uttered the words, they played Bertie false. True, at first she saw only her exotic reflection as the Mistress of Revels and the child Queen dancing with impatience behind her, but then a water-wavering form flickered in the glass. "I see . . ."

"Yes?" the Queen asked, her reflection also wavering.

It was Ophelia, staring back at Bertie, though her gaze didn't register the presence of her daughter. The water-maiden sat at the table in her Dressing Room, flowers, perfume bottles, and makeup scattered before her. Soft electric lighting poured down upon her from the unseen rim of her mirror.

"That's my mother," Bertie whispered.

Someone stood behind Ophelia just as the Queen stood behind Bertie: a tall, dark form that could only be the Scrimshander.

"And that's my father." Bertie wanted to look away, but she couldn't turn, couldn't close her eyes. "This is when they met, when she left the theater with him."

As if cued by the explanation, Ophelia turned about in her chair and began a conversation with the newcomer. Though Bertie couldn't hear it, she could tell by the Scrimshander's expression that the scene was unfolding just as the puppet creatures had performed it in *The Big Pop-Up Book of Scenery*.

"You see, Your Majesty?" Bertie struggled to pull the words from a mouth seemingly filled with saltwater taffy and secrets. "It's all as I told you."

"Ah," said the Queen, "but you were missing a piece! And it's within my power to give you the bit you didn't know!" The mirrored sections of the floor shifted, carrying them forward until the Queen pressed Bertie's palm flat against the glass. The gleaming surface wavered, becoming a waterfall of mercury.

"Stop!" Bertie tried to pull back. "That's not my place!"

But the Queen's hand upon hers was a vise, her will ironclad. In the intervening minutes, she'd aged another few years and more greatly resembled the monarch of yesterday. Her clothes transformed with her, the lengthening of her skirts and the stiffening of her lace collar reflected countless times around them. "You must step through and collect the missing piece of your mirror."

The past had a grip upon Bertie now, pulling from the other side, sucking her in before she had the chance to scream. Traveling through time and space in such a fashion twisted her inside out and upside down before the Queen's mirror belched her out upon the dressing table. Ophelia's makeup and hair combs and crystal perfume bottles scattered in every direction. There wasn't enough room to balance herself, so Bertie half jumped, half fell to the floor.

"Your Majesty!" Scrambling to her feet, Bertie spun back to the mirror with undiluted panic aflame in every vein.

Barely visible, the young Queen waved to her. "Go find your missing piece!" she mouthed.

The light on the other side of the mirror faded, like stage lights behind a scrim curtain, until everything beyond the glass was dark. Bertie smacked her hands against the mirror once, twice, though she knew somehow it was too late. Left to stare wild-eyed at her own horrified expression, she was well-trapped now, eighteen years or so in the past, and right back where she'd started.

At the Théâtre Illuminata.

CHAPTER TWELVE

I Summon Up Remembrance of Things Past

*T*his is *where* it all began. With Ophelia. With the Scrimshander.

She had two choices now: pound her hands on the looking glass, demanding the demented child Queen permit her return, or stay. Stay . . . and perhaps better understand what had really happened, without the story filtered through memories and the telling of it.

With one last glance at her own face in the mirror's silvered surface, Bertie turned and ran for the door, jerking it open in time to see her mother gliding through the Stage Door with the Scrimshander at her heels. Bertie managed to keep pace without them catching sight of her, ducking around the usual bits of scenery, unable to believe she was back and similarly unable to spare a moment's joy at the homecoming, however unexpected.

Ophelia led her consort in front of the proscenium arch, where *The Complete Works of the Stage* bathed in a pool of its own golden light. The water-maiden turned the pages, the movement marked only by the whisper of paper, until she found what she sought.

"'Do you doubt that?'" she said, quoting her entrance line before she smiled and tore her page out.

The Scrimshander shifted uneasily. "Are you sure you ought to leave?"

"I ought to have left a long time ago," Ophelia murmured, "but now's as good a time as any, I suppose."

Green and gleaming, the Exit sign in the back of the auditorium flickered to life. The water-maiden tucked her page into her bodice, smiled up at the Scrimshander, and took him by the hand. Together, they ran down the stairs, up the aisle, and to the lobby door. There, they disappeared into a swirl of color and light that gave every indication a crowd was gathered for the evening performance.

"What are you doing backstage?" demanded a familiar voice.

Bertie nearly swallowed her tongue at the Stage Manager's shout. Ducking her head and muttering uncharacteristic apologies to her nemesis, she wove a path through the scenery pieces and coils of rope.

"Come back here and show your face," he commanded. "I would let the Theater Manager know who is ignoring the proper calls!"

"No time, so sorry!" Bertie dove for Ariel's trapdoor, disappearing into the darkest bowels under the stage. She could hear the Stage Manager stomping about overhead, muttering curses and then giving up to summon an ocean scene. The gentle lap of mechanical water filled Bertie's ears.

The Little Mermaid. *The night Ophelia left, they were— are!—performing* The Little Mermaid.

With a delicacy that recalled Varvara's dainty steps en pointe, Bertie tried to pick her way through a darkness relieved only by the narrow slats of light easing fingers through the stage's floorboards. Negotiating the maze of pulleys and lifts proved more difficult than she remembered, especially when she reached the tooth-and-claw machinery that rotated the ocean waves. Her skirts snagged on a splintered corner—*Mr. Tibbs should attend to this at once!*—and she was still jerking upon them to no avail when a familiar form appeared next to her, his cherry-tinted lantern driving back the gloom.

"Here now, ye'll rip it like that," Nate noted, the gentle chiding containing none of the tolerant exasperation he normally used with her.

Because he doesn't know who I am.

As he worked to loosen her petticoat from its moorings, Bertie couldn't help but stare up at him through the fall of her silver hair, the realization dawning that he looked much the same as he did now. . . .

And I haven't even been born yet.

"Th-thank you." The moment she was free, Bertie shrank back into the shadows, certain it would be a very bad idea indeed for anyone in this time and place to see her face.

"Yer not in th' first act." Nate peered at her, the lantern in his hand swinging to cast erratic illumination over the area under the stage. "What are ye doin' down here?"

"I was summoned by accident." Not even a lie, though the next bit of explanation would be. "A mistake with the Call Board, I assume."

"Ye ought t' get back t' th' Dressin' Rooms, then. Ye don't want th' Stage Manager discoverin' ye wandering about." With a cavalier salute, Nate dismissed her and turned back to check the various bits of rigging that helped the *Persephone* dock after her flight.

"Right then." Bertie remained rooted, fighting the urge to rush forward, to cling to him like a painted barnacle, to explain everything that had happened, to force their future friendship upon him this second. Adrift in this place that was strange and familiar all at once, she yearned for his steady words and steadier gaze, not the passing courtesy due a stranger. Realizing she had her hand outstretched toward him—the hand marked with his handfasting scar—Bertie forced herself to take a deep breath and a step back, then another breath and another step. The greater the space between them, the harder it was to move, and she emerged from the same side door Ariel always used, a sob climbing the back of her throat.

The chaos in the hallway thankfully smothered the noise. In the short time that had passed since she'd followed Ophelia, the corridor had filled with dodging mariners and the members of the Ladies' Chorus wibble-wobbling down the hall in pearl garlands and fish tails, trailed by the tap-dancing starfish. None of them paid Bertie any attention, and she had to be quite literally on her toes to avoid getting jostled or stepped upon.

"Ophelia?" The Call Boy's shout carried over the noise. "You're wanted in the Theater Manager's office at once!"

With muttered apologies she wished could be swear words, Bertie pushed and shoved her way through the Players, ducked into Ophelia's Dressing Room, and slammed the door shut behind her. Wheezing, she turned the key over in the lock and ran for the mirror.

"Your Majesty!" Bertie's palm met the glass with a smack, though she didn't dare raise her voice above a harsh whisper. "Open the mirror, damn it all!"

But the only response was a knock at the door. "Ophelia?

Is everything all right in there?" A pause, then the door-knob rattled. "I would have a word with you, please."

The Theater Manager.

Bertie scrabbled through the pots of rouge and tubes of greasepaint for something she could use to disguise herself. Her fingers closed around something cold and familiar: a faceted perfume bottle that felt quite at home in her hand. The crystal glimmered in the lights surrounding the mirror, producing a rainbow that snaked over Bertie's palm. Not quite the "Drink Me" bottle from the Properties Department, but she could imagine that it was, could envision it labeled as EAU D'OPHELIA.

Even as she removed the stopper, Bertie concentrated on the scent that naturally enveloped her mother: water lilies and white roses and the pale moss that clung to the rocks of an ice-fed stream. There was the salt of tears shed as well, and under that something wistful, something longing, something dark that lurks in the shadows below the water's surface.

Bertie had the bottle to her lips before she could think twice. There was no triple apple this time, no coffee, no buttered toast, just the taste of the ocean, salty as an oyster swallowed straight from its shell. Turning back to the mirror in desperation, she concentrated upon her image: so like her mother's, and yet not.

I have my mother's eyes. Let's see what I can do about the rest.

With salt water still spangling her lips, Bertie smoothed a hand over the mirror, recalled her mother's delicate features, and shaped her own face into something more of a heart.

Now to do something about my height.

Placing a hand atop of the reflection of her head, Bertie pressed down until she shrank, reducing the inches bestowed upon her by the Scrimshander. Stature adjusted, she set about removing the rest of the bits he'd gifted her until almost-Ophelia gazed back at her from the surface of glass.

That which I inherited from my father is gone; I am my mother's child only.

"Ophelia?" Another knock, and a rattle of the doorknob. "Please let me in."

All that was left was her hair. Imagining a dye brush in her hand, Bertie traced over her bedraggled silver locks, reshaping them into curls the hue of dark honey. With a few last finger-strokes across the mirror, she exchanged the Mistress of Revels's bright skirts for a trailing gown of pale green.

Hardly able to breathe for looking at her reflection, Bertie turned, crossed the room, and unlocked the door.

The Theater Manager stood in the hallway, forehead crinkled into a mighty frown. "You're here. Thank goodness!" He caught Bertie by the hands and squeezed, his relief grinding the small bones in her fingers nearly to dust. "I knew there must be a mistake!"

"A mistake?" Wisps of water crept into Bertie's voice, wetting the words with Ophelia's inflections. "Where did you think I would be?"

"I was told . . . that is to say . . ."

As he stammered, Bertie summoned one of Ophelia's flickering-faint smiles. She knew why he'd panicked, why he'd hammered upon the door as though the building was on fire. Mrs. Edith had told him Ophelia was gone, and he'd raced down here to investigate.

But Bertie had given him an Ophelia to find.

"I know I wasn't summoned tonight," Bertie improvised, gesturing to the Call Board on the wall behind him, "but there was so much water on *The Little Mermaid* set. It calls to me, you know."

"Yes, I'd heard that." The Theater Manager must have realized he still had her by the hands, for he dropped them with a muttered apology and colored up to the tips of his ears. Though he looked much the same as he would in Bertie's time, it wasn't only the blush that suggested a greater youthfulness. He had the green air of an unripe apple, an uncertainty about what to do with his feet and his hands, and his gaze leapfrogged over Bertie-as-Ophelia's face.

"I'm terribly sorry you were interrupted without reason," Bertie said.

"Ah, yes, well . . ." He cleared his throat and summoned

a smile. "I will excuse myself, then. I was working on my opera, and I'm afraid one of my characters isn't behaving as she ought to. She's a fire-dancer, you see, born of the flames. . . ."

With the least bit of encouragement, he might have continued, filling Ophelia's sympathetic ear with his current artistic tribulations, but Bertie only gave him another half smile and tried to close the door. "If you are reassured that I haven't disappeared into thin, thin air, I hope you will excuse me."

"Ah, yes, but of course. My apologies." He made her a stiff bow and checked his pocket watch. "The performance is about to begin, and I ought to check the Box Office, in any case."

Bertie nodded and waited for him to turn the far corner of the hall before she closed and locked the door again. With fear and adrenaline subsiding, the potion had yet more room to wend its way through her body. As the familiar strains of *The Little Mermaid*'s overture drifted from the speaker in the corner, Bertie's mind began to go blank, as surely as a bit of blackboard wiped clean. Every worry was a rainbow bubble that bounced against the inside of her skull, popping, fizzling. Nothing seemed to matter anymore, nothing save the need to drown herself in gentle currents. An invisible tether tugged her toward the stage, but she knew it wasn't her play, wasn't her call, that the mermaids and starfish wouldn't appreciate her presence backstage during a performance. With a sigh, Bertie crossed to the basin in the corner of the Dressing Room, poured the contents of the ewer into the flower-rimmed bowl, and bent forward until her face was submerged.

"Not as good as a bathtub," she murmured as the welcome liquid poured down her throat, "but it will have to do."

Some days were better than others for remembering. Some days, there was yet a Bertie, pounding against the mirror and calling to the Queen, a Bertie who wondered if the miniature monarch would remember she'd shoved the Mistress of Revels through the looking glass, a Bertie who schemed ways to return to the Distant Castle and wring that child devil's royal neck. But more and more often, there was only Ophelia staring back at her from the mirror, Ophelia drifting down the corridors to mingle with the Players, Ophelia, not at all interested in the offerings in the Green Room unless sushi or watercress sandwiches or oysters on the half shell were in the offing.

"What is *wrong* with you?" Hamlet demanded, having cornered her there one inauspicious morning.

By now, Bertie had lost track of time. The theater was deep into a season of classic Shakespearean performances, so Desdemona and Othello bickered in one corner of the tiny room while Miranda nibbled at bread and butter and tried to pretend she wasn't eyeing Ariel with all the keen interest of an island-banished virgin.

Ariel. There was something about Ariel that this Ophelia remembered, a secret that none of the other Players knew. Sitting in the corner of the Green Room, the air elemental ate nothing at all, spoke to no one, and only responded when Prospero commanded him to prepare a plate of refreshments. This Ophelia thought him beautiful, noting the translucence of his skin and the wild silver of his hair, but the haunted look in his eyes unsettled her, as did the way he shrank into himself whenever anyone approached him.

In another lifetime, he will be brash. Fearless.

The thought came unbidden, and it confused her. How could he be anything more than his written part? The sort of hapless, hopeless character for whom she had no patience at all?

Pity he cannot escape through the water as I do.

A bit of wind ruffled the edges of her gown, mimicking the ripple of a swift river current. Through her eyelashes, she could see Ariel staring at her, a most curious expression on his face.

"You think to pity me?" His voice wrapped about her, a silk streamer fringed upon the ends.

"I did not say so." Feigning great interest in a bit of

cake frosted with sea-salted caramel, Ophelia reached for excuses and a fork.

"Your expression said as much, if not more." Ariel was on his feet now.

Looking down, this Ophelia wished her teacup were big enough to fit her nose and mouth inside it, but drowning again would have to wait until later. "You seek escape, but cannot find it."

"And what would you know of escape, precious mad thing that you are?"

"Only that it's not hard to find if you know where to look." Unable to bear the excess of air in her lungs for a second longer, this Ophelia set down her cup and slipped from the room. A glorious drowning she wanted this time, to feel herself drift through water without end. More than a teacup or washbasin or even a copper bathing tub could provide.

A copper bathing tub? When have I ever used such a thing? Mine is porcelain.

"Wait, I would have a word with you!" Ariel gave chase. Perhaps it pained him a bit, with the call on the board for *The Tempest* and the second act about to begin, but still he followed her, past the Stage Door and down to the Scenic Dock. It was dark there, and quiet, and this Ophelia had discovered a new set in progress only a few days ago. The magnificent tiled tub was part of a glorious Turkish-Bath scene, and though the flats about it were only half painted and the dome tilted against the wall awaiting frescoing, this Ophelia didn't mark them. She cared only for the pool, the nearly bottomless pool, and the sensation of water against every bit of her skin at once.

Before she could clamber over the side, Ariel caught her with a strand of wind and held her back. "Is this where you've been seeking freedom? In an oversize bathtub?"

"It's not the container, but what fills it." She struggled against his winds, now joined by his arms, almost remembering in that moment that she, too, was a shell that contained more than this Ophelia and the need to drown herself over and over again. "It's what fills it that matters!"

That time, when she spoke, the voice was Bertie's own.

Ariel let her go, backing toward the door as though afraid of what she might say or do next. "They underestimate you, I think." Then, because he could resist no longer, he disappeared down the corridor to answer Prospero's summons.

"Indeed they do," said the fading strains of Bertie. "They underestimate both of us."

The call for *Hamlet* came sometime later. How much later, this Ophelia had no idea, and by then, she didn't care. What was left of Bertie was a tiny mewling thing trapped in a great darkness somewhere deep inside, silenced over and over again by the water, and so this Ophelia answered her call upon the board with cheerful good grace. She applied her makeup with deft hands, donned her costume with the aid of Mrs. Edith's minions, and tried to ignore the sound of distant ocean waves crashing in her head.

"The sea," she murmured into the folds of her costume. "I can smell the sea."

She could also hear a man and a woman whispering to one another in the night. Water poured in about the lovers, and this time it was horrible, evil stuff, black and choking.

"I suppose I'm imagining things." Puzzled, she stood waiting in the wings without the slightest flutter of nerves. The Danish Prince lingered about her before the curtain rose, trying to wheedle a kiss, a token, a favor of some sort, but she hardly marked him. The play was the thing, and she had a part to play.

A part to play.

This Ophelia licked her lips and tasted greasepaint. Something felt amiss as she listened to the opening of the play unfold. There was something she knew, something important about her first line. . . .

But before she could puzzle it out, the Stage Manager gave her an encouraging sort of nudge, indicating she'd nearly missed her cue. Gliding into the scene with her brother, Laertes, this Ophelia could hardly hear for the wind roaring in her head.

"Do you doubt that?" she said, just as she ought.

The words echoed through the auditorium, and then memories, Bertie's memories, slammed into her with the force of the tsunami.

Ophelia's opening line.

I'm the one who said it. I'm the one who acted her page back into The Book and pulled her here.

Bertie thought she heard her mother's wail as the real Ophelia was transported into the theater and away from the Scrimshander. Despite wanting to flee the stage, Bertie was still too much Ophelia. She had to stay, to finish the scene, but the moment it was done, she ran for the door and down the dimly lit corridor.

Somewhere, a bird called out as it fled into the night.

Somewhere, a baby took its first breath and screamed.

Along with her disguise, the rest of Ophelia's madness fell away from Bertie the moment she spotted her mother at the far end of the hallway. The real Ophelia stood, eyes vacant, a single diamond-tear clinging to her cheek.

"Mom—" Bertie choked out, but the water-maiden drifted past her in silence, stepping through the Stage Door, making her next entrance as though she'd not just given birth, as though she'd never been gone.

The distant figure of Mrs. Edith carried a blanket-wrapped bundle the opposite direction, and the child's cry echoed in the corridor. Bertie took one step toward the

Wardrobe Mistress—*toward myself*—but was stopped by the faint summons of an imperious sovereign.

"Beatrice Shakespeare Smith!"

It was Her Gracious Majesty, finally recalling her through the looking glass. Torn, Bertie turned first one direction then the other, unable to know what she would be able to change, if she stayed, or if it was really possible to change anything at all.

One step made her decision, another cemented it. She ran, Ophelia's drowning dress falling away in tattered strips to reveal a new gown underneath, one of diaphanous black, cut from shadow-cloth and stitched together with secrets. Properly attired for mourning, Bertie burst through the door to Ophelia's Dressing Room, reaching for the mirror and the beckoning hand of the child Queen who pulled her back through the glass.

CHAPTER THIRTEEN

Like Bubbles in a Late-Disturbed Stream

Regurgitated upon the floor of the mirrored room, Bertie felt as aged as the Queen. Now a sulky teenager, Her Gracious Majesty was dressed tip to toe in melodramatic black also and had her lace-mitt-covered hands planted upon her royal hips. Hauling Bertie up, she kept a death grip upon her subject and kicked the door open with one foot.

"You've been gone—"

"Months." Almost nine of them, exactly, from the time Ophelia had fled the theater to the day she'd been pulled back.

By me. It was my fault she was separated from my father. That was the missing bit of the story. The missing bit of my mirror. The reason Her Gracious Majesty thinks we can't ever be together as a family.

Shuddering, Bertie wished the Queen wouldn't hurry them so. Thrust into the brilliant corridor that led back to the breakfast room, Bertie could hardly see for the glare of sunlight through the glass, could hardly hear for the echo of the ocean's roar in her ears.

The Queen shook her head. "Maybe there it's been months. Here it's been less than two hours. But what hours!" Now the approximate age of sixteen, Her Gracious Majesty had a tiny pimple on the end of her nose and a vicious temper, as evidenced by the pinch she gave Bertie's inner arm to hurry her along. "I am most peeved, forced as I was to call you back before you learned the whole truth of it, but someone is seeking you."

The Queen gestured out the largest and clearest of the windows. The view fell away from them in tiers, the Distant Castle flowing into the territories of the unicorn and the lioness, the surrounding countryside a never-ending cake platter. The river coiled about them, sandy banks churning with waves and its waters rising to batter against the outermost gates.

In case Bertie missed it, the Queen jerked her chin at the Reine with a forehead-knotting scowl. "Whatever that is came here for you. When I stand upon the terraces, I can hear it calling your name."

Bertie could guess easily enough who had come calling.

"It's the Sea Goddess, Your Gracious Majesty, the one from my life tale. She must have given chase up the river."

"I don't care *who* she is! She's ignored two very pointed proclamations to depart, and she's ruining my birthday celebration." The Queen pointed at an impressive archway and the balcony beyond. "Tell her to go this instant."

Having worn her mother's face for so many months, Bertie's mask was now thick enough to hide her irritation. "Of course, Your Gracious Majesty. At once."

Because Sedna is so very likely to obey me.

The wind that whipped across the terrace was heavy with moisture, stirred by the very ebb and flow of the sea unnaturally driven to the Distant Castle's gates. When the Sea Goddess spoke, it was a salt-spangled whisper against Bertie's skin.

"Beatrice . . . Shakespeare . . . Smith."

Bertie wiped it away as best she could, trying to not flinch. "Sedna."

"You escaped."

"I survived, as you did, because I must." Bertie remembered the rocks of the cavern pinning her to the floor, the movement of water and sand up her nostrils and in her lungs, the welcoming arms of the earth that had enfolded her and given her a loamy passage back to the surface. "You have no right to follow me, to threaten me again. The Queen wishes you gone, as do I."

"You do not command me, Daughter of the Earth, and the Queen passes into the dust every nightfall. What care I for the wishes of dust and yet more dust?" The water's laughter sloshed over the gates.

"You forget," Bertie breathed, suddenly inspired, "that earth controls the path of the river." Concentrating upon the area nearest the bottommost glass archway, she held out her hand. "I call upon the dirt, upon every speck of sand and silt. Remake the landscape so as to drive this impertinent water back where it belongs."

And the land did so, by inches, until the gates no longer creaked upon their joints. Bertie would have smiled, save for the sweat running down her forehead and into her eyes, burning like fire and sun together.

Sensing a weakness, the river surged forward again, turning everything to mud that oozed between the glass bricks.

"The water cuts a path where it will," Sedna purred. "It is steady. Patient. It washes away everything in time's slow path."

"Slowly it might, but for now you will be corralled." Reaching out again, Bertie called to the deepest roots, to the largest boulders and the smallest stones. One by one, massive oak trees toppled before the gates, driving the river back to its banks. Bertie fortified the boundary with rocks, rolled into place like stalwart soldiers. The water hammered at the walls of its improvised playpen, cursing Bertie to the blue, blue skies, rising as though in a fist before smashing back into the riverbed.

"Yet another battle goes to you, then," Sedna snarled. "But while you protect this place, you leave another defenseless. Rivers lead to cities, cities with pipes, pipes that snake directly into buildings. Your precious theater will suffer for your insolence."

Sedna turned the tide, her waters rushing away from the Distant Castle in search of a more vulnerable target. Nearly hanging over the stone lip of the balcony, Bertie screamed a wordless threat at the disappearing Sea Goddess before whirling about to face a most flabbergasted Queen.

"That was quite something!" Her Gracious Majesty sounded a bit awed before she remembered just who she was and to whom she was speaking. "You will be suitably rewarded! Gold, perhaps, or jewels. A royal appointment as my personal Mistress of Revels—"

"My thanks, Your Gracious Majesty, but I would be remiss if I permitted harm to come to the Théâtre Illuminata while I lingered here in safety and comfort." Bertie hoped interrupting the Queen wouldn't result in a beheading just when she most needed to keep her wits about her, and she curtsied as far as her shaking knees would permit. "Can you send me back to the theater with your mirrors?"

"In the present?" Scowling, the Queen shook her head.

"I'm afraid not. Their magic only reflects the captured images of events past."

It seemed hardly prudent to argue, but Bertie couldn't stop herself. "If not the mirrors, what about a wish-come-true? Would that send me there?"

"No doubt."

When Her Gracious Majesty said nothing further, Bertie pressed her only advantage. "You did say I would be suitably rewarded for turning the Sea Goddess away from your very gates."

"So I did." The Queen reached out her hand, and pressed the largest and most impressive of her rings to the center of Bertie's forehead. "I would have you consider a few things, though, before I bestow this upon you. Wishes are not mere trinkets and trifles, nor are they a way for us to wriggle free from our troubles. Reflect hard, Beatrice Shakespeare Smith. A wish-come-true must be worthy of the wisher, and the wisher must be worthy of the wish."

"I understand," Bertie said, nearly cross-eyed from trying to look up at the massive sapphire digging into her flesh.

"You don't," the Queen retorted, "but with luck you might someday."

Then Bertie's head filled with light, the sort of brilliant silver illumination that suggested sunshine reflected off all the Grand Hall's mirrors at once. By the time she drew a breath, the radiance of the wish-come-true was reduced to a lingering smear of sparkling light that danced behind Bertie's eyes when she blinked or turned her head too quickly.

It was, she realized, a thing too weighty, too precious to waste on something as simple as mere transportation. "If you fetch my friends and my carriage, I will find another way to get us back with due haste."

Her Gracious Majesty hiked up her royal skirts and scampered down the corridor, revealing dainty ankle-strapped Mary Janes under the yards and yards of silk petticoat and embroidered black velvet. "Fenek!"

The servitor appeared around the very next door. "Yes, Your—"

He didn't get the chance to finish the royal address, for the Queen bellowed as she passed, "Come! The Mistress of Revels demands her cart and her companions at once, do you hear!"

"Of course!" His own voice raised, amplified by unseen means as he kept pace with them. "Calling the many-liveried butlers! Calling the ostlers! Calling the courtiers!"

They converged in groups of three or four, pouring in from the various corridors until the massive tidal wave of personages convened in the Grand Hall. Bertie was most relieved to see the members of her own company standing Center Stage.

Nate leapt at her, his face a study in panic and relief at

once. "Bertie! Sedna's here, in th' river surroundin' th' castle—"

"Not anymore!" the Queen crowed, victorious. "The Teller of Tales banished her!"

"Ding-dong, the Sea Witch is dead!" Moth crowed, waving his tiny hat overhead.

"Not dead, stupid!" Mustardseed jabbed him with an elbow. "Just banished!"

Ignoring the byplay, Her Gracious Majesty issued orders like rifle fire. "Open the gates! Prepare and pack the Mistress of Revels's caravan! And SOMEONE bring me an omelet!"

Nate drew Bertie off to one side as the Queen shouted and jabbed her finger at various members of her court. "Is it true? Sedna's gone?"

Bertie wanted to rest her head upon his shoulder, but she didn't have that luxury right now. "Yes, but I drove her away from the castle only for her to turn toward the theater." Four horrified gasps from the fairies, and Bertie could only nod in acknowledgment. "She's rushing there now, determined to clamber up the plumbing and no doubt flood the building to the rafters again. We have to get back. Immediately. So I can protect it."

"You think we can protect the theater from an angry Sea Goddess?" Ariel's soft question attacked from behind.

Both Bertie and Nate turned as one, though she spoke first. "I don't know if I can, but I'll try. I have to."

"And I stand wi' her." Nate almost didn't need to say the words, so aligned with her body was he.

"You're both fools," Ariel said with the sort of sigh he might direct at a pair of children playing in the mud. "And in great want of a babysitter. I suppose I have no choice but to accompany you on this mad journey."

Not about to let him get away with using such a tone with her, Bertie shook her head. "Don't be bound by a false sense of obligation, Ariel. We've no more need of your company than you have of ours, it seems. Stay here with the Queen, or visit the other Twelve Outposts of Beyond if you prefer."

"I could never desert you, as well you know." The air elemental's hair coiled about his shoulders, drifting around him like wisps of smoke. Varvara, as yet silent, hovered just behind him, her own hair moving in superheated currents. "And Mrs. Edith would never forgive me if I left the two of you . . . to your own devices."

Wishing she could understand just what he was playing at now, Bertie shook her head. "A pretty argument, except you've already deserted me thrice in anger, once upon the Innamorati's train, just days ago at the Caravanserai, and again on the road. And so I tell you this: Leave again, and you needn't ever come back."

Fenek squeaked an interruption before Ariel could respond. "It is as you wished, Your Gracious Majesty! Their caravan is ready!"

"There now!" The Queen beamed, and as an unseen clock struck ten, time advanced upon her face; her pimple disappeared, and the roundness of her cheeks melted away until a beneficent woman of perhaps one-and-twenty stood before them. "To your carriage, good Mistress of Revels, and safe travels to you!"

Bertie paused long enough to curtsy—*may it be the last time!*—before she ran for it with her friends at her heels. Pirate, air elemental, fire-dancer, and fairies negotiated the hallways, clattered into the courtyard, and clambered upon the caravan. Ariel looked ten sorts of sour to see Nate in the driver's seat, a position he had once occupied with grace and skill, though he made no comment.

"Ye might want t' hold on to somethin'," Nate warned Bertie before he signaled the mechanical horses.

The clockwork steeds launched themselves forward with matching pewter whickers, hurtling toward the bottom of the hill and the newly cleared opening just beyond the gates. Bertie squeezed the armrest hard enough to coax sap from the wood as the road leveled out. Passing under the glass archway, the caravan nearly overturned as Nate tried to avoid the felled trees and boulders that littered the road.

"Bertie—" he cried, guiding the horses around the worst of it. "Do yer best t' clear th' way!"

Concentrating until she was nearly cross-eyed, Bertie struggled to move the wayward branches and massive stones from their path. A particularly large specimen wiggled mica ears at them as they passed. It had, she realized, the sort of face worn by Pan and Puck. The sort of face that would be carved in the bark of a tree. The sort that *had* been carved into one of the trees in her dreamland forest. Leaves of ivy formed his features then; granite trapped him now. He taunted her from the heart of the stone, beckoning with loam-encrusted hands and moss-tipped fingers.

There are faster ways to travel, Daughter of the Earth.

There were indeed . . . like a wish-come-true. But Bertie resisted the lure of the glowing, magical thing lingering just behind her eyes; she couldn't bring herself to use it just yet.

"I can skip us ahead," she shouted into the winds. "A stone across a pond, like I did aboard the circus train!"

Mustardseed squeaked with apprehension. "You melted the train's engine!"

"I don't want my guts turned into warm nougat!" Cobweb shouted.

Bertie reached out and jerked the reins from Nate's grip. The caravan swayed wildly upon the road. Ariel was knocked back among the luggage with a curse. The fairies clutched her hair, screaming, "AAAAAAAAAH!" until they ran out of breath. Moth even went a bit blue, trying to keep it going. Then they all sucked in another breath and started again. "AAAAAAAAAH!"

"Careful, lass!" Nate admonished after one of the wheels

hit a particularly large rut. "Ye'll knock th' pins right out o' this thing!"

Bertie shook the hair from her eyes, scrutinizing the rocks that rose on either side of the road like needles poked through embroidery cloth. "Quiet. I need to focus, unless you want your innards to end up somewhere other than where they ought to be."

The fairies immediately ceased their screaming as Bertie guided the caravan between another series of boulders that formed an ever-narrowing alleyway. Focusing upon the stones, she allowed the rest of the world to blur into an Impressionist canvas of blue and gray and green paint splotches. The tunnel that formed ahead was like the yawning mouth of a mountain mining shaft. The road under the caravan sloped down.

"Bertie—" Ariel started to warn her, but too late.

Daylight disappeared as the earth swallowed them, leaving only Varvara's soft glow bathing Bertie's shoulders. With grace almost impossible for their circumstances, the fire-dancer leaned forward and lit the caravan's lanterns with a snap of her fingers. When that was done, she held out her hand until it skimmed the tunnel's walls, causing heretofore unseen and ancient torches to spark to life.

"That's a bit better, I think!" Her triumphant laughter caused a flare of heat and light around them.

The road ahead no longer a gaping void, Bertie could

now see the tiny, uncut jewels studding the rocks, the gold-filled fissures in the walls, the brilliant and sparkling bits that suggested the Queen's fantastically studded crown. The rock faces still appeared at intervals, beckoning them deeper into gloom, and Bertie had no choice but to obey; even if she stopped the caravan, there was no room in which to turn around, nowhere to go except forward, racing toward a theater that might be smashed to the ground before they arrived. Gauzy cobwebs drifted over them like tattered lace, and she had to swallow a scream when something with skittering legs crawled over her right shoulder.

"I got it!" Mustardseed grasped the uninvited passenger and flung it into the darkness.

"How long will this take?" Nate had both his booted feet braced against the floorboards. In the intermittent flashes of torchlight, he managed to look pale despite his tan.

"I don't know. I should do something in the meantime. Something else to keep Sedna out." If Bertie had had the journal, she could have written something and instantly made it so, but all she had now was her spoken words. . . .

And the wish-come-true. The Queen's words echoed in her head:

"A wish-come-true must be worthy of the wisher and the wisher must be worthy of the wish."

Surely it was worthy to protect the Théâtre Illuminata

from the Sea Goddess! Except small cracks immediately appeared in the surface of such a notion. Could Sedna penetrate the theater's defenses? Would the Sea Goddess even reach the grand building at all? A waste of the wish-come-true would be a terrible thing indeed.

I can think of another way to protect the building and all the Players, surely.

Bertie closed her eyes and cast her thoughts far ahead of them to the theater. Her connection to the grand building was thin but powerful, strengthened with memories and obligation and love, and so she summoned all that was earth to protect it. Cold iron answered her call in the form of bars upon the doors and locks upon the windows. Dirt clogged the pipes, and tendrils of every growing thing fortified the very timbers of the building. But those measures did not feel like enough.

"Faster," Bertie said, though not to urge the horses, who were already running at a flat gallop. She reached out a hand, trailing her fingertips over the surface of the rock, gathering the heat of the earth: the tiny chemical reactions of mold lying against loam; the exertions of every root and branch simultaneously reaching down and pushing up. Catching them like green and brown ribbons, she wove them into something hot and bright. "Let all that is rough and rock be smoothed."

"I can help with that," Varvara murmured, placing her ruby-tipped fingers upon Bertie's shoulders. "We are growing quite proficient at this party trick."

In moments, the stones and dirt on which they traveled were transformed into glass. The walls flattened into dim mirrors, their silvered backing scratched and pockmarked with eons passed. It was as though they traveled the halls of the Distant Castle, but in a kingdom the sun had forsaken.

Except the princess isn't asleep in a tower . . . she's drowning herself over and over again, waiting for her prince to return.

When Bertie squinted, the torchlight blurred. Marked by wet, green trails, water trickled down walls reminiscent of a moldering dungeon. The damp pooled on the floors, and the caravan's wheels splashed through puddles with increasing frequency.

"What's happening?" Peaseblossom cried.

Bertie had no answer for her. Behind them, she could hear the building rush of a tidal wave. Over that, a voice called to them, growing more shrill with each passing second.

"I can hear her!" Nate leaned forward in the seat. "Move yer arses!" he shouted to the horses as water now poured down the tunnel walls.

"I don't wanna diiiiiiie," Moth wailed into Bertie's ear like a tiny, demented ambulance siren.

"It's not my destiny to go down with the ship!" That was

Mustardseed, who had donned a tiny life preserver stamped RMS *TITANIC*. He clung to her bodice like a buoyant, beaded broach.

Another noise, somehow worse than the fairies' screaming, started off low and built upon itself one decibel at a time. Varvara's eyes had gone black, corner to corner, and her banshee shriek summoned another wave of heat to counter the water. Steam enveloped the caravan, thick with the scents of salt and seaweed.

Bertie would have jammed her fingers into her ears in an effort to banish the screaming, the rushing water, the stone walls that shuddered like an old man with rheumatic fever, but it was too much to manage while yet holding the reins. She gestured frantically to Ariel. "Help her dry some of it up."

Winds answered his immediate summons. Kneeling behind Bertie, he held his arms out so they passed over her shoulders, crowding the fairies but shoving the worst of the water out of their path. It sloshed up the sides of the tunnel and poured in atop their heads, but still they raced forward. Light appeared in the distance; their luck being as it was, Bertie prayed it wasn't the Innamorati's train. The glittering star-promise expanded and then went supernova with golden brilliance as the caravan hurtled into its very heart and landed hard upon the cobblestones of a topside thoroughfare.

CHAPTER FOURTEEN

Come Not Home in Twice Six Moons

*C*areful now!" shouted a curiously familiar pedestrian as Bertie pulled upon the reins with all her might. The mechanical horses' shoes sent up sparks when they dug in. The caravan rocked left, swerved right, and narrowly missed both the curb and the sneak-thief who bounded up to greet them.

"Such impeccable timing!" he crowed, clapping Bertie upon the arm and shaking Nate's and Ariel's hands in turn.

"Waschbär!" Bertie reached out to clutch at his sleeves. "Did you get the journal?"

"I tracked the brigands back to the theater," he answered, expression suddenly pained, "but I've been as yet unable to reclaim the purloined tome."

"The brigands are *here*?" Bertie gaped at him. "But why?"

"I know not yet, but when they left you upon the road, they headed straight for the Théâtre Illuminata, and I followed. Just as they would have entered, iron bars grew over the windows and massive bolts locked the doors in place. Such fortuitous magic warned me you might be nearby, and here you are!"

"Where did you last see them?"

"Circling around the back of the building, no doubt contemplating their lock-picking options."

Peering down the alley in search of the brigands, Bertie couldn't help but also gape at the city that surrounded them. The troupe had departed via an ill-lit boulevard, nearly deserted save for the rubbish collectors and a stray cat. The buildings had been like night-painted scenic flats, one-dimensional shapes propped against the backdrop of a star-splashed sky. Today the main avenue swarmed, overrun with people and conveyances of all sorts: Dickensian-era shoppers perusing wares from the open-air fishmongers alongside grinning short-skirted teenagers carrying slim cell phones in candy colors. Horse-drawn cabs maneuvered between motorbikes and automobiles of every make and model. Looking at the street was like peering through one of Mr. Hastings's stereoscopic viewers at countless picture cards taken at different time periods and layered one atop the other.

Sitting at an apex of space and time, an intersection of

all the years, the Théâtre Illuminata loomed over every-thing. The only steadfast point in a whirling world, the façade mirrored the ivory of the scrimshaw hanging, in-nocuous, about Bertie's neck. In turn, the medallion echoed the theater's domed roof, its gracious statuary, the wrought-iron flowers and vines, each detail rendered in miniature upon its surface.

Then everything shuddered, and chaos erupted. Gush-ing geysers of water exploded from the manholes. Seawater flung the circular metal disks skyward before they hit the street, an unoccupied automobile, and a cart filled with apples with a series of heavy thuds. Screams rang out as people scattered. Angry waves gave chase, shoving men and women into buildings, picking them up like rag dolls and tossing them aside.

"Run for the revolving door!" Bertie's shout almost didn't carry over the bedlam, but every member of the troupe heard and obeyed. A gust of wind indicated Ariel was right behind her. Varvara and Waschbär kept pace, marked by the thud of his feet and the tippity-tap of her toe shoes. Nate was next, moving uncommonly fast for a man of his stature. The fairies careened ahead, their wings a blur as they flew backward and upside down, facing Bertie so as to better coax her forward.

"You can run faster than that!"

"My grandmother can run faster than that!"

"You have a grandmother?!"

At the next gush of water, they adjusted formation with screams of "Help, she's going to eat me!" that echoed off the flower-crowned statues, the portico, the dome. One enormous wave after another smashed into the steps behind Bertie. Currents swirled about Varvara's toe shoes, staining the red satin tips two shades darker than blood and eliciting a whimper from the fire-dancer.

Taking pity upon her, Waschbär lifted her onto one shoulder before catapulting them forward. "See to your craft, wordsmith, before Sedna has her way with all of us."

The wish-come-true glowed white-hot behind Bertie's eyes as the Sea Goddess rose, huge and terrible, from the waves churning at the base of the stairs. Water sluiced off Sedna's brackish-green skin and seaweed hair. She stretched out scaled arms, reaching for them with hands that were yet starfish.

I could wish her gone.

I could wish her dead.

Sedna's cruel mouth twisted into a smile of triumph, revealing jagged shark's teeth. "Yes, wordsmith, do your worst."

Bertie's anger, her rage, her nearly futile hope that she could save them consumed her, and there was no room left in her head for wording the wish. Fueled by the memories of her mother and father, almost killed by the Sea Goddess's water, of Nate kidnapped, of the brutal swordfight Sedna had orchestrated between Ariel and Nate on a distant beach, she pointed a single finger at the Sea Goddess and called upon all four of the elements: her own earth, her father's air, her mother's water, and a new understanding of fire.

"Get you gone!"

Her words caused an explosion of light and sound unlike anything Bertie had ever experienced before. Even when their page from The Book had fused into the journal, even when she'd been trapped, drowning, in Sedna's cavern, she'd been able to think; now there was only pure energy using her body and mind as a conduit. Sedna's screams filled the street, and still the fire and water and air poured through Bertie's earth, consuming every shred of her consciousness and sanity and reason until there was only darkness.

From a distance, she could hear the others, could feel their hands upon her and a blood-flower of pain blooming on her skull. When the energy faded away, Bertie found she was flat on her back at the top of the stairs, head pounding harder than the time she'd gotten into Mr. Hastings's rum, eyeballs one size too large for their sockets, and every inch of her body aching.

"Lass!" Nate looked as though he was shouting, but his

voice was wrapped in wet muslin and his face had gone swimmy about the edges.

The distant suggestion of friction hinted Ariel might be chafing her hands. Bertie blinked, looking at both pirate and air elemental, wanting to reassure them but unable to summon the words.

"Ye know a part o' me dies every time I see ye hurt like this?" Nate shoved his hands under her shoulders and knees, heaving her from the ground in one smooth motion. Someone or something had bloodied his lip, though the water had washed the worst of it away. "Ye keep this up, ye'll be th' death o' me yet."

All Bertie managed in reply was a soft wheeze. The entire street below was in chaos, but the Sea Goddess was gone. In her wake, rivulets of damp worked their way down nearby walls, and scum-bedecked puddles lingered between the lower-set cobblestones.

"Will she be all right?" Peaseblossom's voice was as tinny as a singer on an antique gramophone record.

"She's not talking," Mustardseed said in funereal tones. "That can't be a good sign."

Bertie managed to say, "S'all right," with the vigor and conviction of a newborn bunny.

Twitching at the noise, Nate shifted her in his arms, the damp linen of his sleeves pressing water into her bodice. "I don't know how ye vanquished her, but ye best remember th' way o' it."

"Where did Sedna go?"

"Back into th' water lines." He shifted her weight so she was more firmly hugged to his chest. "Most o' her, anyway. Th' rest evaporated."

Bertie tried to speak again, but found she couldn't and, what's more, wouldn't bring herself to care about the absence of words.

"Let's get ye inside." He moved, swift and sure toward the glass revolving door. Neither of them expected it to give only an inch before slamming into some sort of obstruction. Bertie's shoulder cracked against the door before they fell back with a spine-jarring thud. Nate cursed in a half-dozen languages, easily switching among them as he struggled to his feet again.

Bertie staggered up, dazed and dizzy. "I locked us out." She mustered the ghost of a laugh, reaching out a hand and coaxing the iron bar to fall from its brackets, the locks to slide from their tumblers.

Nate pushed on the door again, to no avail. "Ye forgot t' undo somethin'."

Peering up at the stern façade, Bertie shook her head. "I don't think so. The theater protects itself and its own. It's sealed itself off somehow." So presumptuous of her to think a magic as old and as powerful as the Théâtre Illu-minata's would need her meager assistance!

"We're friend, not foe." Waschbär turned Bertie to-ward the ticket booth and the woman who stood inside it. "Maybe she will have a suggestion as to how we can gain entrance."

Startled, Bertie leaned forward to address the stranger before realizing it was a wooden figure, life-size and cun-ningly carved. The red paint upon her lips formed a per-fect bow, and dark curls were piled atop her head. "How is a mannequin supposed to explain anything?"

The sneak-thief reached into his pocket, pulled out a silver coin, and dropped it into a slot. There was the sound of metal gears grinding to life, then the woman in the ticket booth looked up with a mother-of-pearl smile.

"No play tonight." *Click. Whirr.* "No play tonight. The season is finished until the Touring Company returns."

"Touring Company?" Bertie gaped at the figure. "But *we* are the Touring Company."

Shhhhh, click. Shhhhh, click. Whirr. "No play tonight."

"Ye just said that," Nate muttered. "Tell us somethin' we don't already know."

The figure shook her head, massive earrings glinting with dull warning in the booth's half-light. "Come back in a day." *Click.* "A week." *Click.* "A month. Perhaps they will have returned with the Brand-New Play by then. I'm certain it will be a wonderful piece!" Her programmed enthusiasm peeled the paint off her mouth. "All lights and flash bangs and people shouting speeches at each other." *Click. Click. Whirr.* "You'll love it."

A wooden hand flicked a switch, and the electric lights of the marquee sizzled to life; white, ruby, and amber luminosity spread across the sidewalk before dribbling into the gutters. Bertie's eyes filled with water and then overflowed. Though the colors blurred, she could still make out the words emblazoned overhead:

Coming Soon!
FOLLOWING HER STARS
A Brand-New Play
By Beatrice Shakespeare Smith

"Yer play?" Nate frowned. "Th' one th' Innamorati are performin' right now?"

"No." Bertie could taste panic and bile in the back of her throat, knowing somehow that she was responsible for this new twist of fate and yet unable to pinpoint what she'd done or how to fix it. "*Following Her Stars* is the name of the play I started so we could exit the theater. The one that's been appearing in the journal."

"But you haven't finished it yet!" Moth said, whizzing forward to collide with a similarly inclined Mustardseed.

233

"He's right," Bertie told the wooden woman in the booth. "And I can't truly finish it unless we get the journal back!"

False eyelashes fluttered, and the figure's bloodred lips dribbled rhinestones as she said once more, "No play tonight."

Out of patience for the automaton's punchcard-programmed answers, Bertie pounded her hand on the glass. "Let us in!"

"You'll love it," the woman only repeated before her mechanisms ran down with a *whirrrrrr*. Her eyes closed, her head lowered. Matching her dismissal, the marquee flickered off, and the rest of the theater's exterior lights faded to a blackout.

The darkness was a perfect foil for a sparkle like moonlight upon the water, and Bertie glanced at the revolving door in time to see Ophelia. The hem of her mother's dress was ragged, her hair tangled about with tattered ribbon ends, bits of shell, tiny silver charms.

"Beatrice." Ophelia's whisper was no more than one fish speaking to another underwater, the glass trapping the words in rainbow prisms and almost denying Bertie the chance to hear her at all.

"Mom." The word rasped like the rough edge of Waschbär's obsidian knife.

For the briefest of moments, the water-maiden's features sharpened. She was Ophelia of the Outside, the woman who had torn her page from The Book and run away with the Mysterious Stranger, the woman who might have lived with the Scrimshander—and Bertie—in a cave high in the cliffs, had it not been for the vengeful Sea Goddess.

Had it not been for me, taking her place by accident, calling her back to the theater by saying her opening line.

Ophelia's eyes were full of tears, her lips faintly blue when she mouthed her questions. "Did you find your father? Is he with you?"

"I found him, but he's not here . . ." Some combination of desperation and compassion compelled Bertie to add, "Not just yet. Can you let us in?"

"Something happened soon after you left." The hem of Ophelia's gown began to unravel, fraying in a dozen spots along the waistband, pinholes appearing throughout the skirts so that she looked progressively more tattered and timeworn. "I heard your voice, as though amplified by every speaker in the building. 'Following her stars,' you said."

The realization was like a punch to Bertie's gut. "That's when I read our entrance page into the journal."

Ophelia nodded, though she couldn't possibly comprehend. "In a trice there were two theaters; the one you left, and this empty shell. I am trapped between them, walking twin hallways, pulled without conscious thought or desire between the two."

Bertie could guess why: Ophelia was a Player, bound to

The Complete Works of the Stage, and yet the most important scenes in her life had played out in the world beyond the theater, the part of her story told in the journal. "You belong to both worlds."

"I think it's killing me." Ophelia was no more than a ghostly apparition now. "It grows harder to remember you. Harder to remember myself. Something is towing me away with the drowning tide."

When next she spoke, Bertie felt the diamond-tears fall again. "I'm so sorry. This is all my fault."

But Ophelia didn't mark the confession. "Would that I had seen your father once more—"

Bertie could not bring herself to tell her mother that the Scrimshander had been here but could not find his way in, that he could not see anything save a deserted building.

There was nothing for me there.

She wanted to scream with the unfairness of it all.

The water-maiden flattened her hand against the glass. "Promise you'll remember me, Beatrice—"

Bertie's palm met Ophelia's, one gesture the mirror reflection of the other, and though she refused to blink the tears from her eyes, the water-maiden still disappeared. When Bertie screamed, her "No!" echoed from the columns and the statues. She shouted again, hitting the glass door with both hands. "Mom!" No response. "Ophelia! Come back!"

"It's killin' her."

Whirling about, Bertie irrationally wanted to hit Nate for speaking the truth. She started to call upon the wish-come-true, had indeed already strung together the words to set everything to rights. At the last second, Bertie remembered the Queen's warning that it couldn't be used to reunite her family.

"Not even my magic could help you with the way things are right now," Her Gracious Majesty had said.

"We have to save Ophelia before she disappears completely. There has to be another way inside. A window. A door." Bertie lunged at Waschbär with such speed that the sneak-thief hadn't the time to dodge or evade her.

"What are you doing?" he demanded as she wrestled the pair of dazed and sleepy ferrets from his jacket.

Peaseblossom hovered just behind her, keeping well out of reach of Pip Pip's and Cheerios's paws and teeth. "Whatever are you thinking?"

Bertie didn't answer as she peered closer at the ferrets, realizing her mistake in casually dismissing Waschbär's companions as potential slippers, as food thieves, as pests. She set them gently upon the ground at her feet. "Single-minded, aren't you, with noses meant for tracking and eyes good for peering into dark and forbidding places?"

In musky agreement, the ferrets sat up on their back legs.

"They can scent anything," Waschbär said.

"I have something specific in mind." Bertie tried to imagine it into being: a forgotten tunnel, darker than the earth portal they'd used to travel to the theater, older than the bricks of the Théâtre Illuminata itself. "What if I asked you to find a crack in the theater's magic . . . could you do such a thing? Could you find a way in?"

The ferrets peered at her, so still they might be mistaken for bookends perched upon one of Mr. Hastings's shelves. Turning, they regarded each other, entering into a silent conversation that ended with twin squeaks and a sudden leaping down the stairs.

Nate's hand came to rest upon the small of Bertie's back. His touch startled her, recalling the time they'd cranked a vintage wall telephone in the Properties Department and accidentally electrocuted Mustardseed, who'd been licking inappropriate bits of the wiring. "They're headed fer th' Stage Door."

Indeed, the ferrets led them down the narrow alley that ran alongside the theater, but they passed the Stage Door, scampering instead to a crumbled and forgotten corner. Shoving at loose brick and primordial mortar, they soon nosed into a tiny opening. Lying on her stomach upon the cobblestones, Bertie could barely make out the glint of light upon two sets of black-beaded eyes.

"Come back—" she started to call, just before the wall

above her groaned an ill omen. Scrambling away, Bertie stifled a shriek as the bricks shifted to open a small but definite passageway. The darkness beyond the portal was a gaping, hungry mouth. Dank air swirled in tidal currents, and the moist breeze held notes of Sedna's mocking laughter.

"I am *not* going down there," Mustardseed announced.

Bertie very much wanted to flee, but to show cowardice now would admit defeat. "That's the way in."

Nate shifted, his cutlass drawn. "I'll go first." He slanted a quick look at Ariel. "Unless ye'd like th' honor."

Crouched next to the opening, the air elemental didn't respond at first. "Something down there wishes to speak with you, Bertie."

"Of course it wants to talk to her," Moth said, his little teeth chattering. "It wants to get acquainted before it eats her!"

Refusing to imagine herself as someone's supper, Bertie ducked her head and wriggled her way in. A ragged brick scraped down the length of her back, a tooth eager for a taste of her. When she stood, the weight of the air inside the tunnel was heavier upon her skin than the stage's velvet curtains.

"Nate?" The word was muffled, nearly smothered by the utter darkness. "Ariel? Are you coming?" No answer. The path led downward—*to the very underworld*—and Bertie held her hands out before her. When she heard the telltale *drip! drip! drip!* of distant water, her limbs froze like birch branches in an ice storm. "Sedna?"

The tunnel exhaled, a monster waiting for the right moment to close unseen teeth upon her. Heat replaced cold, Bertie's blood encouraging her to retreat. Galvanized by panic and adrenaline, she might have obeyed the instinct, save for Ophelia's voice, calling to her through the darkness.

"Bertie." The name brought with it the bleeding-water promise of her mother shredded to nothing.

Stiffening, Bertie summoned vines to wrap about her nerves, wood splints to straighten her spine, enough courage to spur her forward. Just when she thought the tunnel couldn't grow any narrower, steeper, darker, her reaching hands met a curved stone wall and torches all around her flared to life. Momentarily blinded, Bertie ducked her head and covered her face, cowering back until her eyes adjusted to the flickering light. The passing seconds slowly revealed that she stood in an unknown chamber carved in the shape of a half-moon. Resting against the deepest part of the curve was the elaborate mosaic she'd last seen in the Turkish Bath: a slab of tile-inlaid marble portraying the Greek Chorus in all their robed dignity. Also taken from that scene was the elaborate clepsydra. Mr. Hastings surely suffered fits over the loss of the water clock, equipped as it was with silver bells, small brass gongs, and doors that would open and shut to reveal dials, pointers, and figurines. The water in the uppermost vessel flowed to those below with a *drip! drip! drip!* that intensified until it echoed throughout the room.

The rest of the troupe crowded in behind Bertie until she could hardly move.

"A dead end," Cobweb said, the disappointment evident in his tone.

"Not hardly. This is where secrets are stored." Ariel touched the mosaic, tracing the gracious curves of a Greek woman's face with near reverence.

"Would they could whisper them to us," Bertie said. "No doubt they know the way in."

As though in response, the mosaic tiles before them shifted so stone mouths could move. "Welcome home, Beatrice Shakespeare Smith."

CHAPTER FIFTEEN

The Next Tile That Falls

"We have only as long as the water clock lasts," the Greek Chorus rasped, each stone-against-mortar whisper accompanied by the orchestration of flowing water. "Then our purpose shall be served."

"What purpose?" Bertie moved forward until she could make out the stone furrows in their flesh, the bits of glass that glinted in place of their eyes.

Drip! Drip! Drip! With each fallen droplet, the chorus shifted their tiled limbs to form various poses and attitudes. "There is a bit of your mosaic yet missing."

Not again. Bertie had heard much the same from the Queen before she'd been shoved through a mirror and into the past. This time she wouldn't go without protest. "You think part of my story is yet untold?"

"We do not think—we know." They shifted again with the sound of jade mah-jongg tiles against an ancient table, then each member of the Greek Chorus lifted a tiled version of Melpomene's tragedy mask to their faces. Jagged-edged or missing stones resulted in vacant eyes or noses, while others were completely without mouths and therefore unable to do more than moan. "We can see your story laid out before us. Only when you discover this lost scene from your script, the lacking piece from your puzzle, will you be able to connect what happened beyond these walls with what transpired within."

Bertie suppressed the overwhelming urge to sigh and glare at the ceiling. What atrocious acts had she committed in a previous incarnation to doom her to battling cryptic riddle askers and gatekeepers?

"I am most peeved, forced as I was to call you back before you learned the whole truth of it," the Queen had also said. The story revealed by Her Gracious Majesty's looking glass, it seemed, wasn't yet complete.

"Do you know what's missing?" Bertie asked the Greek Chorus.

"We do."

The bits of stone and glass rearranged themselves with the hiss of a Caravanserai sandstorm to form the picture of a familiar yet foreign hallway. It was, Bertie realized, the backstage corridor, its mahogany paneling and the floral pattern on the wallpaper rendered with colored glass, travertine, and river rock. Glittering mica and mirror composed the Ophelia leaning against the Stage Door.

"The performance is done. I didn't miss my call. I did what was expected of me."

The stones shifted so that the Theater Manager's door now stood before them, thick with bubbled glass and black lettering. Tiny rubies marked the water-maiden's trail—blood droplets, Bertie realized—but Ophelia paid them no attention at all.

"My child. I held her but a moment—" Though it was unlocked, the water-maiden barely managed to turn the knob before her strength gave out and she fell to her knees on the carpet.

Glowing amber light poured out of the mosaic's version of *The Complete Works of the Stage*. It sat upon the desk, open to a blank page. Next to it lay the opal ring, already sparking with trapped fire.

"Ophelia!" A flint-chiseled Theater Manager jumped up in reluctant greeting.

"Where is my child?!" Grasping a chair, the water-maiden levered herself up from the floor.

"You're speaking nonsense. . . ." But he was no actor, and he couldn't deliver the line with any sort of conviction.

Ophelia lunged over the desk to clutch at him with

fingers like talons. "Do not lie to *me*. I will have her back, or I will scream this building to the very ground."

"Speak reason, I beseech you," he pleaded. "You are a Player. Daughter of Polonius, sister of Laertes, betrothed to Hamlet. You cannot fulfill these roles with a child clinging to your knees! A child who never should have existed! It was all some dreadful mistake—"

"You will not call her a mistake again if you hope to keep your tongue." Grasping an obsidian-sharp letter opener, Ophelia pointed at the microphone that controlled the backstage loudspeakers. "Instead, you will call the Wardrobe Mistress. You will instruct her to return my child to me." She brought the weapon around to aim it at his chest. "Or I will cut the beating heart from you."

"What will you do with the baby?" The Theater Manager gaped at her, wild-eyed. "Things cannot remain as they are!"

"I will quit this place with her, and you will not stop us."

He hesitated a moment, then nodded. "If that is your wish, of course, I will have the child brought to you. At once. I will write the order this second. . . ."

"Nothing written is needed here. Call her to me." But Ophelia's legs, though stone, were unable to support her a second longer. She fell back into the chair, and Bertie saw her strength had waned, that she could do little more than pant her river-tainted breath in a mist before her.

The Theater Manager saw it as well. Reaching past the microphone, he picked up his pen and slowly, deliberately placed it upon the blank page of The Book.

"Let all that happened outside these walls be cast aside," he whispered as he wrote.

A terrifying flash of light filled the room to the rafters as The Book rendered his words as truth. It snatched Ophelia's memories with golden, greedy fingers: a chance meeting in her Dressing Room, a handsome stranger, a daring escape, a cliff-side sanctuary, a flood, a flight, a child born. The images waltzed away like so many ghosts, shrinking down to nothing, tiptoeing into another, smaller leather-bound tome upon his desk, wrapped about with a scrap of silk that could have been torn from Ophelia's gown.

The journal . . . it holds all that happened outside the theater's walls. It somehow contains the lion's share of Ophelia's memories.

But how could that be when it was blank when I got it?

Now in possession of yet more questions without answers, Bertie stared at the mosaic's version of the Theater Manager. If nothing else, she knew now who had hired the brigands to steal the journal back.

Sitting empty and spent in her chair, Ophelia smiled blankly at the Theater Manager. "Did you want me for something, sir?"

"No, my dear." He shook his head gently. With trembling fingers, he moved the journal next to the opal ring.

As Ophelia drifted to the door, Bertie caught muttered sentences, snatches of a conversation he held with himself: "Not what I'd intended," followed by "There's no changing it now," "That's two mistakes I've had to correct today," and "Truly, these are both unwanted things," but the water-maiden paid him no mind, and Bertie knew why. Ophelia's Dressing Room called to her mother with a siren song, and she wanted nothing more at this moment than to put her face in the washbasin and drown.

Secrets told, the mosaic seemed to sag under its own weight. The droplets falling from the clepsydra suddenly gushed forth as though from a killing wound.

"Our allotted time is done, the ages call us back to dust," the Greek Chorus said with crumbling lips. "Up the Charonian stairs you must go, from the depths of this underworld."

With a final exhalation of ash, the mosaic crumbled in upon itself and snuffed out the torches. Bertie coughed and covered her streaming eyes. When the dust settled, another tunnel yawned before them, another demon's mouth that would spit them out into a new, fresh hell at the top of the stairs.

"Can someone manage a little illumination?" she asked.

In response, thin golden light seeped outward from the bodies of the fairies, all four of them concentrating with their faces screwed up. Varvara added her rosy glow, revealing the remains of the mosaic, lying scattered on the floor about them.

Bertie looked to the others. "What came to pass . . . did you see it all as I did?"

"Everythin', includin' th' Theater Manager's betrayal, th' bastard." Nate looked very much like he wanted to punch something or someone. "Don't ye think he tried t' make ye disappear int' th' journal along wi' Ophelia's memories?"

Bertie didn't want to defend the Theater Manager, but she knew how tricky it could be to find the right words, especially where the journal was concerned. Despite herself, she was unable to believe he'd known all that would happen as a result of his actions. "I think he was probably trying to fix matters as best he could, though I marvel that Waschbär didn't take me from this place, since I was the truly unwanted thing."

The sneak-thief shook his head. "Not possible. You were wanted—and loved—by plenty of people here. Besides which, I wouldn't have known what to do with a small, willful girl, would I? I'm not in the habit of carrying jam-faced urchins away from their homes."

Bertie didn't answer him, didn't return his coaxing smile, instead focusing her thoughts on the journal. Hard to believe the story of its creation and harder still to believe that they might never recover it. But recover it they must. . . . It was the center strand of her story, stretching between her and Ophelia, between the theater and the outside world, between the past and the present. "We'll have to track down the brigands and steal the journal back somehow."

"We ought to find a place to rest and plan beyond 'somehow.'" Ariel turned to consider the way they'd come in, then the path that lay before them. "If I'm correct, these stairs should lead straight up to the stage."

"An' just how do ye figure that?" Nate stared into the tunnel, his distaste all too evident.

"I know every false wall and trapdoor in this building. I think this may lead to the solitary one I was unable to broach in my time here."

"So the only way onward is up." With a shuddering breath, Bertie put a hand against the wall and started to climb. She forced herself to hold her panic at bay.

We'll find the brigands, and they will rue the day they twice over stole what was mine: the journal and Ophelia's memories of everything that happened outside these damned walls.

Much as Bertie would have liked to curse the Theater Manager to the skies, she had to focus her determination and rage upon the brigands. With every step, she painted a mental picture of them: the woman who'd murdered Pease-blossom, the snatch-purses and cutthroats, the glint of gold-capped teeth by firelight. Then she focused on their Leader, on the sour stench of his clothes, the reek of his breath next to her face, and the secret pocket in which he'd hidden the journal. The image of him swam before her in the darkness, so real that she might have reached out and grasped him by the throat. Feeling the wish-come-true pressing behind her eyes, Bertie waged a fierce internal argument with herself: She might not be able to reunite her family by using it, but surely she could wish the journal back into her possession.

That wish-come-true isn't doing any of us any good lingering just behind my eyeballs, and Ophelia can't last much longer, trapped between worlds.

Thus preoccupied, she nearly stepped upon the four glowing lights that were the fairies when her little friends collided with something blocking their upward path and, sparking and sputtering, bounced back down the stairs.

Trying not to curse, Bertie scooped them up. "Are you all right?"

Cobweb rubbed the top of his head. "I think we found the trapdoor."

Nate shoved past them. "Let me take a look."

Bertie held up her fairy-filled hands so he could see the irregular, puzzle-piece shape of the door and the massive bolts locking it in place.

"Ye try t' unlock it wi' yer thoughts," Nate said, bracing himself, "and I'll push."

Obeying, Bertie shoved at the thing made of earth and

metal, commanding it to yield. With the screech of rusted iron, the first bolt slowly slid back.

The fairies clapped their hands over their ears. "It's like nails on a chalkboard!"

"The wail of undead spirits—"

"Bertie singing in the shower!"

Three more bolts, each more stubborn than the last. The moment the final lock gave way, Ariel hit the wooden panel with a massive blast of wind, throwing it wide-open.

"Stay here a moment," Nate managed to say through a wheeze. Taking the last of the stairs, his head and shoulders immediately disappeared.

"Like hell I will." With a withering glance, the air elemental ducked in behind him.

Swallowing, Bertie transferred all four of the fairies to her shoulder and followed.

"I'm right behind you," Waschbär said cheerfully. "I can pull you back if need be."

"Thanks," Bertie muttered. "I think." The last few stairs were the steepest, and she had to look down to keep from barking her shins against the stone. It was only when her right foot hit familiar wooden floorboards that she realized she stood onstage. Letting her gaze flick over the cavernous darkness of the auditorium, she caught broken-glass glimpses of empty seats and the glittering chandelier. The room was as hushed as a Player behind the scenes waiting for a cue, the empty eyes of the footlights staring at them in the darkness. Bertie's pulse was like the slamming of doors in her ears as she looked to the proscenium arch, Downstage Left, where *The Complete Works of the Stage* should have been sitting. Its pedestal stood empty, the chill of its absence silvering her breath to match her hair.

"So we meet again, and under such unusual circumstances," said a disembodied voice. "I must admit, I was perturbed to have been locked out. I'd never before encountered a building we could not breach."

Bertie whirled around, eyes adjusting enough to realize the brigands ranged before them, standing so still as to nearly be lost in the darkness. In the tunnel, Waschbär froze; when Bertie gave him a nearly indiscernible nod, he retreated with the fire-dancer in tow.

"How did you get in, then?" Bertie demanded, hoping her voice covered whatever telltale rustle might give them away.

"Transported as though by sorcerer's wand," their Leader said. "One second we were on the roof, the next on the stage as you entered like little mice."

"Not a sorcerer's wand," Bertie said. "I summoned you here with my thoughts."

He raised an incredulous eyebrow. "Is that so? Then

you have our thanks and my utmost attention to assure neither you nor your friends do anything stupidly heroic."

Nate and Ariel raised reluctant hands to prove they were no threat, reinforced by a brigand's swift removal of the pirate's cutlass from his belt. With matching squeaks, the fairies disappeared into the curtain of Bertie's hair and clung to her like tiny, teeth-chattering barrettes. Contrariwise, Bertie hadn't the presence of mind to be scared, not with the new bit of her story swirling about her head, not with the knowledge that she had to get the journal back if there was to be any hope of reuniting the theaters and saving her mother.

"You have something that belongs to me," she said.

The brigands' Leader ignored her, turning instead to the three largest of his band. "Fetch the Theater Manager." Without a word, they disappeared in the direction of the Stage Door.

"Best of luck with that," Bertie said. "I'm curious myself to know if he's here."

"He was most anxious to recover this tome," the Leader said with a snarl. "Something about settling a small matter of a wayward child who should have never existed . . . I assume that wayward child is you."

Chilled through by the words, Bertie did her best not to quail before him. "I am not easily erased, as well he knows."

"Nevertheless, your Theater Manager will answer my summons, if he wants to remain in good health."

"Your threats aren't going to mean much if he's unavoidably detained in a parallel dimension. Would you care to leave a message for him, should that be the case?"

"Stop speaking rubbish, or I'll cut the tongue from your mouth." The room seemed to darken a bit with the threat.

"And how are all your small, squishable friends this fine day?" the lady brigand asked, peering pointedly at Bertie's neck.

Peaseblossom cowered back and buried her face in Bertie's collar before bursting into tears. The blood raged in Bertie's veins, sending angry heat rushing through every limb.

"If you touch any of them, I'll personally break every one of your fingers."

With a bark of laughter, the lady brigand feinted toward her, cackling again when Bertie recoiled.

"Enough!" her Leader snarled, stepping forward with his wicked knife already unsheathed. "You can have your fun once we've been paid for our troubles."

"I assure you that I'm the only one interested in acquiring your wares at the moment." In a show of bravado, Bertie forced her stance wider, her voice louder.

"In exchange for what, I'd like to know?" The Leader

raised his nose to the air and circled the troupe, sniffing at them. "We left you with nothing of value."

Bertie hoped that he wouldn't be able to detect the wish-come-true lingering just behind her eyes, not just yet, not so early in the game. Her fingers clamped down upon her other gift from the Queen. "I've this broach. It's a token from Her Gracious Majesty and worth quite a lot."

"A paltry bit of jewelry isn't worth anything close to what we were promised."

Suddenly suspicious, Bertie narrowed her gaze at him. "What *did* the Theater Manager offer in exchange for the journal?"

His answering smile was a fearsome thing indeed. "A fortune in gold and jewels. A prince's ransom, he said."

"And just where do you suppose he was going to get such a sum?" Bertie tried to sound reasonable and soothing, to convey as much goodwill and *don't stab us* as she could manage rather than the dripping condescension boiling up the back of her throat. "There's never much money in a theater's cash box."

"He paid us each a coin on tick," the lady brigand purred. A metal disc flipped through the air and landed at Bertie's feet with a *ping!* "He said there would be more when the job was done."

"And when did he enter into such a contract with you?"

Under no obligation, the Leader nevertheless answered, "A week or so ago."

"About the same time we departed the good theater," Ariel noted. "That's quite the coincidence. But the Theater Manager couldn't have known that Waschbär had stolen the journal, nor that he would give it to us. How did you track it down, without any idea who had it or where it might have been taken?"

The Leader flipped his knife about one hand with silver slices of reflected light. "Magic that strong leaves a trail, and we followed it as surely as a hound scents a stag."

"A rheumatic bloodhound with a bum nose," Bertie said with a sniff. "We wended our way over half the countryside, and it took you that long to catch up with us?"

The Leader scowled his displeasure, but before he could punish Bertie for the insult, the brigands returned without their quarry.

"His office was empty," the tallest said. "There's no one at all in the building, save this motley group."

"What are we to do about our fee if our hire is nowhere to be found?" The brigands' Leader didn't address the question to anyone in particular, though his snarl raised considerably in volume.

Sensing his distraction, Bertie dared to pick up the bit of money. She noted the weight of it, the imprint stamped on the front and back. Though lacking the necessary filing

cabinets and reams of provenance paperwork, she still recognized its general origins. "This is from the Properties
Department. I wonder if Mr. Hastings knew it had been
taken."

"The Properties Department, eh?" The Leader leapt
upon the information as a starveling mongrel dog would a
scrap of meat. "I think you ought to take us to this place.
We will collect our payment, and you can have your little
book back. How does that sound to you?"

It sounds too good to be true.

Bertie knew the chances were far greater that they'd
lead the brigands into the Properties Department only to
have their throats slit ear to ear, once the thieves realized
the nearly boundless store of priceless artifacts contained
therein could be theirs. She gathered her courage to her
like armor. "I don't think so."

The Leader's expression shifted from false amiability to
undiluted malevolence. "Kill the tall one. It will give our
hostess something to consider as we continue negotiations."

"Which is the tall one?!" Mustardseed squeaked in
alarm.

"Not I!" yelled the other fairies in one voice, even as
the most likely candidates immediately backed up against
each other, Nate with his fists at the ready and Ariel pulling a tempest from the space about them with both hands.

As the storm gathered strength, Bertie remembered

she had her own source of power. Instinctively, she backed into the circle the boys had started. "If the mosaic can pull bits of my story forward, then I can do the same." Even as she thought of the forest, of the trees, she directed her words to the brigands' Leader. "Do you remember the first time we met?"

But it was Waschbär who answered, emerging from the tunnel to add his feral strength to their group along with the words, "I do, though it was many years ago."

"Welcome to the party, turncoat," the Leader said, offering cheerful hospitality at knifepoint. "I see you no longer travel alone." Though he did not shift his eyes for more than a half second, Bertie knew he'd spotted the opal ring upon Varvara's finger. "How much does that sort of companionship cost?"

Standing behind Waschbär, the fire-dancer's eyes were dark and her expression carefully blank. Fed by Ariel's windstorm, her hair blazed about her shoulders; only then did she bestow a vicious smile upon the brigands' Leader. "You couldn't afford me."

Two livid red patches appeared on his cheeks and mottled his neck. Signaling to his comrades to close in, he hissed, "Let's finish this."

"Yes, let's. When you liberated the journal from my possession, didn't you recognize the caravan?" Bertie recalled the details from her own play *How Bertie Came to the*

Theater. "It was many years ago that you tried to steal from a child traveling with her guardian, the previous Mistress of Revels. I was too young at the time to realize your coldness, your cruelty."

Advancing as a group, the brigands hesitated.

"Candy fell from the sky that day." The lady brigand finally remembered a girl who could make something of nothing with only a piece of paper and a crayon. "Peppermints and chocolate humbugs rained down on the road and fields."

Now it was Bertie's turn to smile. "Yes."

"You wrote it and made it so," the Leader said, the second to remember. "No wonder you want this!" He jerked the journal from his pocket and brandished his knife over the pages. "A pity it's in my possession instead of yours."

"The years have taught me many tricks," Bertie said, "but the greatest is that I don't necessarily need the paper. My power comes from the source itself now, from the trees. . . ." She had barely finished speaking when they answered her call: the great gnarled oaks pushing up through the floorboards, towering pines splintering the wood and popping nails from their places. Branches clambered over one another to reach a sky not there until the brigands were forced back, away from the holes opening underfoot, away from the tightly knit group gathered Center Stage.

"Stay close," Bertie warned the troupe. "The trees will protect me, but they don't care about anyone else."

As one, Ariel and Nate took another step back, their shoulders meeting hers and Waschbär's, Varvara pushed to the middle like the jelly in a doughnut. The five of them braced against one another for the next spurt of wild growth, and the sound of running sap was more thunderous than the rush of blood in their veins. Vines clambered up through the cracks in the stage next, unfurling leaves and trumpet flowers with choking puffs of pollen.

"Get to the tunnel," their Leader wheezed. "We'll leave them here to be buried!"

Bertie countermanded the order, summoning an errant green tendril to tangle about his ankle. The rest of his crew pushed and shoved their way to the open trapdoor, despite the ominous rumble that issued from within.

"Call them back," she warned.

"Witch! Sorceress!" He raised his fingers in a ward against evil.

Bertie had to concede that's probably what it looked like, given that the very forest primeval crept up around them, but still she protested, "This isn't what I wanted—"

"Don't apologize t' th' likes o' him," Nate said. "He would ha'e killed us wi'out thinkin' twice about it, an' may try it yet, given half th' chance."

"What would you say now to a trade?" In the

green-filtered half-light, Ariel's smile was unholy. "Your life for the little book?"

Before the brigands' Leader could answer, the vine dragged him toward Bertie over splintered bits of wood that tore at his jerkin and nearly scratched the eyes from his head. Howling, he dropped the journal and sliced through the tendril with his wicked-sharp blade. With the uneven gait of a drunken sailor, he followed his comrades into the swirling-white storm brewing in the tunnel.

"Don't—" Bertie tried to stop him, but too late. The forest closed ranks to stabilize the floor while everything else in the theater heaved and buckled and broke. The noise of it nearly deafened them as the stone walls of the tunnel turned to snow and tumbled inward. Tiles broke into jagged chunks of ice and shifted to fill the spaces between until not a single particle could be coaxed from its resting place.

"He didn't remember," Waschbär said softly with a twitch of his nose, "that the word-threat you used to banish us long ago was 'avalanche.'"

CHAPTER SIXTEEN

For a Fantasy and Trick

Leave it to you," Ariel said with a shake of his head, "to conjure snow indoors."

Bertie retrieved the journal and pressed it tightly against her chest. "Leave it to me to nearly kill us all in the process."

Indeed, most of the troupe stood, silent and shaking with various amounts of residual fear and adrenaline. Only Varvara, wandering away to pick a haphazard path through the trees, was unperturbed, even when she nearly set a mound of moss aflame.

Nate retrieved his cutlass from the outer edge of the snowbank, in case the ice should not prove to be a sufficient cairn for their enemies. "It's a mistake, havin' somethin' like her on th' stage."

"Here," Waschbär said, guiding the fire-dancer to a small circle of stones. "You can kindle something here, to better purpose."

Standing atop a mound of dry sticks and leaves, Varvara bestowed upon him a brilliant smile, then used her toe shoes to create sparks against the rocks. A conflagration soon blazed merrily with the fire-dancer sitting immediately adjacent, hair crackling to match, hands reaching for the flames.

By then, the grove was as it had been every time Bertie had visited it, whether rendered in scenic flats, painted upon rice paper, or growing from earth so old that it had forgotten time itself. The trees towered over them, wearing their many years like a lush mantle about their shoulders. Sensing relative safety, the fairies emerged from Bertie's hair to discuss important issues.

"I'm *starving*," Moth whined, holding his stomach with both hands. "Near-death experiences do that to me!"

"We need jam cakes," Mustardseed said.

"I propose a run upon the Green Room immediately, if not sooner!" Cobweb said, already flying for the Stage Door.

Bertie reached out and snagged him. "Not just yet. We don't know if it's safe beyond the grove."

With grumbles and threats of mutiny, the fairies retreated to investigate their pockets for residual chocolate crumbs. In the ensuing quiet, Bertie traced the swirling markings on the journal's cover. Frowning, she flipped it open to reveal the first page, which was—as expected—their own exit page, torn from *The Complete Works of the Stage.*

If I created the two theaters by acting this page into the journal, then maybe I can undo the damage I've done by pulling it out.

Her fingers slowly curled about the edge of the paper.

This could work. It could fix everything. . . .

It was true what they said about being able to taste victory: hot buttered toast from the Properties Department and tea poured out by Mrs. Edith. The flavors of home and safety and love she'd known growing up here gathered on the tip of Bertie's tongue. She could taste her desperation as well, the thin acid of lemon juice, the ragged crystals of salt gathering at the corners of her mouth. Licking her lips, Bertie clenched their entrance page and pulled. The journal shuddered in her hands. A glow began to emanate from the binding, a spotlight coaxed to life.

Please let this work.

It has *to work!*

Any moment now the page would come loose from the journal, and everything would be set to rights.

Any moment now.

Sweat popped out on Bertie's forehead and upper lip.

Any moment now . . .

Despite her greatest effort, the page didn't yield. Like a dying lightbulb in the marquee, her hope flickered out.

"I tried something similar, once upon a time. Allow me to remind you of the futility of fighting such magic?" Indeed, Ariel had nearly destroyed The Book, pulling almost everything from the binding but unable to tear out his own entrance page.

Bertie—panting, furious, terrified—gazed up at him and, in the midst of sweating through her shirt, a new and unexpected bit of understanding for the air elemental clicked into place. "You must have hated the magic, the theater, for denying you."

"I hate it still." He covered her hand with his own and stroked the glowing paper. "But one learns to function even in the midst of nearly overwhelming desire when given no other choice."

Bertie pulled away from him and his insinuations. "There's always another choice."

"True, when you're accustomed to paving your own path where no one else can even fathom a road." He accompanied the statement with a snow-tinged wind as he turned toward the Stage Door. "Though I would not do it to fill the bottomless-pit bellies of the fairies, I think someone should investigate the rest of the theater. You're swaying where you stand, which means you need food and some strong coffee. I'll start with the Green Room."

"You're volunteering?" While the idea of food caused Bertie's stomach to turn over, a cup of coffee cradled in her hands might stave off the cold fears uncoiling in her extremities.

"I do have a history of fetching caffeinated beverages for you, milady, and there's no sense sending a pirate for cappuccinos when he would surely come back with rum punch." Ariel gave Nate a small salute and received a dark look in return. "I'll take the opportunity to check the other rooms. The Theater Manager may well have gone into hiding when he heard the brigands coming. If he's here, I'll find him." Without waiting for either an answer or permission, he disappeared into the gloom backstage, his exit marked only by the whisper of the door.

Bertie sank down to her heels. Though she'd started to hate the very sight of it, she couldn't help but open the journal once again. By the mosaic's account, it should have contained all that had happened outside the theater's walls, but nothing preceded the troupe's entrance page . . . no story of her parents' escape from the theater or from Sedna, no watermark illustrations to show all that had transpired at the Aerie. Bertie flipped through the rest of the journal, noting the pages covered in her own scritch-scratching and longer sections of bold, distinct typeface that mimicked that of The Book.

Where have Ophelia's memories gone?

Wanting to howl at the moon, she squeezed the journal hard between sweating hands. "The Greek Chorus lied to us. There's yet another puzzle piece, another bit of broken mirror-story to find if we want to save Ophelia."

Nate crouched next to her. "Did ye stop t' think that mayhap she cannot be saved?"

"Don't say that! It's my fault she's the way she is . . ." Bertie's voice dwindled and died, unable to finish.

Nate chucked her under the chin, coaxing her to meet his gaze. "What d'ye mean by that, now?"

And then the story came pouring out, how she'd gone through the Queen's mirror, how she'd found herself in the theater the night Ophelia had escaped. "You were there. I ran smack into you under the stage during the preset."

Nate's expression shifted from shock to disbelief. "That's impossible."

"You forget who you're talking to," Bertie said, shaking her head at him. "For me, all manner of impossibilities are mere child's play."

"Under th' stage, just before th' show?" Rubbing a rough hand over his stubbled face, Nate tried to bring the memories to the surface through the stern application of force. "I don't remember it at all, but it's most odd t' think I knew ye before ye were born, that's fer certain. What else did ye see?"

"Ophelia tearing her page out of The Book and exiting

with the Scrimshander." Bertie could hardly bring herself to admit what had come next. "I was stuck here, in the past, and so I took her place. Drank her perfume down and wore her face like a mask and nearly lost myself in her madness. I was the one who called her back, Nate. The one who acted her page back into The Book. It was"—here, her voice broke into as many pieces as a smashed mirror—"it was my fault she was pulled away from him. I ruined everything!"

"Ye couldn't know. Ye weren't even yerself, not really." He reached for her hand and gave it a firm squeeze, meant to reassure. "If ye hadn't said her line, an understudy surely would ha'e. What's past cannot be changed."

"Maybe not, but I can sure as hell try to guide what's yet to be." Bertie scowled at the journal. "She's the only one shifting between the two versions of the theater, the only one who's trapped, fading to nothing. We have to restore her memories to her . . . all of them, and not haphazard or piecemeal, but in their entirety."

Ever practical, Nate looked about him as though charting possible locations for wayward memories. "Where d'ye want t' start lookin' fer them?"

"I thought they'd be inside this damn book." A slow sigh escaped Bertie with the hiss of a pricked balloon as she tried to think like her mother, tried to step into her river-slick skin. "We should check her Dressing Room. That's where my parents' story started."

"Hold there a minute, lass. Let's consider some practicalities." Nate led her to the prompt corner. Unearthing several flashlights, he passed her one with a short "Hold this."

Bertie gave the flashlight a hesitant shake. Its luminescence not only held steady but slowly changed from dim yellow to lime green to vibrant lavender with small silver sparks, lighting a narrow pathway between enormous coils of rope and scenic flats lined up like soldiers in a regiment. "Ariel is searching the building for the Theater Manager. Should we get the others?"

Nate glanced over her shoulder at the fairies piled in a heap of moss like a litter of sleepy kittens, unusually quiet and subdued due to lack of sugar, and Waschbär yet sitting with Varvara. The fire-dancer looked at her companion with eyes alight; the sneak-thief had his back to them, so there was no reading his expression just now.

"Let them be fer now. We can manage, just th' two o' us."

It was indeed just the two of them, their footfalls the only disturbance in the otherwise deserted corridors. Everything else was exactly as it should be, the woodwork polished to a rich mahogany gleam and frosted glass sconces rendering the flashlights quite unnecessary.

"It looks just the same." Bertie didn't know why she whispered, nor why she tiptoed, yet she couldn't bring herself to do otherwise.

Despite his sturdy build and boots, Nate exercised the same restraint. "Did ye expect peelin' wallpaper, broken light fixtures, an' a ceilin' drippin' cobwebs?"

"I don't know what I expected." They'd arrived at Dressing Room Four. Anxiety seeped through the spot where Bertie's skull met her spine as she reached for the brass knob.

"Let me go in alone," she whispered, and Nate fell back without offering a protest.

The interior of the room was darker than a night without stars. Bertie skimmed her hand along the wall until she located the key to the gas jet. When she twisted it, a blue-white flare illuminated the rest of the room. Flipping another switch fired the electric lights to life, their additional golden radiance pouring down the walls and onto the floor.

It was as if Ophelia had merely stepped out for a moment. Jars of cold cream, tins of greasepaint, and glittering perfume bottles beckoned from the dressing table. The chaise upholstered in pale princess-blue velvet occupied the far corner, and a folding screen took up most the room behind the door. Peeling paint indicated it had been decorated with a statuesque Grace, holding a leather-bound tome in one hand and a feather quill in the other.

Peering closer, Bertie realized the face of the woman on the screen was her own.

The Scrimshander wasn't the only one trying to recapture my features.

Bertie's breath caught when Ophelia slowly shifted into the here and now, her hands and face paint daubed. All the shades of spring splashed her gown: the pinks and greens and blues of flowers and grass and a sky wedding-veiled with clouds. The water-maiden held a paintbrush in one hand and a tattered bit of cloth in the other. Bertie nearly cried when she realized her mother clutched the cotton-print kerchief that Child Bertie had worn on her journey with the Mistress of Revels, her plummet from the White Cliffs, her rescue by the Scrimshander, her return to the Théâtre Illuminata.

I brought it home with me, and Ophelia found it. Kept it.

Bertie crossed the room with tentative steps, afraid her mother would evaporate like ocean mist into midday sunlight. "I . . ." Her throat was so dry that the words were a frog-croak. "I need to find your memories. Where did they go?"

Ophelia held the scrap of fabric up to her cheek, cradling it as she would a child. "What memories do you seek?"

"Everything that happened between you and my father. Everything that happened at the Aerie."

"The Aerie?" The water-maiden stopped to consider such an idea. "I'm afraid you've mistaken me for someone else. You want the woman who smells of salt and destruction. The one with the starfish hands."

"You remember Sedna?" Bertie took a tiny, cautious step forward.

"The Sea Goddess," Ophelia corrected. "From *The Little Mermaid*."

Not the answer Bertie wanted to hear. "You left the theater, Ophelia, with the Mysterious Stranger. You had a daughter. What happened to those memories after the Theater Manager stole them from you?" Bertie held the journal out to her mother. "Is there anything in here that can help you?"

Ophelia spared it only a glance. "'Tis but paper, and no place for what is water-bound."

"Water-bound?"

"The memories disappeared into the water," Ophelia said, impatience leaching into her voice. "Everything finds its way to the water, eventually."

Bertie felt the same impatience, the same need to reach out and shake someone who couldn't—or wouldn't—understand. "But I don't know what that means!"

In response, Ophelia closed her eyes and faded away. Bertie lunged at the spot where the water-maiden had stood only seconds before, trying to catch hold of her mother's hands, her skirts, anything.

"Come back!" But the words were spoken too late to do either of them any good.

Nate's voice from the doorway startled her. "Do ye see anythin', lass?"

"Give me a moment." Concentrating upon the painted screen, Bertie conjured words like *please* and *return,* but there was nary a shimmer to suggest Ophelia would come back. Wrapped in disappointment as thick as a woolen cloak, Bertie exited the room and addressed her words to the floor. "She was there for half a second, maybe more, but I was too thickheaded to do anything about it."

"What about yer wish-come-true?" Nate asked. "Usin' it t' recall Ophelia's memories t' her isn't th' same as tryin' t' reunite yer family, is it?"

Bertie's forehead puckered as she tried to force reason and logic into her swimming head. "That's splitting hairs, but I think we should try it." Reaching up, she covered her eyes with her hands, willing the silver power to billow, to burgeon, to suffuse her body until every bit of her soul was bathed in refracted light. She tried to conjure the perfect image of Ophelia as she ought to be: solid, serene, and in full possession of all her faculties.

"I wish for Ophelia to remember."

At the last second, doubt seeped in. Perhaps it was the same, wishing Ophelia's memories restored and wanting to see her family reunited.

Perhaps I don't deserve my own happily ever after, after all.

A quaver in her voice sent tremors through the wish-light. Her memory of Ophelia flexed into a funhouse reflection, distorting her mother into something terrifying and nearly Sedna-like before sucking the power back within itself and flinging Bertie against the nearest wall.

"Lass!" Nate caught her before she fell to the floor, but even his solid presence wasn't enough to steady her head or slow her galloping heartbeat.

"That answers that question." She'd wasted the wish. Tears threatened until a dim silver light returned to haunt the space inside her head, as mercurial and taunting as one of Ariel's winds.

Not wasted, then, small thanks for that.

Despite her vicious scowl, Nate looked encouraged. "An' yer breathin'. I don't think yer bleedin' from anywhere, but fer god's sake, lass, have a care wi' that thing!"

"I promise I won't wish for anything again until I can do so with utter conviction."

I will be worthy of the damn wish.

Wondering if she could stand without his aid, Bertie noted her legs wobbled like something turned out of a jelly mold and allowed him to support her as they made their way down the hall. "We'll just have to figure out where her memories are hidden without supernatural aid."

"What did she tell ye when ye spoke?"

Trying to clear the ringing from her head, it took

Bertie a few minutes to recall her mother's words. "She said her memories were in the water."

"Ophelia always did ha'e th' uncanny habit o' turnin' up every time she heard th' water runnin'," Nate said with a snap of his fingers. "Didn't matter if it was th' Turkish Bath or a faucet in th' Wardrobe Department."

Given they'd just reached the massive mahogany door that led to Mrs. Edith's domain, his timing was impeccable. Once Bertie would have bounded in without so much as a knock to announce her arrival. Now she hesitated, trying to gather what little strength she could—from the ancient wood flooring to the creaking timbers that supported the ceiling overhead—before turning the knob. A tiny part of her believed that whatever magic had spliced the theater in twain, it could not have waged a war and won against the formidable Wardrobe Mistress.

"Mrs. Edith?" Bertie's inquiry echoed off the high ceilings and the lead-glass windows. Normally covered in heaps of shining silks and rich velvets, bits of lace like cobwebbing, buttons, bobbins, and bits, the worktables stood empty. The sewing machines sat eerily silent and still. Overhead, costumes swayed like rows of hanged men and women.

"She's not here, lass." Just behind her, Nate nudged Bertie into sacrosanct territory. "So she can't gainsay yer turnin' on th' water."

The scent of lavender yet lingered in the air, suggesting purple-hazed fields and Victorian sachets. "It still feels like trespassing. Like Mrs. Edith might appear at any moment, demanding to know what I think I'm doing." Bertie would gladly exchange a tongue-lashing for the chance to be held by those familiar arms, to be reassured in grandmotherly tones that everything would work out as it ought, that the Wardrobe Mistress felt it in her bones.

Bertie's fingers sought out the scrimshaw medallion about her neck. "Do you think my father would know which waters Ophelia meant?"

"He might, but he's not here now t' tell us, is he?" Nate closed the door behind them and switched on the working lights.

"No, he's not."

There was nothing for me there.

Wishing she could tell the Scrimshander he was mistaken, Bertie crossed to the dyeing vats and opened the spigots to full. Water gushed into the enormous cauldrons, splashing up the sides and spattering Bertie's cheeks and forehead when she leaned over to check the rising level. "Your memories are in the water, Ophelia. Come take a lovely bath and explain that to me."

The minutes passed as the vats filled, but the water-maiden made no appearance.

"I would ha'e thought her enticed by such a summons."

Nate wet his sleeve to the elbow reaching into the tub, splashing the contents about. "Maybe she didn't mean this kind o' water, then."

"She didn't mean seawater." Not a trace of doubt marred Bertie's words. "That's Sedna's domain."

Nate stiffened. "Could th' Sea Goddess ha'e stolen them?"

Sedna kidnapped Nate. She might hold Ophelia's memories prisoner as well.

"Let's hope that isn't the case." Bertie continued to back away from the idea until her posterior activated the brass control mechanism for the overhead costume rack. With the hum and whir of an enormous music box, the conveyance awoke, shuffling the vestments of queen and courtier, lover and beloved past them.

A flicker of palest green caught Bertie's eye: Ophelia's tattered drowning dress, the one she wore in *Hamlet* every time she fell into the river and died. It slid away from them, as though trapped in a dream, and the flower of an idea bloomed in Bertie's head.

"Not actual water, but wooden water, maybe. The river scene." Bertie jammed her thumb against the control. When the gliding dance of costumes came to a standstill, she scrambled from a stool to the top of the worktable. Reaching up, she captured the drowning dress's padded hanger. The garment slithered down her front like a cool rush of water.

"What," Nate asked in a dire tone, "do ye plan t' do wi' that?"

Bertie turned to him, holding the dress up before her. "They say I have my mother's eyes."

"And?" His tone held all the wariness of a soldier facing an unknown enemy.

"Ophelia might come to call if we bring in the *Hamlet* set for her death scene." In the theater's version, Gertrude gave her speech describing the young maiden's drowning standing before a scrim curtain; behind it, bathed in watery light and flower petals, Ophelia enacted the sequence, a ghost before she'd even died. "Especially if I take her part from her. Especially if that's the water where her memories are hidden."

"Yer thinkin' o' drownin' yerself?" Nate shifted his feet.

Bertie thought of all the times she'd drowned while masquerading as the water-maiden, certain she wouldn't be able to manage Ophelia's tranquil resignation now that she no longer wore her mother's face and Eau d'Ophelia no longer flowed through her veins. "I'll do whatever it takes to pull her through." Expecting vehement protests, she put on her most belligerent expression.

"Ye won't have t' do it alone." Nate's quiet reassurance was not dimmed by the distance between them. "I can see if th' Stage Manager's headset will work t' call th' scenery in, but if it doesn't, I know where th' flats are stored."

She couldn't help but stare at him a moment, wondering what had happened to the overprotective streak that ran as deep and as strong as his countless mariner superstitions. "You're not going to try to stop me?"

"If I've learned anythin' in th' last few weeks," Nate said, his voice low, "it's that ye won't be swayed once ye've made up yer mind, an' I can either help ye or get out o' th' way."

Unable to stop the smile that threatened to take over her face, Bertie squeezed his arm. "That must have been quite the epiphany."

"Aye, well, pound a rock against a rock an' one o' them will give eventually." He leaned forward and touched his forehead to hers. "Tell me what ye want done."

"We'll need to get the green lights rigged." Bertie couldn't repress a shudder at the idea, but forced herself to add, "And a scrim." She draped Ophelia's dress over her arm and mustered as much bravado as she could manage on such short notice. "If you'll see to the scenery, I'll fetch the flowers."

Nate saluted and moved toward the Stage Door. Bertie headed the opposite direction: down the hallway, along the path nearly worn into the floorboards by the many times she'd escaped to the Properties Department.

Stepping inside, she hung Ophelia's costume on the side of a massive armoire and turned to study the room. It was as neat and tidy as the Wardrobe Department—she saw this within seconds—and its curator similarly absent. Atop his desk and the adjacent filing cabinets, massive stacks of paperwork awaited Mr. Hastings's return. The teakettle sat on a burner, filled with water but cold to the touch. A paper-wrapped loaf of bread was safely interred in its tin box. A quick squeeze revealed it was only slightly stale, but for once, Bertie had no desire for toast.

A terrible silence shifted around her with the occasional stray dust mote, magnifying the sense of a sanctuary lost. Moving through the dream of days past, she stepped over to the ancient record player, twisted the power knob, lowered the arm, and released music that was the ghost of an orchestra. Not a tango this time, but a slow waltz; Bertie's heartstrings felt as taut as the violin that sang to her from the past. The flesh of her arms rippled with tiny bumps, the hairs on the nape of her neck rising to match, until the recording ended with a hiss, a pop, a whirring of internal gears before the arm lifted and reset to the beginning of the song. Easy enough to imagine she wasn't alone, that the Ladies and Gentlemen of the Chorus whirled past her, faces fantastically masked, hands properly white gloved, fans dangling from delicate wrists and tuxedo jackets impeccably pressed . . .

"Shall we dance?" Ariel said as he entered, not requiring a formal jacket or a mask to belong to the scene.

"No, thank you." Bertie cut the power to the record player. The turntable ceased spinning, depriving the needle of the music's rise and fall, and her imaginings faded into the gloom.

"It seems the Green Room is yet able to produce food, though I question its selection of cherry turnovers alongside a haunch of roast mutton." He offered her a thick ceramic mug, its contents gently steaming. "Coffee?"

"Not just yet." Remembering Ophelia's blooms, Bertie set off down the nearest aisle. Her fingers skimmed the shelves, over ship's lanterns, iridescent carnival glass, brass-trapped globes mapping worlds that didn't exist. "Did you find anything or anyone else?"

"I didn't sense so much as a mouse stirring under the floorboards. It's a safe bet that we're the only ones in this version of the theater." Without effort, he managed to keep up with her rapid search despite the full cup in his hand. "What are you doing here?"

"Acquiring the necessary properties to summon a water-maiden." Bertie turned a corner and tried to leave her prickling worries behind, wedged between stained glass panels and a timeworn carousel horse.

"Without chaperone or bodyguard?"

"Nate is seeing to the scenery, and hopefully the others are helping."

Ariel abandoned her coffee so he could catch hold of

her elbow. "You need to take more care with Varvara. She's dangerous, something neither you nor any of the others seem to grasp just yet."

Bertie shook free of him, impatient to resume her search. "Varvara might be like you in many ways, but she is more human than fire."

"There you are wrong." There was no melodrama in his words, just conviction. And fear. "She is everything that is wild and untamable and burning."

Staring up at him, Bertie realized how very tired she was of fighting with everyone and everything around her. Fighting to bring her family back together, fighting to unite the theaters, fighting to prevent her friendships with Nate and Ariel from crumbling to dust. At the end of the row, practically beckoning with its down coverlet and tempting pillows, sat a stack of twenty feather beds upon twenty mattresses. Certain she wouldn't notice a pea nestled at the very bottom, even if it were the size of a goodly boulder, Bertie contemplated crawling atop it and tumbling into an endless slumber.

When he noticed the direction of her gaze, Ariel shook his head. "You aren't the sort to draw the covers over your head and hide."

"I could be. Give me enough time and pillows."

"Liar." He delivered the accusation with a half smile. "What are you looking for here, besides vindication?"

"Ophelia's flowers."

Ariel slowly rose from the floor, supported by winds that stirred up dust and bits of Mr. Hastings's paperwork. Bertie tried not to cough as he plucked a lidded basket from the uppermost shelf and alighted next to her.

"These are what you're seeking, I think."

Bertie turned back the lid and saw that they were indeed. "'There's rosemary, that's for remembrance.'" *Pray, love, remember.* "'And there is pansies, that's for thoughts.'" They were all there: fennel and columbines, rue and daisies. With a frown, Bertie plucked an unexpected rose from the glorious assortment within the basket's wicker walls, its fragrance more startling than the thorn that pierced her flesh. The bloom tumbled to the ground, blood-red petals yet moist. "They're freshly picked."

"Did you expect different?" Ariel knelt, retrieving the flower.

Looking through the rest of the basket, Bertie saw with growing wonder that the green stems wept a bit of liquid from where shears had parted them from the shrub. "I always thought them clever silk and paper reproductions."

"If that logic held true, the food in the patisserie set would be plastic and papier-mâché." He held the rose out to her. "Is that how you'd prefer it?"

Bertie refused the offering, overly reminiscent as it was of their long-ago tango, and instead heaved the basket onto her hip. "I don't think the Fates are all that interested in my preferences."

"Even if they aren't, I am." Taking full advantage of the fact that her hands were occupied, Ariel tucked the rose behind her ear. His fingers lingered there a moment longer than necessary, straying through her silver hair and coming to rest on the nape of her neck. "If you cannot save her, what is left for you here?"

"Not much." The truth slipped out before Bertie could stop it.

"I see."

"Do you?" Bertie wished she could better read what flickered in the smoke gray of his eyes. "When you look at me, do you see that losing Ophelia in such a fashion might break my heart in a million pieces? Do you see yourself trying to put me back together, like bits of smashed mirror that will always be fragmented and flawed, no matter how careful your work?"

His mouth tightened. "Against my better judgment, I would have you know that your flaws are also your saving graces."

"If you tell me that trials by fire only make one stronger, I *will* hit you." Except, for once, she didn't mean it. She had no desire to lash out at him anymore, no desire to see the bodies—or hearts—of others hurt as much as her own did.

He saw the change in her, as clearly as if she'd removed

her mask again. "While we've been running about the country-side like mad things, chasing your dreams and nightmares, I think you grew up."

"That would explain why I feel so terribly old." Moving as briskly as she could manage with the enormous basket bouncing against her side, Bertie reached out to pluck Ophelia's dress from the armoire. "I'd be surprised if these misadventures haven't put a hundred gray hairs on my head, under the silver."

CHAPTER SEVENTEEN

There Is a Willow Grows Aslant a Brook

By the time Bertie arrived onstage carrying the burden of both dress and flowers, the river scene was not only in place but properly obscured by the spectral wafting that was the scrim. Although never before part of this scene, the ancient trees wove seamlessly into the landscape, supporting the floor and ceiling after the tunnel's collapse.

"Th' headset works," Nate noted in passing.

"The lights are all rigged!" Mustardseed said, clapping his hands.

"And gelled Lagoon Green," Moth said.

Bertie peered past them, suspicions pricked by the air of productivity and goodwill. "Where's Varvara?"

"Hiding in the back of the auditorium." Cobweb jerked his thumb at the farthest row of seating where the fire-dancer was indeed huddled in a chair, looking simultaneously terrified and miserable. "The moment she caught sight of the wooden waves, she fled."

Bertie frowned. "Someone needs to mind that she doesn't set the seats on fire."

"Th' sneak-thief is back there," Nate noted, wiping a trickle of sweat out of his eyes. "Keepin' a wary eye on things."

"That will have to suffice, I guess." Bertie crossed to the quick-change corner. When she snapped on the lantern, bluish light poured over her as though from a fairy-tale moon. She drew up short, realizing this was the place where Ophelia caught the silver fish of clarity. "Pink carnations are for mothers."

"What?" Mustardseed arrived on the scene only to prove he'd never been schooled in the more polite alternative of "I beg your pardon?"

"It's nothing." A little nothing. A revelation so small it would have made no difference to almost anyone but a seventeen-year-old girl. It had not been the sort of discovery that would launch a thousand ships, shake the foundation of an empire, alter the future for all of humanity. No, it had simply changed one life, Bertie's own, forever. "Get out of here while I change."

Peaseblossom herded the boys away with admonishments of "Go on, shoo!" and flapping of her skirts. The fairy returned seconds later to serve as a tiny handmaiden, presiding over the many tiers of silk organza, the laces that ran down Bertie's spine, the minute ruffles reminiscent of ocean ripples.

"It's eerie," Peaseblossom said, "seeing you in Ophelia's costume."

"Trust me, it's twice as discomfiting to be wearing Ophelia's costume."

Again.

Bertie twitched her shoulder blades, startled that the dress fit her own body as well as it did. Her mother was a full three inches shorter, so the gown ended above Bertie's ankles instead of the floor, but they appeared to be built similarly through the waist and bust. "At least I'm not falling out the top."

"Indeed, that's not the sort of show I had in mind!" Peaseblossom stopped fiddling with the dress long enough to add a small wreath of flowers to Bertie's hair. "There you are. Not a carbon copy but certainly an adequate understudy."

"I don't want her part, I only want the performance to pull her through." Gathering the rest of the flowers in her hands, Bertie stepped behind the scrim and took a deep breath. "I'll need you to perform Gertrude's speech, Pease."

"I could totally do it," Moth said, arriving with a sulk already in place. "That's discrimination, casting her just because she's a girl."

"If you want the part, by all means, it's yours!" Peaseblossom put her hands on her hips. "Though I don't know what you're making such a fuss about. You don't even like *Hamlet*."

"Humph," Moth said, because it was true. "Fine, you take it. You look better in long skirts anyway." He flitted away to join Mustardseed and Cobweb, who were loudly partaking of a snack in Bertie's usual seat, Fifth Row, Center. "Hey, save some for me!"

"They're vinegar and salt!" was Cobweb's faint greeting, indicating Ariel had retrieved them a packet of crisps from the Green Room.

Though she didn't think she could stomach food, Bertie's midsection rumbled a bit, matching the last groaning creak of scenery as Nate and Ariel approached. Both sets of footfalls fell suddenly silent when the boys caught sight of her.

"Will I do?" Bertie smoothed a nervous hand over her skirts.

"Ye'll do just fine," Nate said, voice hoarse.

"You would think so," Ariel murmured, "given that it's the garment of a fellow water creature."

The pirate slanted a dark look at the air elemental and added, "Though I wouldn't ha'e ye do this at all, given my preference."

"It's not your decision to make." Bertie carefully leaned against the nearest flat, not quite trusting it with her weight, but suddenly dizzy from lack of food and sleep.

"There was a time when I'd ha'e carried ye off over my shoulder t' keep ye safe, but that was th' child. Ye've grown int' a woman that's mine neither t' command nor t' claim—"

Interrupting, wooden waves slid into the area upstage of the scrim. Bertie had to set all thoughts of commanding or claiming aside.

"You need to take your places in the audience," she whispered. "The show's about to begin."

The men obeyed with visible reluctance; before they'd quite departed, the sound of the water, both mechanical and ethereal, washed over Bertie. A misty spray spangled her face as the wooden river currents twisted about the center axles spanning the width of the stage. Glued along the edges of the waves, tiny mirrors caught the light and cast it back like so much glitter. Bertie could only hope nothing would grasp her, chew up her flesh, grind her bones to dust.

Banish these maudlin thoughts . . . I have a specter to summon and memories to pluck from this place like the flowers I've gathered.

When Bertie concentrated, she could almost imagine Ophelia's soft voice saying, "I heard the water running." But water and wishing were not enough to conjure her.

"Go ahead and start the speech, Pease."

The fairy took her place Downstage, having changed into a regal frock that appeared to have been, once upon a time, an embroidered pocket square. Her whisper pierced the sudden darkness that fell when the stage lights dimmed. "Are you certain you're ready?"

"'Tis time I was ready."

Peaseblossom nodded and began with " 'There is a willow grows aslant a brook, that shows his hoar leaves in the glassy stream.' "

Gertrude's next line was Bertie's cue to make flower garlands, fantastic concoctions of crow flowers and nettles, daisies and long purples. Sitting under the largest of the trees that lined the riverbank and leaning against the paint-rough bark, Bertie hummed while she worked. The wordless song vibrated in the back of her throat, as strong as a colony of bees ensconced in a golden hive. It surrounded her, louder than the workings of the water, echoed by every bough and twig upon the stage.

There was magic afoot, and Bertie twisted her hands

in her skirts, willing Ophelia to appear, willing the memories to waltz out of the waves. The air beyond the river shimmered faintly, the mirrors catching light that was gold and silver and pure diamond white.

She's on the other side.

Rising, Bertie nearly stumbled over a tree root. Filtered by the scrim, the fairies' collective gasp was barely audible, but Nate's curse would have carried to a distant ship. She held up her hand, not wishing them to break whatever magic surrounded her, fearing she'd never reach Ophelia if they interrupted now. She followed that with a finger jab at Peaseblossom, who skipped to the important bit.

"'There, on the pendent boughs her coronet weeds clambering to hang, an envious sliver broke . . .'"

Reaching out her arm to place the flower garland upon the nearest branch, Bertie tried not to look down into the gnashing teeth of the hungry river. As required, there was just enough room to land between the "waves" and disappear from the audience's view.

If she didn't accidentally fall upon one of the rolling columns of wood.

If her skirts didn't catch on a splintered end and drag her into the machinery.

At the far back of the stage, all that was silver, gold, and white wave-reflected light coalesced into the faintest feminine shape.

"Go on, Pease," Bertie hissed at her, "you have to hurry and finish it!"

The fairy obliged. "'When down her weedy trophies and herself fell in the weeping brook.'"

Bertie took a deep breath and let go, prepared to fall, prepared for the possibility of pain if it meant reaching Ophelia. Except the moment she released the branch, the tree that had been her support quivered. Bits of jigsawed and painted wood suddenly sprouted a dozen green tendrils that wrapped about her wrist. The garland she'd hung upon its branches like a funereal wreath trembled as Bertie dangled over the river. Peaseblossom tried to adhere to the adage "The show must go on!"

"'Her clothes spread wide,'" she squeaked, "'and, mermaid-like, awhile they bore her up.'"

Bertie very much doubted she looked like a mermaid, and she could see past the glare of the footlights that Nate and Ariel had abandoned their seats. She had only seconds to free herself and fall, to reach the ghost figure that now held out importuning hands.

"Child of mine," came a fading voice over the rush of the water, and with a surge of adrenaline, Bertie tried to jerk herself free from her leaf-bedecked bonds. Shouting curses instead of the script-required "old lauds," she willed the tree to let her go. A creaking protest emanated from the wood holding her; it seemed the very timbers of the theater itself shuddered until she whispered, "The water is wooden. I'll be safe."

The tree took her at her word, its tendrils giving way, loosing her from its grip as it would a leaf in autumn.

It would have been nice, Bertie reflected, to similarly drift down, swirling in the winds that surrounded her as Ariel tried to rush the stage; instead, she landed hard between two of the mechanical waves. The one behind her immediately caught hold of her dress's long train, chewing through the fabric and dragging Bertie back. Freeing herself with a desperate twist and a rip, she popped up like a demented jack-in-the-box. Ophelia's wraith had solidified, the rear wall no longer visible through her body.

"It's working!" Bertie's bellow was nearly lost, ripped from her mouth and flung at Peaseblossom. "Finish the damn speech!"

"'. . . but long it could not be till that her garments, heavy with their drink, pull'd the poor wretch from her melodious lay . . .'" Here the fairy gulped and shook her head.

Bertie clambered over the next wave and the next, flinching when they smashed into her shins, tripping over the unexpected chains that traversed the stage. "Finish it!"

"'To muddy death,'" Peaseblossom finished, eyes round and lips trembling.

Bertie reached for the water-maiden, clamping down upon Ophelia's wrist as she gasped, "Mom! Stay with—"

The last word was lost when Bertie went down, caught by a piece of unseen machinery and towed under the rotating set pieces. A dozen rusty nails, jagged screws, and tiny mirrors dragged claws across her flesh, their sharp edges recalling the rocks that had pressed down upon her back in the Sea Goddess's cavern. Memory and panic opened a doorway in Bertie's mind, and through it, Sedna finally found a way inside the theater. The world shifted. Everything that had been wood and paint was now moss and slime and sluggish water. All that had been Ophelia evaporated like dew on rose petals in July, leaving the green glimmer-glass reflection of the Sea Goddess free to speak in an eel's hiss, her words the slap of kelp against the skin.

"I told you this place would suffer for your insolence."

The Sea Goddess's minions clambered onto the stage through unseen pipes. Tiny crabs pulled out strands of Bertie's hair, and sea horses nipped at her ankles. A massive saltwater wave picked her up, slammed her into the stage, caught her in a riptide, and dragged her back.

"You will let her go." The command seemed to come from a great distance, but was not issued by either Nate or Ariel. Strong hands clamped down upon Bertie, pulling her free from the water, both wooden and wet, and she was blinking up into the furious face of the Scrimshander.

"How did you get in here?" Bertie sputtered through the mud lingering in her mouth.

"You had as much to do with it as I did," he said. "I gave chase when Sedna entered through your very thoughts."

Fresh disappointment coated Bertie's tongue. "You were following her?"

"I had a message most important to deliver." The feathers fell again as he finished transforming into a human father trying to protect his young. Indeed, he placed himself between Bertie and her foe. "Time has changed us both," he said to Sedna. "For the sake of the people we once were, you must stop playing this deadly game with me and mine."

"You betrayed the woman I once was." The Sea Goddess swelled with malevolence, exuding rage though every pore.

Beyond her, Nate and Waschbär approached at a run while Ariel alighted upon the stage and raised the Stage Manager's headset to his lips. Though he banished the river set, Sedna could not be made to similarly disappear.

Ignoring the others, she cast word-nets at the Scrimshander. "I see heredity at work in your daughter, for she is just as obstinate and treacherous as you ever were. I should have used a swordfish to slit her throat! I ought to have boiled her bones clean and fed her guts to the urchins!"

"Enough!" The Scrimshander's roar filled the auditorium, sending the fairies tumbling back through the air and startling Bertie nearly out of her skin. "Make no mistake, I know my contributions to your cruelty, but my daughter will not suffer again for what passed between us."

"Don't think of it as suffering, think of it as balancing the scales." Hair caught in unseen currents, the Sea Witch jetted forward. The Scrimshander lunged for her, his protest a wordless bird screech, but Sedna had already enveloped Bertie in a dark bubble of squid ink, already wrapped one starfish hand about her neck. "I will have payment for all that was taken from me."

Beyond the swirling black that surrounded her, Bertie could just make out her father, Nate, Ariel, Waschbär, the fairies. Though they tried to broach the bubble's membrane with shouts and fists and swords, the delicate thing was somehow stronger and thicker than even the Queen's glass gates. Bertie held out her hands, tried to manipulate it from within, but there was nothing of earth about it, nothing that could be coaxed or coerced.

Just as there was nothing she could do to stop the inexorable starfish fingers that pried her mouth open.

"I will have payment," the Sea Goddess said, the words creating a tickle in the back of Bertie's throat. "I will have your voice."

"Don't—" With the single word of protest, the tickle unfolded, every edge a cutting one. For a moment, Bertie believed that her tongue had been sliced from her mouth, but there was no knife, no blood, only the absence of screaming. Fear boiled up inside her like one of Serefina's mysterious hearth-mixed concoctions. Trying to escape it, Bertie staggered and fell into the welcoming slick-silken arms of the Sea Goddess.

Sedna cradled her as a mother would, murmuring lullaby threats. "I am not content with just your voice, I think. I will have your word-magic as well."

The Sea Goddess pressed her cold lips to Bertie's in a chaste and horrible kiss, and the pain in Bertie's mouth dilated to fill her entire body with a vast nothing. She had no thoughts, only images: Ariel, iron collar about his neck, head bowed, winds stilled. Contained. Crippled. The weight of regret squeezed her throat, suffocating her. Wishing she could apologize but lacking the voice or words to do so, Bertie vowed instead with her heart and her soul that he would never again be so imprisoned.

The Sea Goddess's voice echoed within their dark cell, tinged with Bertie's own inflections. "Now I've another prize to reclaim."

The bubble burst, catching everyone unaware. One black wave sucked Nate into a riptide while another cast Bertie and everyone else into the orchestra pit. A third picked Nate up and slammed him onto the stage so that the pirate lay crumpled in the exact spot the prince washed ashore in *The Little Mermaid.*

Sedna entered the scene, knelt next to him, and pulled his head into her lap. "My love, you must wake up," she crooned with Bertie's voice.

He twisted about in her arms. "Th' water—"

"Shhh, I have come for you. You're safe. That's all that matters."

Now, if ever, was the time to use the wish-come-true! Concentrating upon the Sea Goddess, Bertie grasped at the silver light just behind her eyes, imagined it transformed into a sword, an explosion, a trapdoor of epic proportions that led into the very pits of hell. She swallowed hard, and with the pain in her throat came every skulking doubt, every crippling fear. Sensing weakness, the wish evaded her, dancing back like an opponent in a duel.

When Bertie lunged after it, the Scrimshander's arms wrapped around her waist. "Little one." He pulled her against his chest, though the hand that clamped down on her trembled. "You must stay back until I think of a way to stop her."

Bertie struggled, but she was no match for him, his strength tripled by his determination to keep her safe. There was nothing to do but watch the scene playing out upon the stage. Nausea sloshed in her middle, murky green and foaming, but she was unable to look away.

The Sea Goddess murmured to Nate, starfish fingers splayed over his face. "We'll rule the sea together, my love, you and I." Her voice wavered, roughened. Once again filled with the low murmur of an incoming tide, it lost some of Bertie's earthbound inflections.

The moment Sedna's concentration faltered, a tiny hope sparked to life within Bertie's heart. She extended the hand marked by the pirate, letting images flicker through her head like a nickelodeon movie: the knife, the vow, the blood. Suffused with memories of Nate, she tilted her head back and cried out to him, heart to heart, unable to use her voice or his name but determined he would hear her desperate summons.

Nate peered up at the Sea Goddess, blinking her dreams and promises from his eyes. "I was yer prisoner once before, an' yer *not* my love."

Sedna stiffened. "I am the voice that calls to you across the waters. I am your goddess, and you will obey me!"

"Yer no goddess o' mine any longer." He twisted away from her reaching grasp, boots scrabbling for purchase on the stage. "I'd rather live a lifetime on land than worship one such as yerself."

"You can't turn your back on the sea," she spit at him with salt spray. "It's in your blood; it's seeped into your bones. You'd wither like a bit of kelp washed ashore and dry out to nothing!" Her anger caused the skin of Nate's face to pucker about the eyes and mouth, the moisture pulled from it like sands baked under a relentless sun.

The sight of Sedna's starfish fingers latched onto the flesh of Nate's arms sparked a sudden and horrible inspiration. Reaching up, Bertie jerked at the scrimshaw necklace, breaking the chain with a golden *snap!* that could be heard all over the auditorium. Holding it aloft, she allowed it to sway to and fro, a hypnotist's coin, a parlor trick without the parlor.

When Sedna whirled about, all the blood drained from her face. Her mouth worked, a landed fish gasping its last breath in the bottom of a rough-hewn boat. "Do you mean to give that back to me?" When Bertie nodded, the Sea Goddess tried to muster venom. "What use do I have for such a thing now? Your father's bird scratchings have violated it. It's less than worthless to me—"

As though he'd taken lessons from the sneak-thief, the Scrimshander suddenly had possession of the medallion and leapt upon the stage to ask, "Is that so?" He twisted his hands about until that which had been a carved circular disk was, in the flutter of an eyelid, a bit of unmolested finger bone. "What about now?"

Sedna leapt for it. "Give it to me!"

The moment the Sea Goddess removed her gaze and her starfish hands from Nate, he scrambled away, half-falling into the orchestra pit on top of Bertie.

"Ah, ah." The finger bone disappeared, once again a medallion on a chain of oldest gold, and the Scrimshander made a tsking sort of noise against the roof of his mouth. "Not for nothing. You will pay to have this back, I think. Pay dearly for it."

"What I shall do is curse you until your innards are scattered upon the shore." Sedna slowly folded in the starfish that were her hands.

"And then?" Only two words, and such soft ones.

Bertie could hardly breathe for the tension between her father and her foe, but when Sedna looked at the Scrimshander, the spark in her eyes suddenly contained untold years of sadness and longing. Bertie didn't intercept the glance so much as it grazed her soul in passing, and she heartily wished she'd not seen it. The emotions were contagious, a black plague of yearning that took root and sprouted tendrils of sympathy, and she didn't want to sympathize with the Sea Witch. It could not be helped, though. Bertie's hand slid into Nate's so that his handfasting scar met furrow to furrow with hers.

Nate spoke, the words burbling like water from his mouth. "I am sorry for her pain." He jerked in Bertie's grip as though he'd been burned. "What did ye do?"

She stared down at her palm, pulse throbbing in her wrist just above the scar. Its twin made itself known on her other hand, and she raised it to the dim light. This time, it was Ariel who met her, palm to palm, without hesitation. Struggling to send her message through him, Bertie's concentration slipped when she looked up into his face, into his eyes. The intensity of his gaze bore through her like a diamond drill, and for the briefest of moments, the connection flowed both ways.

His thoughts were like the air: free, flowing, elusive. Whispers filled Bertie's head, each of them an echo of the words he spoke next. "Let me help you."

Her fingers tightened down upon his, and she tried to show him what she thought must happen next. A moment later, he gave voice to the picture swimming through her head. "Give Sedna back the bit of bone. It's hers. It's always been hers."

Startled, the Scrimshander glanced down at Bertie. "I would have something of her in return."

Sedna scowled. "Beyond the human life I sacrificed to keep you safe?"

"I will have your assurances that you'll quit this place, return to the sea, and stay there. That you will not try to harm my daughter or her friends again."

"Is that all?"

The Scrimshander shook his head. "And you will return Beatrice's voice, her word-magic to her."

"You ask for quite a lot in return for so little." The Sea Goddess allowed her dark gaze to roam over those present, as though assessing her ability to overwhelm and crush them all.

"It is no small thing if it frees you from your prison of anger and hatred." The Scrimshander took a step forward, his expression importuning her. "Perhaps someday you will be able to realize I never wanted you to sacrifice your life for mine. You will understand that while I was prepared to die for you, I would never have asked for you to do the same. You will finally believe I never wanted our story to end as it did."

He reached for her then, cupped her starfish hand in his, and lowered the bone-glimmer of the scrimshaw into her palm. The gold chain melted away, the disk wavered and disappeared. The starfish faded, and Sedna's hands were human once more. All that was omnipotent and sea-powerful melted away. Her face lost its ghastly green pallor; her hair was no longer the fungal brown of kelp, but rich brown, plaited into elaborate braids. She wore a thick fur jacket, and the edging on her hood moved like anemones underwater.

Forehead creased, the Scrimshander touched her face just once, tracing the planes of her cheek as he would a bit of bone. "Bertie is not the only one who mourns your pain. Did you not think I would rescue you?"

"I knew you would try," Sedna whispered. "I could feel you rushing toward me, crying out my name. My father heard it as well."

The stage filled with the recollection of waves until

Bertie felt that she, too, clung to the side of an umiak. The boat dipped and bobbed. The killing cold numbed her senses and dulled her limbs. She heard the cry of a desperate bird creature, felt his winds stirring the ocean, urging the waves to ever greater heights.

"The waters were so cold that day." Sedna's whisper crossed salt-frosted lips. "I could see you flinging yourself through the sky, and I knew if you got close enough, harpoons and spears would be thrown. It was too easy to imagine them piercing the delicate flesh of your wings, to picture your death spiral. So I let go. Of the umiak. Of you."

Bertie could see the resolution in Sedna's eyes when she gave herself over to the sea and let the dark water close over her proud head.

Though he could have reached out to her again, caught her by the wrist, pulled her back, the Scrimshander only said, "I hope that your heart will heal, that you will find peace once again. I do not think the storm in your soul shall ever abate, nor should it, but when you are angry, may it be righteous instead of vengeful, and when you raise your voice, may it be more often in joyous songs than in curses."

Sedna closed her eyes and exhaled. All that was mortal faded into foam on the waves until only the Sea Goddess remained. She towered over them, a myriad of emotions playing over her face like the wavering sunlight upon the ocean's floor. For a moment, Bertie thought Sedna would damn them to the very skies and surge forward to collect her retribution. Indeed, with a twitch of her fingers, Sedna called forth the tiny currents from the world's forgotten rivers, the dank liquid that pooled in the streets after a rainstorm. They joined to form a stream, the streams melded into a river, and upon the river floated eels of light and color.

Seconds later, the waters slapped into Bertie, as though Sedna wished to hit her one last time, and the eels wriggled up her legs, wrapped about her wrists, wormed their way under her skin. Undiluted word-magic rushed through Bertie's veins, hotter than hellfire, colder than an arctic tempest. When Bertie swayed a bit, Nate caught her under the elbows.

"Are ye all right?"

I will be.

CHAPTER EIGHTEEN

That Thing That Ends All Other Deeds

Bertie's voice vibrated inside her head like a tuning fork, only louder, growing in intensity.

"I will be," she repeated aloud. For all that the words were stilted in delivery and mundane in nature, they rang with the triumph of an opera singer holding an impossible high note.

Nodding to her, one diva to another, Sedna drew the waters about her shoulders like a cloak, melted through the floorboards, and was gone without so much as a word of farewell. Stepping free of the bookends that were Nate and Ariel, Bertie clambered out of the orchestra pit and rushed to embrace her father.

"Dad." She hugged him as hard as she dared, thinking of a bird's hollow bones, its delicate skeleton. His arms similarly tightened about her; reassured by his very human frame, she ceased to be afraid she'd hurt him.

But other fears weren't as easy to banish: that he would leave, that it would take Ophelia's presence to preserve his humanity and hold the winds at bay. Bertie forced her gaze to meet his, to remain steady as she asked, "Will you stay? There's only one missing from this scene, and I believe you're the right sort of bait to catch a water-maiden."

"I will stay," the Scrimshander hastened to reassure her. "But Ophelia will not come when she is called."

"It's not that she won't . . . it's that she can't. Her memories are trapped in the water somewhere, but I haven't been able to find them." As she pondered aloud, the rest of the troupe joined them onstage. "Maybe the trick is to reunite the two theaters first. Then Ophelia won't be trapped between worlds, and she can tell us where her memories are hidden."

Waschbär had his arm wrapped about a shivering Varvara. "And how will you manage that?"

"I caused all this trouble by acting our page from The Book into the journal, yes?" Bertie stumbled over the words, her mouth unable to keep pace with the speed of her thoughts. "Then the opposite must be true!"

Trying to puzzle out her meaning, the fairies looked as though their heads might explode.

"The opposite of what?"

"Was that supposed to be logic?"

Bertie pulled out the journal and flipped through the pages. "Our story is becoming a play . . . *Following Her Stars.* It said so on the marquee."

"Yes?" Suspicion crept into Ariel's voice.

"We'll act the pages from the journal into *The Complete Works of the Stage.* That ought to fuse the two theaters back together."

"So that we're trapped within the walls of the theater again?" Twitching tendrils of air gathered about Ariel's clothes, pleading, plucking at his sleeves, begging him to fly far away.

Bertie's lips went numb, and a faint buzzing filled her head. Hadn't she vowed never to imprison him again? "I will free you the moment Ophelia is safe." When he didn't answer, she swallowed. "Please. It might be the only way to save her." She held the journal out to the fairies, struggling to keep her voice even and her hands from shaking. "Mustardseed, the first line is yours."

"Everyone hold on to your bums," the fae muttered before reading the opening line from the script.

MUSTARDSEED

IT IS A TRUTH UNIVERSALLY ACKNOWLEDGED THAT A FAIRY IN POSSESSION OF A GOOD APPETITE MUST BE IN WANT OF PIE.

There followed the sound of electric bulbs sparking, popping, burning out their filaments, but Mustardseed remained.

"It's not enough," Bertie whispered. "Keep going."

COBWEB

YES, INDEED, THOUGH I AWOKE ONE MORNING FROM UNEASY DREAMS, I FOUND MYSELF TRANSFORMED IN MY BED INTO A GIGANTIC PIE.

MOTH

IT WAS THE BEST OF PIE, IT WAS THE WORST OF PIE.

The auditorium wavered, two pictures rendered on glass, one sliding atop the other.

"Nearly there." Bertie could hardly draw a breath as she turned to Nate. "It's your line."

Eyes widening a bit, the pirate cleared his throat. "It is?"

"She was, apparently, thinking of you from the very beginning." Ariel's voice was distant, though he hadn't stirred from her side.

Bertie shook her head, trying to signal he shouldn't speak, but the pirate reached for her, his hand cupping her face, tracing the line of her jaw.

NATE

(OFFSTAGE WHISPER)

LASS.

PEASEBLOSSOM

(FRETTING)

WE SHOULD HAVE HAD A PROLOGUE, NOT ALL
THIS NATTERING ABOUT PIE.

The air about them shimmered, growing heavy with
greasepaint and the memory of applause.

Peaseblossom's wings fluttered as she clasped her tiny
hands together. "We need something more, something
stronger."

"My line, maybe?" Bertie ran her finger along the page,
wanting to be absolutely certain of the wording. There was
Peaseblossom's valiant attempt at an iambic pentameter
introduction, yes, then her own name stamped out in heavy
typeface:

BERTIE

THAT WILL BE ENOUGH OF THAT, THANK YOU
KINDLY.

She cast her opening line across the stage and waited to

see if the silver fish would bite; in response, feedback crack-
led through the speaker system, accompanied by a whirring noise. The red velvet curtains rustled. Then the magic
paused, as though the theater held its breath, refusing to
exhale.

"What more does it need?" Mustardseed demanded,
his entire face contorted into a scowl.

"It needs me," Ariel said.

Bertie wanted to make promises, to reassure him of
her good intentions. "Ariel—"

He wouldn't let her finish. "Give me the journal."

Forever after she would remember that moment: the
way she hesitated; the look of resignation on his face; how
she handed him the journal and wondered—as all actors
must—what her motivation truly was, beyond her determination to save Ophelia. Bravery, inherited from a woman
fearless enough to leave the theater and her written part
behind? Cowardice, born from the fear that she could not
set matters to rights?

In the end, it mattered not. He spoke with the conviction she lacked.

ARIEL

THIS IS THE FIRST MOMENT WE'VE HAD ALONE
SINCE I RETURNED FROM YOUR DELIVERY
ERRAND.

Everything hung in the balance, golden scales evenly weighted, every member of the troupe holding their collective breath, but still nothing happened.

"Why didn't it work?" Moth stage-whispered to the others. "Did we do something wrong?"

With a sinking feeling in her middle, Bertie flipped through the pages. "It should have worked."

Except there were blank spaces in the journal where not even dark smudges of ink marked the absence of certain words.

> SERAFINA
> (HOLDING OUT A CRYSTAL FLASK)
> FILL THIS.

> BERTIE
> WITH WHAT?

> SERAFINA
> WITH WORDS.

> BERTIE
> (REMEMBERING THE CHANGES SHE WROUGHT IN THE MARKETPLACE: RIVULETS OF RIBBON-COLOR, GOLDEN EARRINGS TRANSFORMED INTO EGGS) JUST WORDS?

SERETINA

(WITH A KNOWING SMILE)
IT'S NEVER JUST WORDS, IS IT?

It's never just words.

"The mistake was mine," Bertie said in disbelief. "Reckless. Silly and reckless. I've done more damage here than Sedna could have accomplished in her fondest dreams." Dizzy with the revelation, Bertie realized there was a very good chance she might faint like any one of the girls in the Ladies' Chorus.

Nate grabbed her by the arm before she could keel over. "An' where d'ye think yer goin'?"

"The journal's incomplete," she said with a stagger. "It's missing the words I traded to Serefina."

Moth clapped his hands. "Back we go to the Caravanserai! I call shotgun on the caravan."

"I call dibs on the contents of the cheesecake-on-a-stick stall!"

"We're not going all the way back," Bertie said, recovering her balance and her purpose all at once. "Waschbär?"

He snapped to attention. "Yes?"

"I need something from your pack. That vial of sand?"

Dropping to one knee, the sneak-thief set to rummaging, locating the requested article with haste. "Here you are. You want to be careful with that."

"I know." Bertie pulled the drawstring and immediately scented the many years contained within the leather pouch. The sands of time, he'd called it, but she knew better. Sand itself was time incarnate, microscopic particles of stone worn down by weather and years.

And Bertie could command the stone.

"Don't move." She walked around them, dribbling sand to form a ring. In an instant, it transformed into rich, brown loam. Moss bloomed upon it, and mushrooms opened like tiny parasols upon the green carpeting.

"A fairy circle," Peaseblossom said, delighted, and began dancing behind Bertie. Her every hop summoned a fat toad until each fungal throne sat occupied. "'Come now, a roundel and a fairy song.'"

"I'll manage the circle if you can manage the song. You know my opinion about musical numbers." Bertie completed the first loop and began the second, willing the earth to respond to her, willing a tunnel to open between here and there, then and now. After the third time around, the air within the circle shimmered. Scrims surrounded them, the iridescent netting trapping them like fish in golden mesh.

"This is no fairy circle." Waschbär tried to take a step back, but he could not move beyond the boundary created by the mushroom-squatting toads. "It's a witch's circle. A *hexenring*. Will you gather your sisters here?"

When shall we three meet again?

Bertie shook her head and dismissed the witches from that Scottish Play. "I'm an only child."

"Are you certain about that?" the sneak-thief asked with a sly glance at the Scrimshander.

Bertie's father colored up to the roots of his hair. "She is . . . to the best of my knowledge."

Having imagined six or seven siblings in *How Bertie Came to the Theater* along with the Family Dog, Bertie similarly blushed. "Don't be ridiculous, Waschbär."

"Can you imagine?" Mustardseed stared at her, goggle-eyed. "Half a dozen crazy-haired troublemakers? They could beat up the Von Trapp kids without thinking twice!"

"Be still." Sweat gathered at the small of Bertie's back, and she concentrated on the shifting curtains of light. This was no time to lose focus, especially not to the ridiculous notion that she had unknown brothers and sisters somewhere. Holding out her arms, Bertie tried to fix a picture of Serefina in her mind, painting a portrait of the herb-seller: skin roughened by sun and wind, hands stained green with herbs, robes the color of emeralds at midnight. Bertie struggled to remember the exact shade of Serefina's eyes, the years of knowledge that lit their depths, each amber fleck in the iris a philter strained, a draught concocted.

The imagined eyes blinked slowly, pale lashes fluttering like one of Ariel's butterflies as the herb-seller hovered between the two worlds, one foot inside the fairy ring, the other remaining in her stall at the Caravanserai. "It's a fine magic that summons me here. Great must be your need, Teller of Tales."

"The vial of words I filled for you." Bertie wished she could grab Serefina by the robes but did not dare touch her, not with the woman's serpent gaze trained upon her. "Do you still have it?"

For a long moment, there was only the rush and bubble of a dozen kettles on an unseen hearth, the subtle movement of cotton curtains closing off the stall from the rest of the Caravanserai. Then there came the rasp of work-roughened fingers against smocking as Serefina pulled the crystal flask from her pocket. Lifting it to her face, she traced the facets with a fingertip as another woman might stroke the face of her lover. "I keep it with me always."

Bertie trembled with the effort to keep from snatching it like a common thief. "What price would you put upon it?"

The herb-seller laughed low in her throat. "It is a most precious thing."

"As I am now well aware," Bertie said.

"Take care," Ariel murmured. "The more eager you sound, the steeper her price will be."

"Do not take me for a fool, air spirit," Serefina hissed at him. Though she was careful not to move her feet, everything else about her surged forward: her hair, her clothes, the dagger gaze that could sever a soul from a body. "And do not interfere in this transaction."

Ariel gave her a low bow, though arrogance prickled from every angle of his body. "I apologize, madam, both to you and"—here he bowed to Bertie—"to the young lady. Were it not for me, she would not have had reason to trade with you in the first place."

"You speak the truth with a tongue more forked than my own," Serefina said. "Now . . . shall we speak again about a price?"

Bertie hadn't the patience or, judging by the fading glow of the curtains about them, the time to dance a buyer's waltz. "What is it you want?"

"You know what it is I want."

"The idea of a child," Bertie remembered, feeling suddenly hollow and glass-fragile. "The child I will never have."

Behind her, the Scrimshander squawked a single protest. Nate's breath left his lungs in a rush, and Ariel caught hold of Bertie's wrist, twisting her away from the herb-seller's sharp gaze.

"What does she mean by that?" he demanded. "The child you will never have?"

"A dream-child," Serefina answered for Bertie. "With every breath taken, with every decision made, the girl sets her course. Untold paths are left unwandered. I would have a child from one of those paths."

"It's not much, is it?" Gaze fixed upon the glittering contents of the crystal vial, Bertie spoke to no one in particular. "Trading something that will never exist for a mother I will otherwise never see again?"

Now Nate stood alongside her, shaking her roughly as though to jostle her from a nightmare. "Ye don't rightly understand th' terms o' th' bargain! She's askin' ye fer too much—"

"A small nothing," Serefina argued.

Raising his cutlass, Nate took a step toward her. "We want different terms."

"Terms?" The herb-seller raised her voice until the trees trembled. "Do you think me addled? The girl summoned me through time and space for this flask; she will pay what I ask, or she will not have it."

Bertie had spent seventeen years trying to learn the trick of thinking before speaking; for once she was thankful the lesson hadn't stuck. "Done."

Serefina held up the mirror once more. "For your eyes only."

Though she didn't want to look, Bertie couldn't help but obey. In the surface of the glass, she did not see her own reflection, but the wavering outline of a much smaller form.

As she watched, it coalesced into bone and flesh, sturdy legs that lengthened with every passing second, arms that reached for the sky.

When the child's eyes fluttered open, they were unmistakably Bertie's eyes. Ophelia's eyes.

The herb-seller lowered the mirror, revealing the wavering suggestion of a person that now clung to her skirts. Made entirely of fire and air and earth and water, the child peered up at Bertie with those familiar eyes, moonlight surrounding its head like a halo. Serefina held out the crystal vial, and Bertie's fingers clenched about words and rainbows. She cradled it in her palm as she never would that little one's cheek. Then the tears slid down; the last of the stars fell from Bertie's eyes, drifted through the air, and settled into the child's. Seeing them sparkle there, knowing that once Ophelia must have cried her star-tears into the infant Beatrice's eyes, Bertie couldn't stop a sob before it escaped her. The noise pushed the herb-seller and her prize out of the fairy circle and back into the Caravanserai, their forms gone in an instant.

What have I done?

Filled with sick regret but unable to turn back the clock, Bertie opened the vial and drank the traded words down, tasting sour cherry syrup over shaved ice, bitter lemon peel, and spices that recalled a nameless sorrow.

I should have found another way. Remorse stabbed at her

middle with every swallow. *I should have used the wish-come-true instead.*

But it was too late for that, too late to do anything save watch the words reappear on the pages of the journal:

RARERIPE, HORBGORBLE, MOONGLADE, CURL-IEWURLIE.

Never again would she underestimate the power of a single word.

Every word is a magic spell.

At the very least, she thought they would have to recite their lines again; a second, terrible idea followed, that perhaps they'd need to summon every new Player they'd met along the journey: the Innamorati, the characters at the Caravanserai, even Her Gracious Majesty and all the court at the Distant Castle.

And how could the brigands possibly recite their lines when they're dead and snow-packed?

But the journal shuddered in her desperate grip, wavered, and disappeared like a conjurer's trick. The next instant, *The Complete Works of the Stage* appeared with a thunderclap and a lightning flash upon its pedestal Stage Left, its glow twice as brilliant as before. The theater surrounding them reverberated with the shift, the double images solidifying into one: the very place they'd left not so long ago.

Bertie reached out to squeeze Ariel's hand, not surprised to find it cold and unresponsive. He didn't move, but every bit of his attention was focused upon the Exit door, and his eyes had the haunted expression of a trapped bird, a wild starling caged for market.

"Ariel—"

As though relishing the opportunity to interrupt her, a tinny voice came over the loudspeaker: "All Players to the stage, please, all Players to the stage."

"Th' Stage Manager," Nate said with a bit of a laugh. "Now I know we're home."

"And my guess is he knows we're back." Ill-tamed bits of Ariel's wind escaped him, as though trying to drag him from the room before it was too late.

The wisps of wind carried something else upon them: Ophelia's perfume. The water-maiden shifted quietly into the here-and-now. At first she was as worn and faded as a bit of sheet music left carelessly in the sun, her limbs transparent, her dress no more than the suggestion of fabric and thread. Then corporeality spread like a warm flush, a waking dream made tangible.

"Ophelia." Moving faster than a bird of prey, the Scrimshander caught her in his arms. "Before you disappear again, I would have you know that I still love you!"

When the water-maiden lifted her eyes to his, something about her face changed. Her expression sharpened, her mouth opened just slightly, and the smile she bestowed upon him was far more brilliant than the dream-lulled expression of a delusional maiden. "I know you, sir, I think."

More than seventeen years had passed since they'd last seen each other, since they'd last spoken, since they'd been torn from each other's arms. Bertie had regained her voice, but watching her father gaze down upon her mother, she was still speechless.

The warmth of Ophelia's expression flickered. The Scrimshander stared back at her, a man stricken, and he held very still as she reached up with a hesitant hand to trace a finger down the bridge of his nose, along his high, curving cheekbones, down the length of his long neck to the swirling tattoos that decorated what was visible of his chest.

"I don't remember these," Ophelia noted, her nails skimming his skin until she raised gooseflesh.

"Those," he said, sounding strangled, "are new since we last parted."

Ophelia frowned. "Why would you do such a thing to yourself?"

His throat worked. "Punishment for my weakness. I should have found the strength to remain human—"

"You speak such nonsense," Ophelia said with a faint laugh. "If you'll excuse me, though, I will go in search of the healing waters." When she pulled away from him, the hem of her gown fluttered, the Cobalt-Flame silk water-patterned and droplet-spangled.

"Waschbär," Bertie whispered, hardly able to speak for the idea crowding into her head alongside the wish-come-true, "hand me your satchel."

He obeyed, moving slower than she'd thought possible though her own hands fumbled as she reached down to the bottom of the bag for a piece of forgotten fabric. Wrapped about the journal, tossed aside as less important than the pages within . . .

It was the most important bit of all.

Bertie held it gently between her fingertips, noting its delicacy, catching the faintest fragrance of water lily for the first time. Turning, she offered it to her mother. "This belongs to you, I think."

Puzzled, the water-maiden reached out to take the scrap of silk. "What is that bit of nothing?" But there was no need to answer. As soon as Ophelia's fingertips brushed over the fabric, the confusion in her eyes dissipated, and all that had been clouded green was now faceted emerald. The bent reeds of her limbs straightened until she was as Bertie had seen her in the Queen's mirror world: a woman whose strength and determination was balanced by mischief and perhaps even a bit of the reckless daredevil. Staring at her mother, Bertie saw more of herself in the water-maiden than she ever had before.

In the next instant, Ophelia had her arms about Bertie, murmuring apologies and seventeen years' worth of motherly endearments that ended with "My darling girl, can you ever forgive me?"

"It's I who should apologize," the Scrimshander tentatively put forward. "For leaving you here, alone, to bear our child."

Bertie dropped Waschbär's bag to better enfold both her parents in the sort of hug she'd dreamed about for as long as she could remember. They stood that way, heads bowed toward each other, breaths exhaled as tiny laughs, tears flowing as free as the rivers until the reunion was interrupted by a hoarse choking noise.

"What is the meaning of all this?" The Theater Manager stood in the gloom of the wings, features half obscured by shadow. His gaze traveled from Bertie to Ophelia's joyful but defiant face, to the Scrimshander, his muscles knotted with righteous anger.

"I'm afraid your brigands didn't quite manage to get the journal back to you," Bertie said. "And it's been returned to its proper place within The Book. I would know what your plans were for it, given that I know *everything else* you have done."

Cheeks blotched with anger, he stepped forward. "I ought to have destroyed it years ago."

"And me?" Bertie demanded. "I am part of what

happened outside these walls. Destroying the journal might have killed me!"

"Would that I had had the courage!" His carefully constructed mask slipped. "I knew you would be the downfall of this place! It was a mistake to let you live, a greater mistake still to let Mrs. Edith bring you back here. The moment she returned, I should have taken the journal from its hiding place and burned the cursed thing—"

"Why didn't you, then?" Bertie flared in return, equal parts sick and relieved to finally know his true feelings toward her. "Why did you wait for me to leave, for the journal to go missing?"

"I can tell you," Varvara said, stepping forward.

At the sound of her voice, the Theater Manager looked as though his collar strangled him. He took several involuntary steps forward, pulled by invisible puppet strings. "What are *you* doing here?"

"The wordsmith freed me from my prison." Hair flaming with temper, the fire-dancer scowled at him. "Tell her how you've always feared the flames. Feared anything you could not control. If the journal's destruction required fire, you would have never managed it unless driven by desperation greater than your cowardice—"

Her creator did not deny it. Instead, he clamped unforgiving fingers around her wrist. His other hand twisted the opal ring from her finger faster than any of the fairies could have downed a cupcake. Varvara began to shriek the moment the metal left her skin, an unholy wail that recalled the death of anything that had ever perished in the flames, but still he did not let her go.

"I've courage enough to return you to your prison."

Varvara's skin glowed white-hot, and he was forced to release her with a curse. "I will not be held captive again!" She turned and leapt through the air, fear and fury consuming her so that only flames were left for the split second when she passed, not by Ariel, but through him.

Wholly unprepared for the assault, he could not stop her from drawing all the winds of the world within herself as she glided through his body. Shirt charred and expression stunned, he teetered and fell into the orchestra pit as Varvara's air-fed flames exploded from the stage in a thousand directions at once.

CHAPTER NINETEEN

So Do Our Minutes Hasten to Their End

"Ariel!" Bertie's shout was lost to chaos.

Within seconds, fire had consumed the lacquered wood paneling and stripped the flocked wallpaper from the walls of the auditorium. Crystals in the chandelier shattered and rained down like fireworks; in the center of it all, Varvara stood on her toes, spinning madly, sparking yet more fires upon the rug and walls as glowing tears streamed down her cheeks.

"Make it stop," the fire-dancer pleaded. "I can't—"

Wishing she could punch the Theater Manager, Bertie instead wrested the ring from his grasp, running forward only to be thrown back by a wave of superheated air and thick, black smoke. The sprinklers that should have poured blessed water down upon them by now only hissed steam like red-hot radiators on the boil. Flames licked eager tongues over the velvet curtains.

And Ariel is caught in this inferno.

Bertie pulled her sweater up until it covered her nose. Creeping forward on her hands and knees, she tried to ignore the tears streaming from her eyes. The speakers overhead clicked on again, and the Stage Manager's panic fanned the flames.

"All Players to the stage!"

Bertie could hear the alarmed screams of the approaching company, the rustle of costumes in the hallway, the frantic footfalls headed their direction.

Nate's determined shout carried over the assembling crowd. "Open th' smoke doors!" Climbing the rigging, the pirate opened the first of the tiny vents above the stage. Right behind him, half a dozen mariners did the same. Nate twisted about on his rope to point at a blue-painted lever. "Activate th' deluge system an' call in every water set we have!"

His voice had a captain's bellow about it now, and the company fell to their tasks, shoving at waves, pulling in rivers, lowering blue-gauze scrim, reaching for buckets of glitter-infused water. The tin handles were passed hand to hand, the contents sloshing over to decorate flame-licked hemlines and smoke-bedraggled stockings.

"Someone lower th' fire curtain so th' flames don't spread t' th' stage!"

A member of the Gentlemen's Chorus ran for the heavy lever in the Stage Manager's corner, pulling it with a grunt. The iron curtain began to slide along the steel channels that would hold it in place.

The theater might well be doomed already, but I'll be damned if it takes Ariel with it.

Bertie threw herself under the yet-moving curtain, skidding to the front of the stage as it slammed down behind her, nearly felling half the Ladies' Chorus.

"Ariel?" With a grunt and a heave, Bertie slid into the orchestra pit, bouncing off a chair and a music stand, scorched sheet music fluttering around her like autumnal leaves. Though he was only a few feet away, it took countless precious breaths to find him, to crawl to his side, to drag him into her lap. The burning in her lungs was even worse than when she'd drowned. Everything about her was going hazy around the edges, but when Ariel exhaled a ragged breath, it cleared the worst of the smoke around them.

"You have to make her stop," he managed to say between wracking coughs.

Trying to escape her own flames, Varvara leapt from the dress circle to the ledge on the upper balcony. Framed by an enormous glittering window, the fire-dancer twisted about to face them. Shooting-star sparks fell from her hands, and the truth raged from her lips like so much lava. "This was not my choice."

"The Theater Manager can't trap you again, Varvara!" Bertie screamed in return, holding up the ring. "But you have to stop, before you destroy everything!"

"He'll use a different word-spell to put me back in the dark. I'd rather perish!"

"*I* can use the words to free you!" Clutching Ariel, Bertie tried to summon the silver light that yet lingered behind her eyes. "I wish for your freedom, Varvara! You will never be a prisoner again."

The Queen's gift swelled, filling her entire head, the words swirling like ink on the surface of a scrying mirror. Sweat poured down Bertie's face; when a ruby droplet spattered her right hand, just over the handfasting mark, she realized her nose had started to bleed.

"Perhaps," Ariel managed to wheeze, "it's not as easy to use a wish-come-true as I thought."

"I can't force it to obey me," Bertie said, falling back against the wall. "The Queen said the wish had to be worthy, but I'm the one who's not worthy! I'm not strong enough!"

"You are!" Ariel gripped her shoulders, trying to transfer his strength to her, though it too was flagging. "You have to be!"

"I wish for your freedom, Varvara!" But Bertie's ragged

scream was lost to the back draft of heat and light that enveloped them. Wrapping her arms about Ariel, Bertie built a tiny shelter from the pieces of theater not yet burning, their world reduced to bits of oak and mahogany, splinters of cherrywood and pine, fitted together like a puzzle with all its pieces. Tiny vines unfurled from the wood, releasing precious oxygen, and Bertie managed to draw half a breath.

"I always knew it would come to this," Ariel said finally.

Bertie couldn't see his face, sensing instead when he rolled over onto his knees. As another bit of the theater's ceiling landed somewhere nearby, she knelt next to him, unable to feel anything more than numb. Face pressed against Ariel's shoulder, Bertie wished for Nate, for the cool waters of the ocean, even for Sedna, who could have saved them all and must be laughing somewhere.

"What did you know?" When she spoke, it was into the silk of his sleeve. "That we would die today? Did that information come in a misbegotten fortune cookie?"

"Leave it to you," he said with a wheeze, "to summon sarcasm at a time like this."

The shelter about them fractured, its destruction held at bay only by the matrix of vines running through the wood like stitches. Firelight wormed through infinitesimal cracks, waltzing orange and yellow and red over Ariel's face like a lighting special. Blood trickled down his cheek, dark in the unreliable illumination, and his eyes sparked with something far more frightening.

Bertie wanted to scream, but air was too precious for that, and so she whispered instead, "What did you know, then?"

"That you would be the one to free me someday." When their handfasting scars met, there was no misunderstanding his excitement; it took flight alongside his butterflies, painting their wings silver to reflect bits of his face on fluttering mirrors. "I can stop the fire as surely as I fed it: with the winds. Release me. Take from me this flesh, the blood and the bones. I will suck the air from the room and smother her flames."

Bertie jerked back as though he'd struck her. She could hardly fathom what he was saying. "What insanity are you mouthing?"

"The theater was never my prison. My *body* is the prison. 'What dreams may come, when we have shuffled off this mortal coil?'"

"Don't you dare quote at me now!" Around them, the shelter continued to fragment, the cracks between the protective wood planks widening. Smoke reached wispy fingers through the plants as though hookah-sent to fetch them, but Bertie wouldn't heed the call. She fed her soul and her strength into the vines, willing them to hold, coaxing them to release more precious oxygen.

Ariel pressed his forehead to hers, the words spoken into her mouth. "It is not death I ask you for, but life. Life eternal. Life unfettered by anyone or anything, as I was meant to be. I am the only one who can stop this. I am the only one who can save you, but you are the only one who can free me. You are the one with the power over words."

Bertie tried to twist away from him. "I will not."

"You will do as you must." Ariel's other hand threaded through her silver hair so she could make no escape.

She circled the idea in her mind, unable to contemplate letting go of someone as much a part of her as Nate, as dear as any of the fairies, less of a stranger than Ophelia or the Scrimshander. "This is not the ending I wanted."

"Nor I." For a moment, Ariel saw not the destruction around them, but something very different. "What was in the mirror might have been for your eyes only, but I saw the dream-child clinging to Serefina's skirts, Bertie. It might have had your eyes, but I think its silver hair was mine." Here his voice broke, as though dropped from a great height and shattered upon marble.

"You can't know that for certain." Bertie stared at him, rage pouring through her; in turn, she fed it into the silver cloud of magic behind her eyes. "My hand will not be forced by something as heartless as Fate . . . I am not Juliet, even if you pine to take Romeo's role!" Shoving him back, she broke free from their meager shelter, held her hands

out to the flames, and screamed to the very heavens, "I wish you forever-free, Varvara!"

Unhindered this time by doubt or fear, the wish's light poured out of Bertie, finally released to do her bidding. The hellfire surrounding the fire-dancer dwindled, drawn out of her like a fever. Within seconds, Varvara's face was pale where it had been unnaturally flushed, her limbs trembling with shock instead of rage. Freed from the prison that was the flames, she faltered and collapsed in the upper balcony.

The fire consuming the auditorium immediately died, the various conflagrations snuffed out like a series of candles upon a windowsill. Wisps of smoke marked their passing, wending gray ghosts that gathered in the balconies and trailed faint fingers over the painted frescos. Where there had been the spitting and splintering crackle of flames, there was now only silence. Though something told Bertie that Nate called to her from behind the fire curtain, she couldn't hear him, couldn't hear anything save the rush of blood through her ears.

She turned to Ariel, giddy, filled with triumph that tasted of champagne bubbles breaking on her tongue. "I did it!"

Crouched in the wreckage, head bowed, he didn't answer at first. When at last he spoke, anguish tinted his words. "Indeed you did. My heartiest congratulations, milady."

The champagne went flat, its sweetness turned to

vinegar. "Are you hurt?" Scrambling back to him, she searched his face and limbs for blood, for wounds.

"Yes."

"Show me where..." Her voice trailed off when he lifted his head and she saw his eyes. "You...you aren't bleeding. Nothing's broken."

Both lies, she realized as another layer gathered upon her mask. He bled from a soul-wound, and she had one to match. "You scented your freedom in the smoke, didn't you? It was the one-in-a-thousand wind."

Several impossibly long seconds passed before he rose and answered her. "Yes."

"Ah. I should have guessed as much." Heart aching as though it had been burnt from her chest, Bertie reached out a hand and caressed his face. She couldn't stop the tears, hot and stinging, from pouring down her cheeks.

"Come now, why are you crying?" Soot-smudged, Ariel still managed to summon the ghost of a smile for her. "The theater is saved. I'm still here with you. Isn't this the happily ever after you wanted?"

Leaning forward, she rested her forehead against his chest. "Whatever happens next, know that I love you."

His hands tightened upon her. "What are you going to do?"

Bertie pressed a hand against his mouth, certain that if

he said another word, she wouldn't have the strength to do what she must. "'My Ariel . . .'"

So began Prospero's speech at the end of *The Tempest*, delivered by the magician to the airy sprite he'd ensorcelled and enslaved. Such a short monologue to mean so much; spoken untold times upon the stage, it never before had the effect it was having now, and Ariel trembled as the winds rushed forward to collect him.

"I will give you your freedom," Bertie said, her words a fierce challenge. "Not because my hand was forced to it, but because it's the right thing to do. Because I love you."

He cupped her face in his hands. "And I, you."

"Enough to harbor second thoughts?" She held close the hope that he would tell her it was no longer a gift he wanted.

"No," was his softly whispered admission. "Make no mistake, I want this. I've always wanted this." The way Ariel clung to her almost belied the words. "But you must know that I will hold your memory fast within my heart and soul. And you will feel me in every wind, every breeze, every exhalation of air from your lungs."

"'Then to the elements be free.'" Bertie choked upon the quote, trying to hold on to his hands, to press a final kiss to his fingers. The chandelier was broken, there was no one manning the spotlight, and yet illumination traced the beautiful planes of his face and neck, turning his hair to liquid mercury and lightning. "'And fare thou well!'"

For a moment, everything about him that was silk and silver lingered in the air, the echo of laughter, a gentle touch upon the cheek. Then Ariel dissolved into a whipping rush of energy. The Exit door exploded outward and all the air in the room gave chase, desperate not to be left behind on this, his next grand adventure.

Bertie couldn't breathe. There was no air left for her. Ariel was gone, and with him part of her heart, part of her very soul.

CHAPTER TWENTY

Of These Most Brisk and Giddy-paced Times

With the slow stagger of one bereaved, Bertie made her way down the carpeted aisle, into the lobby, and pushed through the revolving door. The air outside was blessedly clear and clean, like a sip of water to her parched throat. A snippet of crimson ribbon fluttered past her, most likely the lost hair bow of a child. It tumbled and twisted in a dying breeze, down the stairs, into the streets, lost between the cart wheels and the clopping hooves of a streetcar's horse team.

"He could come back. I could find a way to make him human again."

Except she knew such dreams were folly, that he'd never been human to begin with, and therein lay all the trouble between them. She stood with her arms wrapped about her for untold minutes, waiting for a whisper of wind that would suggest that Ariel yet remembered there was a Beatrice Shakespeare Smith.

You will feel me in every wind.

Closing her eyes, she shut out the sights of the city, the acrid scent of smoke, the shouts of passersby until nothing remained but the gentle breeze passing over her skin. At once snow driven and summer warmed, it contained the promise of rain and sunlight, the perfume of arid desert and salt breezes. It roused all her father-bestowed avian instincts so that when Bertie blinked, she suddenly viewed the world behind the graceful curvature of a sharpened beak. Fingernails transformed to talons. Her arms prickled with the possibility of feathers even as Ariel's voice echoed in her head.

"Have you ever seen a falcon, hooded and jessed for the hunt?"

"It's love that tethers me to you."

"And I, you." After all they had been through, Ariel would not want her trapped as he had been, bound in servitude to a body not truly her own. Bertie's hands dropped back to her sides. When next the air caught hold of her clothes, her hair, she felt no need to succumb. She was herself again.

There's another way to fly. Steeped as I am in fairy dust, all I need is my "happy thought."

She set her memories of Ariel in stone: his beautiful face, the movement of his hair, the yearning for freedom that was his very soul. To embrace everything he had been, Bertie stretched her arms out wide and let the wind carry her skyward. Gravity had no hold upon her just now; she was a child-loosed balloon, held aloft by wistful joy.

"'Farewell,'" Bertie whispered. "'Thou art too dear for my possessing.'"

A single tear fell, recalling gravity, and she drifted down, aided by the weight of her grief. When her feet touched the ground, she took a moment to breathe, to simply be. With the passing seconds, the world coalesced around her, the buildings sliding into place like set pieces, the traffic resuming its frantic pace. Inside the ticket booth, a woman of flesh and blood had replaced the automaton.

"You're back!" She flashed Bertie a crimson-painted smile. "Is the rest of the Touring Company with you?"

"They are." Bertie stepped closer to the window and caught her reflection in the glass.

So this is what grief looks like.

Ash smeared her clothes, now darker than widow's weeds. Her hair was twisted into a silver tangle, her eyes two holes burnt in a blanket. No doubt her appearance would send Mrs. Edith into an apoplectic fit.

"Shall I put the tickets to *Following Her Stars* on sale?" The woman's eager hand hovered over the switch that would ignite the marquee lights.

"Not just yet," Bertie said, drawn like a magnet to the revolving door. "There are still a few loose threads to tie up."

Inside the lobby, the theater already sought to heal itself: wood had regenerated, the sparkling glass windows overhead wiped clean. Beeswax polish and roses couldn't quite veil the acrid stench that clung to the drapes and the carpets, though Bertie had no doubt the scent of smoke, too, would soon fade to nothing, as though it had all been a Puck-induced dream.

"For once," she murmured, "that menace had no hand in the mischief."

Feeling much like a ghost, she entered the auditorium.

"Thank the heavens you're all right!" Waschbär cried, meeting her halfway down the aisle. His coat yet smoldered but from it he drew *The Complete Works of the Stage,* thoughtlessly abandoned when the fire curtain had slammed shut. The skin on his hands was angry pink, blistered, and weeping clear fluid.

Bertie's skin felt just as raw, though her wounds were deep inside her. "What are you doing with The Book?" Better to focus on such a curious anomaly than on what had just happened.

The sneak-thief swallowed hard. "I . . . I stole it. Snatched it from its pedestal when the ceiling started to yield to the flames."

"Why would you do such a thing?"

"I could not let it burn. I waited as long as I dared, until ash drifted down like snow, and I could hardly think or breathe. At the very worst moment, I thought it would be destroyed, and then I broke my vow. I took a wanted thing." With trembling hands, he held The Book out to her.

She accepted it, careful not to touch his tender skin. "It seems to have cost you dearly." *We've all paid harsh prices on this day, it seems.* "But you have my thanks, Waschbär, and that of the theater. It was a hero's deed."

If possible, his nose turned even more pink. "I would not say that."

"I would, and my word seems to be gold just now." She hugged him then, as gently as she could, and led him onstage.

"I would have a small measure of forgiveness as well," said a small voice behind them.

Bertie let go of Waschbär to better address the once fire-dancer. Deprived of her flames, Varvara ascended the stairs with great uncertainty, her loveliness perhaps more apparent now that she no longer threatened them with annihilation. Though Bertie wanted to condemn her, wanted someone to blame for everything—the destruction of the theater, Ariel's absence—she knew such blame would be misplaced. "There is nothing to forgive, I think. It was an accident that Ariel's winds fed your fire."

"It was certainly not my intention." Varvara indicated a small pile of ash at the base of The Book's pedestal. "Yet there is no excusing murder, I think."

The tarnished-gold gleam of the Theater Manager's pocket watch glinted in the half-light, cover open, glass face cracked down the middle. Bertie stooped down; though she did not touch it, she noted the watch had ceased *tick-tick-ticking*. Like the clepsydra, it had marked the minutes of something now finished.

"It was self-defense," she told the fire-dancer. "At last you'll be safe from his machinations. As will my parents."

"As will you," Waschbär noted.

Behind them, the fire curtain began its unhesitating ascent, revealing a group of sodden but triumphant Players. Nate stood in a massive puddle, shirt hanging in tatters, eyes bleak. The moment he spotted Bertie, he crossed the stage at a flat run.

"We did it, lass, th' fire's out." Jubilant, he embraced her, only realizing when she pulled away that something was very wrong. "What's happened?"

Bertie swallowed, too tired to recount all that had transpired, too heartsick to say the words aloud. Yet certain things must be explained. "Ariel's gone."

"Again?" For a moment, it seemed Nate couldn't decide if he were furious the air elemental had abandoned Bertie during the crisis or thrilled to be rid of his rival. The dark horse of that particular race revealed itself as wry resignation, winning by a nose. "Don't let it trouble ye, lass. I very much doubt it's th' last we've seen o' him, despite what ye said."

"What I said?" Bertie repeated, parrot to his pirate.

He quirked an eyebrow at her. "That if he wished t' abandon us a third time, not t' return?"

The irony of it grated on already tender flesh. "I did say that, didn't I? It seems I have the 'spirit of deep prophecy,' if not palmistry." She turned her hands over, cursing the secretive scars upon her palms.

What would I have done differently if I'd known how all of it would end?

Nate nudged the thought aside, though he was careful not to crowd her. "Ye think him forever gone, then?"

"I am certain of it."

I released him from his prison of flesh and blood.

She was spared saying it by the appearance of the fairies. Utterly bedraggled, Peaseblossom and the boys resembled nothing so much as four airborne filthy handkerchiefs. Behind them hurried Ophelia and the Scrimshander, their hands yet clasped, looking for all the world like the young lovers Bertie had long imagined.

"You disappeared!" the water-maiden accused before Peaseblossom could. Ophelia let go of the Scrimshander to embrace Bertie again. "We were so worried!"

Nearly suffocated by wet chiffon, Bertie had no time to make excuses before Mrs. Edith entered, skirts hiked up above her ankles to allow for her brisk pace, followed by Mr. Hastings coughing his way through the residual smoke.

"Oh, my dears!" The Wardrobe Mistress gathered both women into her arms. "Are you all right?"

"We're—" *Fine,* Bertie started to say, except it was a lie.

"But you're home! And safe, praise be!" Mrs. Edith backed up far enough to clasp Bertie's chin, to take in her bedraggled costume, and her glance fell upon the broach pinned to the bodice. "You visited Her Gracious Majesty . . . well, well, well!" Each successive "well" rose in pitch and volume until they rang out across the stage; even the Scenic Manager took note of it.

"No doubt she didn't wreak this sort of havoc in the Distant Castle, or her head would be on a pike instead of her shoulders!" In light of the recent destruction, Mr. Tibbs was conspicuously without his usual cigar, though he roared twice as loud to compensate for his loss, urging his crew and the Players to clear the worst of the mess off the stage.

"You were missed," Mr. Hastings said, adjusting the spectacles over his suspiciously moist eyes.

"While I appreciate the sentiment, there's more that must be said." Bertie twisted away from her guardian to address the Players and the various Managers present. "You all acted valiantly, and the Théâtre Illuminata already heals itself, but we lost one of our own today. It is with regret that I must tell you that the Theater Manager was killed in the inferno."

She saved her condemnations, forced herself to swallow the words that would wipe the shock and dismay from their faces. Half the Ladies' Chorus already sobbed loudly into their handkerchiefs, while members of the Gentlemen's Chorus loudly alternated between exclamations of "It can't be true!" and "What a damn shame."

"There is more indeed to say." The Stage Manager joined her at the front of the crowd.

"Oh, crap," said Mustardseed. "This isn't going to be pretty."

"The truth is never pretty," the Stage Manager said. The usual roar of his voice dialed down to a near whisper, he asked, "Aren't you going to tell them the rest?"

"I am not," was Bertie's soft reply. "No one would benefit from such a revelation."

Nonplussed, the Stage Manager stared hard at her. "I heard what he said. He tried—"

"He tried," she interrupted, "in his own misguided way,

to preserve the theater. It's better that he be remembered for his quiet dignity, for his tireless efforts."

Goggle-eyed, the Stage Manager seemed to see for the first time the woman she was rather than the child she had been. "You would give him that charity?"

"I would give that charity to those who remain." Clarity of thought came as though Bertie peered through Her Gracious Majesty's golden binoculars, the truth brought magically into focus. "Such news would fracture the company and allow chaos to descend. Contrary to popular belief, I want what is best for this place."

"There we are in decided agreement." He produced a rusty half smile that surprised Bertie and terrified the fairies. "Most unsettling, this finding of common ground."

"Indeed," Bertie said, borrowing some of Her Gracious Majesty's inflections. "This place requires a new Theater Manager, one who can temper what is good for the Théâtre Illuminata with what is best for the Players. Someone who cares as much for this place as its people."

"Someone like you," the Stage Manager said, his words startling the both of them.

Two could play this game, though. "Someone like *you,*" Bertie countered.

The Stage Manager blinked, mouth working without words for several seconds before he managed a sputtered "Me?"

"Him?!" Moth squeaked.

"Abandon ship!" Cobweb added.

About to tell them to shut up, Bertie suddenly found herself at a rare loss for words. A woman had joined them onstage, and she was in all ways Ophelia's double, possessing the same sweet face, the same dreamy expression but without the signs of age or mother wisdom upon her face. This water-maiden took no notice of Bertie nor her former incarnation, drifting instead nearer a vaguely perturbed-looking Hamlet.

"One Player was too much altered to continue in her part," the Stage Manager said. "I took the liberty of placing a call upon the board." He glanced into the wings and beckoned to someone standing in the shadows. "And not just for Ophelia."

A second newcomer stepped into the light, revealing herself as a slim girl of perhaps twelve, fey of face and silver-white of hair. There was no mistaking the character, even in this altered form.

Bertie could hardly speak the name without choking upon it. "Ariel."

The Stage Manager nodded. "It seems the theater decided this time to cast the part with a girl child, though we know such creatures are hardly less willful than the Ariel who preceded her." With an eye twitch at Bertie most likely meant to be a wink, he sent the girl to mingle with the rest of the Players.

"Speaking of girl children . . ." Bertie handed him *The Complete Works of the Stage*. "Intact once more, with no pages missing, you'll find. All that happened outside these walls is now transcribed within, under the title *Following Her Stars*. You'll have new Players turning up soon, I'm guessing. Best of luck with a certain blue-haired girl."

He looked perturbed and bemused all at once. "And you? Where will you go?"

Bertie tried not to think about how she'd left the first time, with Ariel at her side, but the comparison was inevitable. "Roaming, I think. A journey to the other Twelve Outposts of Beyond. Nate's coming with me, as are the fairies. They've only a few lines between them. I think understudies would be most glad for the opportunity."

"Will you go as the Mistress of Revels again?" Mrs. Edith asked, drawn into the conversation by the possible need for a costume.

Mistress of Revels, Teller of Tales, Forest Queen, wordsmith, daughter . . . "I think I'll go as myself. For a while anyway."

"Yourself!" Mustardseed screwed his face into a monkey's fist. "What kind of costuming does that require?"

Mrs. Edith's mouth quirked with approval, though all she said was, "Follow me, my dear, and I'll see you properly outfitted."

"We'll need provisions, too!" Moth clapped his little hands. "And lots of them!"

"To the Green Room for pies!" Mustardseed said, sounding his battle cry.

"Shouldn't pies be Mr. Hastings's department?"

"Not if I hit you in the face with one!" Cobweb said, rocketing to the Stage Door. "Then it's makeup!" The other fairies pursued him, arguing whether the pancakes should be buttermilk or buckwheat, served with butter and syrup or chocolate hazelnut cream.

"For my own part, I am less interested in food than frolicking." Ophelia glanced up at the Scrimshander, the beginning of a smile playing about her mouth. "Do you think yourself ready for another adventure?"

"I do." He tightened his arm around her, as though not quite able to believe she wouldn't once again be wrested from his grasp. "This time, neither success nor failure will be due to the machinations of others."

Bertie reached out a hand to each of her parents and gave them a parting caress. "Overdue for a honeymoon?"

"Indeed," the Scrimshander said. "Bertie, please think of the Aerie as your home. Seek it out when you're ready for a rest from your travels, and don't keep your mother and me waiting overly long." Trying to sound stern and fatherly, he almost managed it.

It was so much easier to let them go, knowing they went together! "I will."

The Scrimshander swept Ophelia into his arms alongside his daughter's promise-made, carrying her like a newlywed bride down the stairs, up the aisle, and out the Exit door.

"What about you?" Bertie turned to Waschbär. "You've seen this thing through to the end. Wither wilt thou go?"

The sneak-thief scratched the ferrets under their chins and smiled. "I'm with you. You'll need a navigator and a roustabout, no matter what trade you undertake."

Varvara had already gone to join the other dancers in the Ladies' Chorus; though she'd almost destroyed it, the fire-dancer recognized the theater as her home, and Bertie couldn't gainsay such a decision.

I did manage to set the fire curtain on fire myself, once.

The Stage Manager lifted a hand to Bertie as he issued a quiet command into his headset. The Players disappeared during the scene change, and then she and Nate stood where it had all started, amid the blue-green lighting and pearl strands of *The Little Mermaid* set.

"Are ye sure ye want t' leave again?"

Surrounded by coral and tap-dancing starfish, Bertie slowly pivoted on her heel. The journey had taken them to the sea and back, to the Distant Castle of the Queen, and through countless looking glasses, but Nate had weathered it all, his presence as steadfast as his gaze, the scar upon his hand proof that he forever belonged to her.

"I couldn't stay," she finally admitted, "not surrounded as I would be by memories of things that can't be changed."

He coughed lightly and gestured to her head. "Will ye want t' dye yer hair before we leave?"

"I think I'll wear it this way for a while, in memory of someone departed." She slanted a look at him through her eyelashes. "Will that bother you?"

"Nay, lass, I've more important things t' consider."

"Such as?"

"How best t' acquaint myself wi' th' person ye are now, at th' end of one grand adventure an' th' start o' another." Nate hugged her, just long enough so she could feel his heart beat, then started to let go.

Bertie didn't let him pull away, not wanting or needing more space between them than the linen of his shirt. "Promise me something?"

"Anythin'."

Nothing she liked better than a challenge. "Promise me pie."

Nate's mouth twitched. "As much as ye can eat an' yer pockets can hold."

"Promise me you won't let Mrs. Edith put me in a corset again."

Eyes widening a bit at the idea, he nodded anyway.

"Though there's no chance o' hemmin' ye in, even wi' fabric an' cords, I'll give ye my word on that as well."

Bertie took the deepest of breaths before issuing the last and most important of the three demands. "Promise you'll stay with me as long as you want to, but not a moment longer."

His hand slid into hers, and he raised them as one to his heart. "Ah, now, lass, there ye've done yerself a mischief."

"I have?" Her pulse thudded twice in quick succession.

"Aye. Now yer stuck wi' me forever, an' perhaps even a bit longer than that." Nate made her a gallant bow. "'Beyond all date, even t' eternity.'"

"Quote all the Shakespeare you like at me," Bertie countered as she led him toward the Wardrobe Department in search of appropriate adventuring attire. "I've words enough when the Bard's run out."

CURTAIN

Acknowledgments

The Management of the Théâtre Illuminata would like to extend roses, glitter, and thanks to the following people:

First and foremost, the readers, for accompanying Beatrice Shakespeare Smith & Company on their grand adventure. Your enthusiasm and applause are greatly appreciated, and the performers reserve their deepest of bows and widest of smiles for you . . . except the fairies, who pelt you with sprinkles and might also waggle their naked bums in your general direction.

The wonderful team at Feiwel and Friends for their continued efforts on behalf of the series, especially Jean Feiwel and Rebecca Davis, for their tireless editorial work.

My family, a constant source of support, joy, and dessert. My husband and daughter, whose conversations over

Legos, Wii, and the ridiculous eight-foot inflatable pool kept me laughing and provided the rhythm for many of the fairies' exchanges. My son, who winked into existence before I'd even completed the first draft, kept me company throughout revisions by pushing on my ribs and sitting on my innards, and arrived the very day I turned in the manuscript. My mother and my sister, who show up at bookstores for the readings and still ask me to sign their copies.

Siblings, friends, and beta readers Lori Diana Hunt, Sunil Sebastian, and Jenna Waterford, who read the various drafts of this manuscript on computer screens, paper, and various handheld electronic devices so they could offer up notes, encouragement, and threats.

Tiffany Trent and Chandra Rooney for their readily offered information about the Japanese tea ceremony, and the insight that green tea does indeed taste a bit like grass.

Shannon Messenger and Sara McClung, who Did the Write Thing for Nashville and bid high on my particular brand of craziness. Whenever I am in need of pirate rubber duck cupcakes, Nutella, enthusiasm, and support, I know I can count on both of you.

And finally, the wonderfully inspiring folks at the Black Phoenix Alchemy Lab, for the insight into the actual scent of Eau d'Ophelia.